Lost Souls

Also by Michael Collins

The Resurrectionists
The Keepers of Truth
The Man Who Dreamt of Lobsters (stories)
The Life and Times of a Teaboy
The Feminists Go Swimming (stories)
Emerald Underground

Lost Souls

Michael Collins

VIKING

VIKING
Published by the Penguin Group
Penguin Group (USA) Inc., 375 Hudson Street, New York, New York 10014, U.S.A.
Penguin Books Ltd, 80 Strand, London WC2R 0RL, England
Penguin Books Australia Ltd, 250 Camberwell Road, Camberwell, Victoria 3124, Australia
Penguin Books Canada Ltd, 10 Alcorn Avenue, Toronto, Ontario, Canada M4V 3B2
Penguin Books India (P) Ltd, 11 Community Centre, Panchsheel Park, New Delhi - 110 017, India
Penguin Group (NZ) Cnr Airborne and Rosedale Roads, Albany, 1310, Auckland, New Zealand
Penguin Books (South Africa) (Pty) Ltd, 24 Sturdee Avenue, Rosebank, Johannesburg 2196, South Africa

Penguin Books Ltd, Registered Offices: 80 Strand, London WC2R 0RL, England

First American edition
Published in 2004 by Viking Penguin, a member of Penguin Group (USA) Inc.

10   9   8   7   6   5   4   3   2   1

ISBN 0-670-03328-6
CIP data available

This book is printed on acid-free paper. ∞

Printed in the United States of America

5/5/05

To my babies, Nora and Eoin

Nobody realizes that some people expend tremendous energy merely to be normal.

—Albert Camus

Special thanks to Steve Barnesberger, John Eby, Rich and Teri Frantz, Shawna Frolich, Melinda Iverson, Christian Lee, Richard Napora, Tracy Ouellette, Jim Tyler, and Judy Wesley

Lost Souls

1 It was past midnight when I got home Halloween night. The car lights swept across the yard. The house had been toilet papered. I got out and saw where the kids had burned the word "PIG" into my lawn with bleach. The air smelt chemical clean. I was used to all of it. As the law in this small dead-end Midwest town, I was a target of pranks, of kids' initiation ceremonies, of first acts of rebellion. It went with the territory, especially since my divorce. The kids knew that when my car was gone, the house was empty, except for my dog Max.

I could hear Max barking from his solitary confinement in the basement. I went down and let him up into the house.

It was a night when they say the dead walk among the living, and the evening had passed in a motley assortment of trick-or-treaters going door to door. I'd followed the ghoulish neighbor spectacle from my cop car, kids dressed as ghosts with shackles and chains, witches with warts, devils with forked tails, skeletons with scythes, sorcerers and wizards, monster brides, along with the usual superheroes: Superman, Spider-Man, Batman, The Incredible Hulk. I'd turned on my siren and lights from time to time, just to add to the phantasmagoria of the evening.

The crime of the night had been some kids tying a string of firecrackers to a cat's tail, that and a bogus incident with some loser kid reporting he'd found a razor blade in an apple.

Max was groggy, though he came and licked my hand. I'd given him a sedative, since he was a barker. I'd not wanted the kids harassing him while I was on duty. He growled a bit, like he was mad at me. I told him about the cat. The word "cat" made his ears point. Just hearing my voice made him pant. He looked to the window like there was a cat in the vicinity. It was good to get that kind of loyalty, even if it had to come from a dog. You hang on to whatever is thrown to you.

I opened the refrigerator. The kitchen filled with the smell of meat-loaf. I put ketchup on it, the way he liked it, and fed him.

I drank a glass of milk just to kill the time. I wasn't sleeping well. My reflection stared back at me in the window—like looking into an old memory.

I was two years on from a divorce that had blindsided me. My wife, Janine, had left with my son. I'd not learned to inhabit the silence of the house. I missed my kid is what it was. Holidays could do that. For some, they represented happiness; for others, regret.

Earlier that night, I'd seen my kid at the mall where the town held its official trick-or-treating. It was two years after the Tylenol murders in Chicago in '82, the case still unsolved. I'd set up a metal detector at the mall, to scan all the kids' candy. I was dressed as Obi-Wan Kenobi, and this kid dressed as ET came forward and emptied his stash of candy. I scanned his candy with my metal detector made up to look like a light-saber. The disguise was complete—that is, until I saw my kid's eyes staring through the eyeholes of his mask, and then I knew, but Eddy said nothing. He turned and looked back. He didn't know what to do, like he was going to get into trouble just speaking to me. It wasn't my day to be with him. He was more lost than that alien he was pretending to be, but I didn't blow his cover. He wasn't the problem.

As he walked away I simply said, "ET, phone home."

In the background, I saw my ex-wife with her new husband, Seth Hansen. They were dressed as ghouls, chained together, each carrying a ball and chain, pretty much how I saw them in real life.

The line for receiving Scare Packages snaked all the way back to the Food Court, our mayor, master of ceremonies, dressed as Gomez Addams, trying to bolster his personal profile in the community. His face shone with perspiration. I could smell his aftershave from fifty feet away—his signature smell, optimism overlaid with desperation, a tangy ripeness of someone having just finished running. He radiated heat when you got near him.

The mayor was in a struggle with the powers that be in the next town over, Elkhart, Ind.—the RV capital of the world—regarding a proposed rezoning ordinance that would put the mall under their municipal control, siphoning tax revenue away from us.

Knowing this might be the last year I would be working the mall added to my own sense of depression. There are times when you are a victim of circumstance, or that is how I rationalize my own personal decline.

That Halloween night would prove to be one of the longest of my entire life, a slur of exhaustive hours. All I got as a memento was a photo of Eddy receiving a prize from the mayor for his costume. Eddy was hidden by his mask, looking out at Janine. I hoped he was looking for me too, there amidst the onlookers.

We ended up having to keep the mall open past ten just to accommodate all the kids getting to shake hands with the mayor.

For my efforts at the mall that night all I found was one razor blade in an apple, and I knew it was a hoax because I knew the kid, Bobby James. He kept looking back into the crowd behind him. Bobby James's older brothers were losers. They'd put him up to it. I swear to God, I didn't want to be part of all that bullshit. My kid was roaming the mall. I was legally bound to keep away from him.

We ended up questioning Bobby James because I had to treat the hoax as something real. Arnold Fisher, a rent-a-cop at the mall who worked part-time for us, had to find out which houses the kid had trick-or-treated at. The kid got his photograph taken holding the apple and the blade.

That image was going to define Halloween for our community, one of those set pieces about our vanishing innocence. I always wondered how the most depraved tapped into our psyche, how they sensed the undercurrent of our lives, anticipating our decline.

I watched Max slobbering at his bowl. His black muzzle pushed the bowl across the floor, his dark pinkish tongue showing. On the table was a *National Enquirer* I'd picked up at the supermarket with a piece in it about a hot dog vendor in New York who'd taken the door off a microwave and, over the course of a few months, cooked his hand from the inside out.

It's how I might have described my marriage.

I yawned and my eyes teared. I put the backs of my hands to my eyes, smelt nicotine in my pores. I had quit smoking a few days prior, something I did from time to time, but with no real conviction. I went and got a carton I'd stashed away, pulled off the ribbon of golden plastic and broke yet another promise. I drew in that first breath the way people coming up for air in swimming pools do after they've held their breath too long. I felt the smoke burn my lungs. It was a satisfying feeling. There are worse ways to die. I know. I've seen them in my line of work.

I got up, feeling the nicotine ease the tension. I was ready for bed. I had a few days off, a long weekend planned at my hunting cabin. But while Max was out doing his business in the cold night air, I got the call about the missing little girl.

The dispatch operator, Lois Gains, said she figured it was just some mix-up, some kid who'd decided to stay at a friend's house, given it was Halloween.

I just listened to her talking.

"I hate to get you out like this, Lawrence, but you'll be back in bed before you know it." She was talking fast. "That kid is probably at someone's house at a sleepover. She just followed kids into a house, that's what happened."

But there was something not quite right in her voice.

I said, "How old is she?"

Lois hesitated. "Three."

"You think a three-year-old could slip into someone's sleepover unnoticed?"

Lois didn't answer immediately. "What with the costumes and masks they got these days, who can tell one kid from another?"

"Whose kid is it?"

"I don't know her . . . some single woman living over in one of those apartments in the old mansion houses on East Pine."

Somehow I knew right then that this wasn't just a kid missing from a sleepover.

I shivered against the night and opened my car door. Darkness was settled in by early afternoon now. Daylight savings had just robbed us of an hour of daylight.

Max barked in the house. He pissed on the floor when he was left alone, suffering from separation anxiety. I could hear him as I backed out of the driveway. I should have put him back into the basement, but I didn't. On a few occasions people had called about his barking, complaining about how he was treated. He had, in some ways, come out worst in the divorce, locked away in the basement during my shifts.

I didn't want to be out looking for a missing kid. I wanted a call from dispatch to tell me it had all been a mistake, but the call never came. In the retelling of things, sometimes I think that if I could get it told right I could change it, I could make it come out different.

I parked at the back of the town hall. The mayor was already there, still in his Gomez Addams costume from the party at the mall. He was drinking black coffee. I saw him through the glass in the chief's office, along with the chief, who was on the phone, and the chief's secretary, who had rollers in her hair, but she wasn't in costume. It made her all the more pathetic.

The mayor was talking out loud, and the chief's secretary was typing up what the mayor was saying. The local newspaper wanted a statement.

When I punched in, Lois told me that the child's mother was being interviewed at her apartment by Arnold Fisher, since he lived close by. Lois said, "The mother's drunk . . . I mean, really drunk."

In the stark light of the break room, which came to serve as a command post since it had the coffee vending machine, we came up with a rudimentary search plan. Some members of the volunteer fire department were already on hand.

Arnold Fisher showed halfway through the meeting and reported that the mother had been rushed to the county hospital after collapsing. He said there were amphetamines in her apartment, that she'd taken them along with the booze. As he talked, his coffee steamed under his chin. I could see his blue striped pajamas under his uniform.

From what he had patched together from the mother, we learned the kid had trick-or-treated with neighborhood kids and had been dropped back at eight-thirty. The mother said she put the kid to bed at just past nine o'clock, then she too fell asleep, admitting she'd been drinking throughout the evening. She didn't wake until she felt a draft of cold air. That was at a quarter to eleven. The door was wide open. She'd left it half-open because of trick-or-treaters and had forgotten to shut it.

Given it was just below freezing, we had to act quickly. The chief cordoned off areas on a map, and we left and began searching the night.

I passed through the old neighborhood lit by the grinning malevolence of pumpkins, the candles licked by the cold wind. I passed lawns laid out like graveyards, tombstones tilted and hands reaching out of the ground. Someone had tied a life-sized witch on a broom to a telephone pole, so it looked like the witch had crashed in midflight.

I shone my spotlight over the gardens, probing the sleeping quiet of 2:00 A.M. I saw the shifting silver of TVs left on, playing those old horror movies, taking insomniacs through the night.

From time to time the dispatch radio in the car hissed a report on the blocks that had been searched.

It went that way through the night, each block checked and accounted for, mapped back at the office, and still no sign of the missing child. I circled through my own street, came level with my house, shone the light on the menace of the word "PIG," on what kids could conjure as evil or malevolent.

They had, of course, no idea, not yet.

I needed an ally, someone to stave off the sadness I felt. Frost covered everything and the temperature had dipped below freezing.

Max was barking. He had heard my car. At least, I hoped it was the car, and that he hadn't been barking like that all night long.

After a night of searching, after hours of exhaustion and black coffee refills back at the station, when I was about to stop searching I let Max out, let him walk beside the car as I drove slowly. We were back on the actual street the child lived on, but up a few houses, when Max stopped in the street and made a whining sound, then barked at something in a pile of leaves at the side of the road.

I stopped the car, got out, and knelt down slowly by the side of the road, brushed the leaves aside to reveal the bent, feathered wire hangers of two broken wings. The yellowish halo of my flashlight lit up the face.

It was like discovering a sleeping angel left between the worlds of the living and dead.

And then I saw where the blood had clotted the leaves. When I touched the child she was already stiff. She'd been dead for hours.

Max sniffed and whined at my coat. He made that huff noise dogs make and settled. I got him back into the car and called for backup.

It was hard just forming the words, speaking to dispatch. The dispatch radio hissed. Lois was talking to me, but I didn't hear what she was saying.

I was looking at a small, sentinel fire hydrant painted like a minuteman.

I got out of the car again and, standing over the pile of leaves, looked back along the street, putting together in my head the terrible truth of what happened, of how this child had died, seeing the tire tracks where a car had come zigzag through the damp leaves.

2 Removing the body took time. The chief had requested help from the coroner's office and the accident investigation unit. It took until almost nine in the morning before the child was removed, but the ghost outline remained, sketched in chalk. I saw the curled pose of the child, like a creature that had set about hibernating, not the sprawled remains of something hit by a car.

I was put on makeshift coffee detail, setting up a table off to the side of the street with Dunkin' Donuts. One of the county's accident investigation experts came and took a cup of coffee.

I overheard him say to a reporter, "Death was instantaneous."

It was a simple consolation. The expert said, "Someone's at home right now, and they probably don't even know they killed a child." He turned and saw me listening, and so did the reporter.

"You found the child?" The reporter directed his question at me.

I nodded.

The reporter wanted my name and a quote on this tragedy.

I declined to comment, just gave the time I found the child.

The expert shook his head. I was culpable in all this—that is what he was intimating—for not keeping the chaos of the previous night in check. He said, "Kids get away with what the law lets them get away with," and the reporter scribbled that down.

The expert looked back up the road, and we followed his stare to the seasonal black and orange garbage bags filled with leaves, some split seam to seam from direct hits by cars, to the orange pulp of smashed pumpkins either thrown from cars or set out like decapitated heads, all there to lure and entice high school kids to run over them. This sort of revelry had become customary, what Halloween represented, the ghoulish haunted houses, the bonfires that lit up the county, a sanctioned madness, effigies of our own fears and superstitions going back to the dark ages of autumnal harvests and ritual offering.

But what adorned this death, this sacrifice, was a yellow police tape fluttering in the cold rain, flares hissing and smoking, giving everything a chemical whiteness that hurt to stare into. It looked like the set of a movie.

I got a call from Lois on my police radio. The school bus was at the top of the street. I was supposed to go to each house on the street and get the kids and take them up to the bus.

Lois said, "The mother's out of danger."

"Does she know the child is dead?"

There was a silence, then Lois whispered, "No."

I said, "How come the people who want to die can't?"

"You okay, Lawrence?"

"No."

I got out of the car again and stood in a cold fizzle of rain.

I went door to door. In some of the houses, I saw the street live on TV. It was weird looking from the TV to the street. I saw myself live on TV at one house. A guy with a camera was pointing it straight at me.

I got the small kids to hold hands, then led the juvenile chain gang up to the school bus. They were like little grubs in their heavy coats printed with their favorite TV characters: Mickey Mouse, Wonder Woman, Superman, carrying lunch boxes with Scooby Doo and My Little Pony painted in bright colors. A camera followed us along the street.

A young woman reporter said, "How do you kids feel?" and one kid said shyly, "I'm not supposed to talk to strangers," and that maybe spoke volumes for the sadness of what we had become.

The reporter said, "I'm not a stranger. This is TV." This other precocious kid said, "No comment," like some seasoned political hack, and that stopped the reporter dead in her tracks. I guess we knew the script. We had just been waiting for the right cue.

The yellow bus waited at the end of the street. I knew the driver, an amateur ventriloquist who always had his sidekick, Lord Marbles, sitting in his lap. Lord Marbles had his hands on the steering wheel. His head was cocked sideways, smiling, belying what had happened outside. The kids scrambled onto the bus and right off started telling him about what had happened.

Lord Marbles had one of those improbably happy faces, but the driver made the eyes register concern by moving them from side to side. Then he pulled the door handle, and the bus pulled away from the side of the road and disappeared down the next street.

There was an eerie silence in the murky corridors of the town hall. It was going on ten o'clock. The police station was an annex of the town hall, a double-wide trailer attached to the main building by a gangway that looked like a ramp for boarding a plane. The trailer was on wheels. We called it the mobile unit. We'd been on the ballot numerous times, petitioning for funds to build a permanent facility, but it was never approved. The force, if it could ever have been called a force, had been slashed in a budget cut and we piggybacked on the sheriff's department for assistance. We didn't even have a jail.

The chief met me at the door of his office. He said wearily, "Come in."

His pomade-combed hair was parted with a severe scar of psoriasis pinkness. He looked like he'd just been washed by a cat's coarse tongue, that characteristic ruddiness of the scrubbed infirm in nursing homes, a scrupulous cleanliness hiding some underlying disease. He looked his age that morning. He smelt of mothballs.

"Sit," he said quietly, and I did.

On the wall behind his desk he had mounted a huge prizewinning openmouthed pike. It was probably the biggest catch the chief had ever made, period, either on the end of a line or in the line of duty. Under the pike, engraved in a gold panel on the lacquered mahogany, were the words "Fish Fear Me."

The chief said, "I hate to ask you, but you think you might cancel your long weekend? We might need you for a day or so. We'll make it up to you, okay?"

"Sure."

"Look, give me a few minutes to wrap up something I got going on here. Get a coffee. I'll come get you in the break room." He walked me away from his office.

Lois was sitting in the break room, looking at the TV. A tendril of smoke was rising from the side of her head. She'd set aside a breakfast of eggs and toast.

The TV was on low, but I could hear screaming. A guy was jumping up and down and hugging Burt Reynolds, who'd helped him win it all on *The Twenty Thousand Dollar Pyramid*. Confetti was falling and the audience was going nuts.

I said, "I wish I could share in other people's happiness like that."

Lois looked at me. "You look like you've been run over by a truck." The metaphor suddenly registered, and Lois averted her eyes for a moment, stubbing her cigarette out in a foil ashtray.

I said simply, "That bad?"

Lois looked up. "Nothing a hot shower and a good home cooked meal can't take care of."

It was the sort of overture I would never have entertained at one point in my life, but I said, "Let's see how the morning plays itself out. I have to see the chief."

Lois started right onto another cigarette, lit it so her face shone against the bowl of her hand. She offered me one, and I lit up from the end of hers.

I sat across from her. The room was windowless. The vending machines shuddered from time to time.

I had nothing to say really. The major news affiliate a few towns over peppered the commercial breaks with a trailer on the Halloween tragedy. I saw myself in the background heading toward the school bus with the kids. It was like looking at a stranger.

When I took hold of my coffee cup, my hands were shaking. Lois looked at them and then looked away.

The news led with a report on the incident, describing it as a tragic sequence of events, how a door left open for trick-or-treaters had allowed the child to get out of her apartment. In the cold and dark, the child had probably become disoriented and just lain down amidst the leaves. In the mere telling, it seemed like a fable, a cautionary tale.

The expert I'd seen at the scene of the accident was working with plaster of Paris, taking a tire impression of the vehicle involved. The camera lingered on him, engrossed in a discussion with another expert. He was shaking his head like there was something wrong. When he saw they were being filmed, he turned away.

I looked at Lois for a moment. "Is something wrong there?" But before she could answer, the camera cut away and found the pile of leaves, then pulled back, putting into perspective the small chalk outline of the child's body against the background of the street, lined on either side with a canopy of skeletal trees, the big manicured lawns raked free of leaves, the pumpkin heads and ghoulish Halloween masks less scary in the daylight.

The voice-over was asking, rhetorically, who of us had not taken store of those memories of our fathers standing against the cold of a clear day raking leaves, who among us had not heard the crackle of leaves burning, who among us had not at one time lain down in a bed of leaves and remembered just how good it felt?

The camera cut back to the studio. The rest of the story focused on the condition of the mother, whose identity was being withheld, but who was described as unmarried and from out of state.

A reporter speaking live from the county hospital began her own synoptic prerecorded segment, recapping the night's events, following in line with what Lois had told me. The mother had been almost incoherent when she placed the missing person call to police just shortly after eleven o'clock. A blood alcohol level of 0.2 had been determined.

The report broke back live to a shot of the reporter nodding her head, taking her cue from the cameraman that they were live again. She was holding an earpiece to her ear and had a pad of paper in her other hand, making her reportage that much more immediate. She finished with the cliff-hanger that the mother was currently under a suicide watch.

A commercial for Rent-to-Own furniture and appliances came on.

———

Just speaking of what I'd seen brought a lump to my throat. I said, "The child never felt anything. That's something to be thankful for." I stopped and took a long hit from the cigarette. "You ever ask why things happen like this?"

Lois took up her cigarette. "I gave up wanting to understand this world a long time ago."

I said softly, "I'm glad you waited." I put my hand on hers for a moment, felt its warmth.

We shared this level of intimacy since we were both divorced, or that wasn't exactly right, Lois's husband had committed suicide. Our relationship hinged on a few nights of drinks and a pot roast, among other things that were best kept between us. What I told myself about her was simply that she got a foothold in my moment of need.

I started seeing her when I was going through my divorce. Her husband was dead by then. Lois gave me one of her husband's suits when I went to court. He and I wore the same size. He'd been a traveling salesman, and he'd dressed sharp when he was alive. In fact, he'd hung himself with one of his fancy ties in a motel downstate.

Somebody passed the door. I could hear voices outside the room. A guy who worked in the town hall came in and got a Coke and a Twinkie and left.

Lois bit her inner lip. She took her hand off mine. She looked right at me.

"What is it?"

She ran her hand through her hair, then took a long drag again, closed her eyes, and exhaled slowly.

"What?"

She opened her eyes. "A neighbor . . ." She cleared her throat. "Somebody saw a truck near where the kid died. He got a license number."

"And?"

"I ran it through DMV, and it came back registered to Kyle Johnson."

Kyle Johnson was the quarterback of our high school team. He was the closest thing we had had to a celebrity in the town for years. He'd taken us to nine and two for the season, with seven straight victories dating back to early September. Listed as one of the hottest quarterbacks in the nation, he'd taken us to the state play-offs for the first time in thirty-six years.

My breath felt shallow. "This neighbor, he saw the truck run over the kid?"

"All he got was a license number."

"Is that why the chief wants to see me? Is that what this meeting is about?"

Lois stubbed out her cigarette. "I don't know."

And then she kissed me on the side of the cheek, which was something she'd never done before in public. I think she did it to stop herself from crying.

3 The chief's secretary told me the chief wanted me to meet him up in the mayor's office. The office was on the third floor, down a long polished corridor in the town hall building.

The whole third floor ceiling was curved and painted in muted brown and green tones with a pioneer motif, men in Daniel Boone hats with axes making houses and canoes.

The curved ceiling amplified the acoustics of the space. I could hear the rapid-fire clicking of the mayor's secretary, Betty Webber, as she typed. When I entered the office, she just glanced up and told me to wait.

Through the frosted glass I could make out two figures.

Betty said, "You want coffee?"

The pot gurgled near the window. There was also a box of glazed donuts, along with condiments. I poured myself a cup and stood looking out the window. The day had changed, a quilted blue sky after the early morning gloom. It made the child's death that much sadder.

I could see down on to the parking lot. Max was still in the car. I knew I should have taken him home before coming to the station, but to what, to silence and isolation? It was again one of those moments that took me under, the strain of living alone. I brought the coffee to my lips. It tasted institutional, strong and bitter—what I needed.

Further along the riverbank sunlight glinted in the broken windows of the old warehouses, now abandoned.

I heard the low sound of voices coming from the mayor's office, aware too of Betty typing behind me. She was a friend of Lois's, a woman who knew more about me than I ever wanted anyone to know. She had organized the local Table of Eight, a marauding Saturday-night Methodist group that scavenged the area, armed with a Crock-Pot, self-righteousness, and a Scrabble board. After my divorce, I'd been assailed with casseroles, garlic bread, and marshmallow Jell-O molds, all left anonymously at my door. I never got to the bottom of it, but I'd always suspected her.

When I turned, I saw Betty looking at me, but she looked away.

These were the waters in which I swam during those years.

The mayor was standing up when I went in, dressed in his signature plaid blazer, the blazer he wore on the car lot he owned in town. His claim to fame was that he could put his whole fist into his mouth. That somehow qualified him for politics.

He smiled at me, but his face was the color of a guy having a heart attack.

The chief looked at me and said my name. He was sitting off to the side when I came in but then he got up, his trousers bunching at his crotch, his tube athletic socks pooling around his hairless shins.

A small portable TV was set on the mayor's desk. They were still broadcasting from the scene of the accident. The mayor came and put his hand on my shoulder. "God almighty, how you doing, Lawrence?"

His asking how I felt made me suppress the urge to yawn, and my eyes watered.

The mayor looked devastated. He turned and sat on the edge of his desk. "You catch any of this yet?"

"I watched it down in the break room."

The mayor let out a long breath. "Let me just say right off, you've done a hell of a job already. We're going to pay you overtime for your trouble." He stopped abruptly.

On the TV at that moment, they were showing the chalk outline of the child. I saw myself again in the shot.

The mayor shook his head, then turned down the volume. "Why do these things happen to us, Lawrence?" He said it in a searching way, as though I had the answers, but of course, I hadn't.

"You know, Lawrence, as mayor, as guardian of this town, I dread nights like last night. There is nothing to come out of such nights except pain and regret."

I didn't say anything.

"It can change the subtle balance of a town, is what it can do."

The chief filled the silence that settled. "I remember hearing about Pearl Harbor on the radio, how things just changed . . ." but the mayor put up his hand and said, "With all due respect, I think I heard that one before, Chief."

The chief's face turned red.

I was looking between them, knew where they were leading me.

The mayor had his head down, like he was at a service. "I don't know where to begin, Lawrence. Let me just say right now, I'm not one to call in favors. I don't keep track of things like that. Friendship . . . friendship isn't the kind of thing you tally up, it's not who did what for whom."

But of course it was.

The mayor was referring to the time he kept me out of jail back when I was getting divorced. I broke down my wife's door at the Motel 6 where she was staying and pulled a gun on her. My only defense had been that the gun wasn't loaded. In the days that followed, in my own despair and facing jail time, coming to terms with the fact that my life was finished, somehow the mayor had gotten the charges against me dropped. He'd had everything hushed up in some backroom deal. I got to keep my job with the department. I never dared ask why or how, as though asking could have undone everything.

So all I could say right then to the mayor was, "If I can help any way here." I left it open-ended.

The mayor took his cue. "I don't have to tell you, Lawrence, what this upcoming weekend means to all of us. We are on the verge of something mythic, a team from the Indiana cornfields that rises up and takes on the city teams. It's that age-old story, David versus Goliath. There are papers from Chicago, Indianapolis, and beyond, coming to cover this story . . ." The mayor's eyes got bigger. He was looking right at me with that same searching concern he used to win people over. It's why he was mayor, that theatrical flourish. It's why he owned the largest used car lot in town. He was a cliché in all ways, but sometimes those are the hardest people to say no to. All you could do in circumstances like that was let him talk.

"We are at the heart of an American dream right here . . ." His voice quivered, his hands became fists. "An American dream, where honesty and hard work are rewarded. We, *our town* here, are adrift in time, in a technological world that is getting crueler with each passing year, but look at us, at our wholesome integrity, at what honest living and faith can let you achieve. We live amidst the Amish, Lawrence! We have a direct bloodline to our founding fathers, to the *Mayflower*."

I could tell it was part of his spiel for the press, though I didn't know if the mayor had all his historical facts straight. I didn't think the Amish had come on the *Mayflower*, but I knew what he meant.

"I'll tell you, Lawrence, you know what it would mean if this game got us on the map, for tourist revenue, for long weekend getaways? I had a market research firm run some figures on the potential boon a major feature in a metropolitan paper can yield for a town like ours, and it's huge. There's been a demographic shift in people's vacationing habits, that's what they tell me anyway. People want more mini-vacations. People are not getting married so young. They want to date, to get away to know one another. They want to escape the bustle of the metropolis. And we can be that escape!"

I just stood there listening. The mayor was talking about the Amish community, not us. They drew the tourists. Our downtown was a wasteland of boarded-up brownstone factories, a museum of failure. The lifeline river that flowed through the town center had been eclipsed during the Eisenhower presidency by a highway that ran three miles to the north of us. That single event had marginalized the town, set us off the beaten track. Life had moved elsewhere, but I said nothing, though the mayor seemed to sense something in the way I was looking at him.

He took a drink of water from a glass jug, letting time hang. Then he started again. "So, you see how what happened last night, how that *tragedy* might put a pall on everything we have worked so hard to achieve?"

The chief chimed in. "A hit-and-run is something we can't have exposed."

The mayor turned in a flare of anger. "Goddamn it, who said anything about a hit-and-run? That's not what this is! Has anybody mentioned hit-and-run?"

The chief looked at the mayor, and the mayor lowered his voice. "I'm sorry . . . okay? Look, Chief, damage control is about semantics, how things are said and perceived."

The chief nodded, and the mayor kept talking. "It has been established that whoever ran this child over probably wasn't aware they even hit the child. I call that simply a *tragedy*. We don't want to connect this with a hit-and-run, because that is not what this is, but if that phrase gets out there, then it takes on a life of its own."

The chief said, "I see what you're saying." The chief was a kind of marginal figure who occupied the position of chief through some long-standing nepotism that went way back to his sister's alleged affair with a former governor of the state, or that is what I'd heard. He'd run uncontested for chief in the wake of the Studebaker factory closing in '63.

The mayor put his hand to the knot of his tie and loosened it. "Now where the hell was I?"

I had this weird feeling I was being played by both of them, that the mayor had demeaned the chief solely to get me on his side.

He looked right at me.

"I'm not trying to play down what happened here, God knows there's a child dead." The mayor hesitated a moment. "What I'm trying to figure out is what the hell did happen. That's what this meeting is about. That's why we called you in here, Lawrence, to try and piece it together. We want to hear about what you saw when you found the child. I'm trying to establish the facts before we do anything. They're reporting on TV preliminary findings that suggest the child was lying in the leaves, that the individual who ran over the child probably didn't even know they hit anything. Is that how it looked to you, like an accident?"

It was one of those leading questions that I knew I was obliged to answer. We were all waltzing around the inevitable, and slowly I told them what they wanted to hear, though I said, "I'm not an expert. I just found the child . . ." I was struggling to say the right thing. I said, "I didn't see skid marks . . . maybe the person never did know what they'd done." I stopped abruptly. "But I'm not an expert."

"There you have it, Mayor. Lawrence didn't see skid marks either!" The chief had ignored my disclaimer.

The mayor went and poured coffee and waited a few moments before turning. I knew he was staring at the chief, that they were checking their own mutual resolve.

"Okay, that's where we are right now, Lawrence. What we have to do is consider the tragedy here, not only for the woman and for the kid, but also for whoever ran the kid over."

I knew they were talking about Kyle Johnson. I said, "I understand."

The mayor looked worn, but he smiled. "You see that, Chief? Lawrence has innate political savvy. You don't teach this sort of intuition. You ever think of running for anything, Lawrence?"

"Running for . . . No. Running from! I've been running from my wife for two years!"

It was just the level of candid self-deprecation needed.

The mayor smiled, then lost the smile again and looked right at me. His voice was serious. "What I'm looking for is that gut feeling, Lawrence. Did it feel like something *tragic*?"

I looked at him, and swallowed. "She was just lying in the leaves, like she'd lain down to sleep." I had to stop talking for a moment, and the mayor seemed to intuit that, and just shook his head, and silence prevailed for longer than three people in a room would ordinarily allow.

When the mayor spoke again, he said, "We got a tip from a so-called witness who said he saw a truck weaving across the street, hitting bags of leaves. He called in to report it."

Again, silence. All I could do was stare at the mayor. He was now leading me to where he'd wanted to go from the beginning. He was shaking his head, dismissing what he was saying even as he was saying it. "This tip, this connection is tenuous . . . tenuous at best. But it was called in, so we have to follow up on it, right? I'm not beyond shirking my political and civic duty here, but what we have here is a simple case of disorderly conduct, some hell-raising kids out having fun, that's all, but it was called in—it's on record."

I waited, knowing what he was going to say next.

And so it
dealings of
I loo
Fish
in

"I'm not going to sugarcoat this, Law make through the DMV, and the truck n Johnson."

I shifted. "Kyle Johnson?"

The mayor lowered his voice. "Look, (play down what happened. We're not. B thing here is how even a mention of Ky mere person of interest in the investigati name is released, he becomes fodder for th media, that constant harassing, cameras in his face, all that stuff, when maybe Kyle didn't do anything. You see what I'm saying, the level of tact I think we need to exercise here? We need to establish the facts, first and foremost. The kid's got the biggest game of his life this weekend, and we owe him that, to investigate behind the scenes before releasing anything to the media. All we're doing here is short-circuiting a media that's way out of hand. It's not the truth they're after, just the sensationalism. They'd love to make us some sideline circus for the week, and then that's that. I think that's the real issue at hand—are we at the mercy of an insatiable media, or do we follow our own investigation and get to the heart of the matter?"

I didn't get to answer, because the mayor started talking again, his face severe. "This is *our* town, *our* lives. We've come through a hell of a lot over the years, the factory closings, jobs moving elsewhere, but now things are changing." He let the sentiment hang. It belied the reality that we were probably going to lose the mall, that we were in the last stages of our final decline, but of course I kept quiet.

"I got a good feeling about the future. We're on the upswing. I truly believe that. Things have a way of aligning themselves somehow. There are intangibles behind success."

The mayor pointed at the chief. "The chief here was thinking about retiring this year. What better send-off could he have than going out riding in the back of some convertible in a parade celebrating a state championship, grabbing onto something for posterity. Why not?"

The mayor came and put his hand on my shoulder. "You know this future includes you, Lawrence. I think I'm looking at the next chief here. I think you have the political savvy for a job like that. Everything in this town works together, or it doesn't work at all."

was that lives and careers were made in the backroom
small town politics.

ed at the chief. I knew that job had been earmarked for Arnold
r, the chief's nephew, who was enrolled in the local college study-
g criminology, but through everything the mayor was saying, the
chief was smiling. There were only so many good jobs left in a town like
this.

The mayor snapped his fingers. "Lawrence?"

I sat up in the chair.

"What we want is for you to go out to Kyle's house and examine his
truck and strike it off as a potential vehicle involved."

I felt my legs sweat. I knew right then Kyle had hit the child, but I
said, "Okay."

"Good. Go out there, say, around . . . what do you think, Chief?"

I looked again at the chief, wanting to gauge his reaction to the
mayor having practically offered me the job of chief, but he betrayed no
emotion, just said, "Around five o'clock should do it."

"Five o'clock then." The mayor cleared his throat and yawned.
"That's settled, thank God."

On the TV they showed the chalk outline of the body again.

The mayor said, "They're going to show that all day long, burn that
single moment into our hearts, stop time, and for what, for ratings?"

He had a way of subtly convincing you of things that weren't exactly
how he described them. I'd seen people come off his car lot with cars
they didn't want, people strapped with payments they were going to
struggle for years to pay off. But despite knowing I was just something
expedient to their cover-up, I felt noble somehow, like this was the only
decent thing to do.

I believed that, right then as I left, or maybe it was what I made
myself believe, because there was no turning back.

Sometimes we can be our own worst enemies.

4 Max was barking at something outside as I finished a grilled cheese sandwich. I got up and told him to hush, then washed my plate and cup, did those divorce things that only heighten the emptiness of the house. I was tired. I kept catching myself falling asleep, my head jerking back, seeing down a tunnel where everything sounded hollow.

The image of the child surfaced from time to time. I recalled a night years earlier with my ex-wife, when things were bad between us, coming home along a stretch of dark road. Amidst our shouting, we felt a dull thud of impact and a rumbling in the undercarriage. I remembered how it stopped us cold, how it made us wince and become quiet, how we held our breath. I got out of the car and, in the crimson bleed of the taillights, I saw this dark mass of possum writhing on the road. I took out my gun and shot until there was no movement. I recalled turning and seeing the interior light on in the car. Janine was leaning out the door, retching. She was six weeks pregnant at that stage with a child she ended up miscarrying.

I called Max in again, went upstairs, and set the alarm clock so I wouldn't oversleep. Tiredness hit me. I went under the covers and slept the afternoon away in one of those death sleeps where you wake up with a stiff neck from having not moved.

———

It was already getting dark outside when the radio alarm went off. I hit the snooze button. Max was lying beside me panting, waiting for me to open my eyes, and when I did, he wagged his tail and licked my face.

I felt I'd resurfaced from a nightmare. The alarm went off again with a static-filled version of "I'm on the Top of the World" by The Carpenters, a strange song, given Karen Carpenter eventually starved to death.

I went downstairs, set down the kettle, and turned on the radio in the kitchen to catch the weather report. The mercury was falling.

I didn't much feel like going out to Kyle Johnson's. The force of the mayor's persuasion had cooled, not that I didn't believe he was right in keeping this hushed up, but I didn't want to be involved. I had my own problems. I wanted to get away to the cabin for the weekend, to escape my life.

I thought of calling up the mayor, telling him I was emotionally involved. Somehow finding the child had unnerved me. It seemed a reasonable excuse. All I had to do was act unnerved, call the mayor up, and tell him I was seeing the child when I closed my eyes.

But I didn't call. I couldn't back out. Having been kept out of jail, I was indebted to him for the rest of my life. That one instance was coming back to haunt me. Despite what I thought, I had not escaped.

Standing alone in the kitchen, I knew my life was about to change, that there was nothing I could do against what I'd heard called Destiny, for lack of a better word. If this went wrong, the mayor and chief were going to deny any involvement. I'd become expendable, somebody to take the fall if necessary. I wasn't in the frame of mind to go out to the Johnsons', but sometimes there are no choices—that is the simple fact.

We do terrible things out of necessity, to survive.

I went out and put out a new salt lick for a family of deer that had been coming to me for the last few years. It was one of the things Janine and I used to do together with Eddy, stand at the window and watch the deer come at twilight. But it was too early yet in the evening for the deer to come.

The sun traveled low on the horizon, looking like it could snare on the bare skeletal trees across in the fields.

I must have been talking to myself, because Max barked like he thought I was talking to him.

I wanted to convince myself that this was fortune shining on me, that out of these most unlikely of circumstances I would eventually assume the chief's job when he retired later in the year. Right here was one of those defining opportunities that you either grasp or let pass you by. It was maybe the main difference between Janine and me. She looked for the silver lining in things. I could never do that. I thought it was a fundamental difference between the sexes. I was never good at admitting my own failings.

But right then, I wanted to see the silver lining. I wanted to think in those terms. With a raise, I could crawl back out of debt, get on a payment scheme, and turn things around. The chief drove a fancy car, had a biggish house, and had the latest fishing equipment that didn't come cheap, along with a boat and a real hunting lodge. I figured he might have been pulling in triple what I was making. Just thinking in those terms made me feel easier.

The furnace kicked on in the basement with a woof of combustion, and that sudden sound made me feel cold. I stayed outside for a few more minutes and watched Max digging a hole at the end of the garden, growling and digging the way dogs dig, with both paws, the hindquarters sticking in the air, tail wagging. He liked me watching. My mere presence made him happy. We all want someone watching over us, to know we are cared for.

The kettle whistled behind me. I went inside and had an instant cup of soup and half a leftover sandwich with coleslaw. I went through the mail, sorting out what needed to be paid and what was crap, wrote out a few bills.

Amidst the bills, I found the envelope from Janine's lawyer, a warning against my nonpayment of last month's child support—what I called Payroll. I had applied for a credit card but hadn't heard back yet. I was planning on getting a cash advance on the card to cover the child support payment, though I was falling further behind financially, paying interest but never servicing the debt on my credit cards.

I don't know how I ended up on that side of life. I really don't, but it had changed me—divorce, debt, lost love, my child. I felt like a fraud after the divorce, dressed in my uniform. I exchanged sunrises for sunsets, working the evening shift. It made me introspective, those long stretches of loneliness in my patrol car, periods of silent self-interrogation, lingering at the chasm of the subconscious, like there were answers there.

I checked out self-help books from the library, got the education I never pursued when I was younger, delved into books like *Stuck Between a Rock and a Prescription Drug*, and others on how to manage interpersonal relationships, pragmatic tracts like *Love Is Never Enough*, *Beyond Codependency*, *What to Say When You Talk to Yourself*, *How to Become Your Own Therapist*, *All Grown Up and Nowhere to Go*, and other books to find out what I did wrong in my marriage.

I read about the psychological stages of divorce, read the clinical details of what I could only describe best as wanting to stick my head down the toilet, but was described in these books as stages like Relinquishing Doubt, Refocusing Doubt, Restructuring Discomfort, Redefining Discovery, Recovering Understanding, and Releasing for Integration—which sounded like an animal program I'd once watched on TV about releasing wolves back into national parks. I believed for a time that I could be reformed. I read a book asking me, *How Much Joy Can You Stand?*

But in the end, all I ever came to understand was that I now knew the opposite of what love was. I think more people live on that side of life than like to admit it.

Just sitting there, I knew I was moving toward calling Lois, toward the tonal browns of her living room, circa fifties decor, and on to her bedroom, with its soft pinks and ruffled lace pillows, that a tug of longing was pulling me under. There was a night after my divorce, when it was cold, and she gave me her husband's pajamas to wear. That one act changed how I felt about myself.

Lois had been a doormat for every man in sight for a long time after her husband's death. She'd even dated the chief, which I found awkward, but in that single night I was with her, we shared something that made me understand who and what she was, that she would have still been married, if not for what her husband had done. I saw in her a willingness to go on. She was a survivor.

I looked up and noticed that the answering machine was blinking. I played the message. It was Eddy. He talked in a whisper. "I saw you on TV, Daddy. I was ET. I saw you at the mall . . . it was me."

There was noise in the background. I heard Janine's voice.

Eddy's voice got rushed. He said, "What's a tree's favorite drink, Daddy?" He waited a moment, then laughed. "Root beer." He went about explaining the joke the way kids did.

The second message was from Lois.

Her damn parrot, Petey, was squawking while she spoke. I could just feel a headache coming on right then. Petey hated me. Just the mention of my name set him rocking back and forth the way parrots do, in a sort of rolling motion, made him fluff up his feathers so he was twice his size.

Lois said, "You hush now, Petey. Mommy can have a *special* friend."

Petey was really Lois's husband's pet, something he took with him on the road when he was a salesman, what he called "an icebreaker." Petey was the sole witness to Lois's husband's suicide. He was perched on Lionel's shoulder when the cleaning lady came in to clean the room. Petey was the sole witness, but he wasn't talking, not about the suicide anyway.

Lois kept talking baby talk to the parrot. "You like Lawrence, Petey," and that caused a commotion, just the mention of my name. I heard Lois yelp. Petey was a biter.

"Damn it, Petey. No!" There was a ruffle of feathers, and then the machine beeped. She'd been cut off.

I pressed the next message. It was Lois again. "You think you can make it tonight? Let me know. I'll have to go out and get groceries if you're able to make it."

I called her and got no answer. I left a message, saying I'd come by at seven o'clock. I'd meant to say I wasn't coming.

I got out my spare uniform, wrapped in plastic from the cleaners. I was scared about what I was going out to do. My life had become a prison, but it was something I'd lived through, an almost imperceptible slide where I could fool myself more times than not that I could recover, that there was something and somebody out there for me. I'd come to live in a perpetual silence, out on my rounds and in the house, where only the tremor of my hands or knees betrayed a current of emotion deep within me.

As I buttoned my shirt, I felt that tremor of nervousness. It was hard doing up the shirt. Beyond the mere fact of helping cover up what Kyle had done, I was seeing again what I'd witnessed in the early hours of the morning. The image of that small child was going to stay with me a lifetime. I thought, why couldn't God have undone that single event? Why was a three-year-old child put on earth to die so young?

But the child was now laid out in the morgue on a cold, stainless steel table, the autopsy already underway, her body cut and probed while I'd been sleeping. I shivered at that thought.

I got Max back into the house, dished out his food, and listened to the sound of my kid's voice again. I had to throw Max's rubber toy bone into the living room to get him away from the door. How many times can a dog be fooled?

The ribbons of toilet paper from the previous night were sodden. The word "PIG" was more distinct, the grass bleached the color of straw.

5 The Johnsons lived on the outskirts of town. They had inherited their farm, but I say inherited like you might say you inherited a gene for cancer. It was a great burden, something that could never even be sold. They survived on the nostalgia of people who bought their roadside produce.

I listened to the radio news on the way out to the Johnsons'. The coverage was more subdued than the TV's, no hint of sensationalism, but it seemed sadder somehow to hear a voice giving a simple account of how the child died.

The report ended with a statement from the chief asking anybody who had driven on the street between ten and twelve o'clock to come forward to help in the investigation.

I thought that was how it should have been handled.

I pulled into the Johnsons' long driveway, felt my wheels catch in the tire tracks. It was raining hard. Night had settled. I arrived into a bleak yard at the end of the driveway, my headlights washing over the dark. Three dogs materialized and started barking wildly. A sea of chickens swept across the beams of my headlights.

In the darkness the barn door opened, and in the sudden brilliance there stood what looked like a space alien in a mask holding a blue finger of flame. The barn glowed.

Earl tempered the flame. I knew him years ago in high school, but not on a first-name basis. He'd been a big-time football player, known as Earl the Pearl, but things never worked out for him. He was just shy of being something great, which was one of the worst situations ever to be in. Now he had a reputation for hard drinking.

He tipped the welding mask back on his head. I got out, despite the dogs, and went to him.

He left me to speak first. "How're you doing, Mr. Johnson?" It was the voice I used when I pulled people over, the formal authoritative voice of the law.

"Hanging in there, I guess." His breath smelt of alcohol. I thought he looked past me to the house. I turned and saw a shadow in one of the upper-floor windows. Then the curtain was drawn closed.

When I turned again, Earl said in this stilted voice, "What brings you out here on a night like this, Officer?" He said it like a guy who needed to take acting lessons.

"Oh, just following up on a few things. I was wondering if I could speak with Kyle?"

"Kyle's in doing his homework." He didn't seem like he wanted us to go over to the house. Instead he turned his head toward the truck, like I should check it out, like that was what had been arranged, so I played along with the charade.

I said, "You know, before I speak to Kyle, you mind if I take a look at the truck he drives?"

Earl answered in that same stilted voice. "What's this all about?"

"Oh, just following up on something, Mr. Johnson. Nothing you've got to be concerned with."

I saw where Earl had been welding the links of heavy chain for his thresher. It had nothing to do with him working on the truck. I spent maybe five minutes looking over the truck. The lug nuts were clean. They'd been taken off and put on again. The tires had been switched. I checked along the bumper and undercarriage for some mark, for any sign of blood or clothing. The undercarriage had been washed down, all traces erased, but I knew the child had died under this truck. I shivered and closed my eyes, felt light-headed.

When I stood up, Earl was standing over me, holding the welder's arc. I could see the blue flame in his eyes. "That it, then?"

"Just about. I need a statement from Kyle."

The rain fell in long silvery needles, lit up by the barn light.

Earl started walking across the yard. One of the dogs came out from behind some machinery and growled.

Earl swung his leg and hit the dog in its midsection, sending it away yelping.

Inside, the house was a dark hovel of connecting rooms.

"Take off your boots."

It smelt of hay on the porch, a fermenting, acrid odor. I heard the scratch of something and saw a set of hutches filled with rabbits.

"You want one? They make good eating."

I didn't answer him. I followed him along a dimly lit corridor into what turned out to be the kitchen, a big open space with a wood fire burning strong. It was like the set of *Little House on the Prairie*.

Kyle was sitting at the table with a math book open and a sheet of graph paper. There were two other kids with him, a girl about fourteen and a boy about seven, also working with pen and paper. The two younger kids looked up at me, as did Kyle's mother, Helen.

Kyle was tapping his teeth with a pencil, pretending he didn't know what this was all about. He had his head down.

Helen said, "To what do we owe this pleasure?"

It was something people didn't say in these parts. And right then I remembered she worked as a cleaning lady at the Motel 6 where Janine stayed in the first days after she left me. It was just another of those awkward coincidences.

"I was wanting to have a few words with Kyle is all, ma'am."

"Is Kyle in some kind of trouble?"

"No . . . No he's not, ma'am."

Kyle reset his feet. He was big like his father, but leaner. He looked up from his homework. That's when I saw how the right side of his face was swollen, the eye a web of broken red veins.

Earl saw me looking. "He got hit good at practice today."

Kyle gave a pat response. "You should have seen the other guy." When he tried to smile, his eye watered. I could tell it was Earl who'd hit him. Earl was fighting his own demons. His son's success only highlighted his own failings. Their personal battles were legendary in the area. Kyle's freshman year, Earl had beaten Kyle in the parking lot after he'd thrown an interception.

I felt sorry for Kyle, just looking at him sitting at the table, poring over his homework. He looked dumb, like school wasn't his strong suit. I'd watched and admired him over the last two years, watching his development as quarterback. I'd taken Eddy to some of the home games. I'd cheered Kyle Johnson until my voice had gone hoarse, but nothing in the house, in that kitchen, hinted at this kid's potential, that one day he'd be signing some contract with an NFL team, that a kid like him might be making over a million bucks a year. Sitting there, he was just one of those improbably good-looking kids that come out of the dung heaps of towns like ours, one of those kids usually destined for a quick marriage, a rash of kids, and a precipitous decline in his mid-thirties.

Helen turned to the stove. "Maybe you'd like to take some coffee? I just put a pot down."

"Fine."

She was relatively young to have a kid going on eighteen. She still had the same shape from high school except for a slight spread of her hips, a few lines around her eyes. But she had turned severe in spirit. She'd gotten religion is how some would have described it—found Jesus Christ. I could see a needlepoint prayer of thanksgiving above the stove. There were no school colors, no trophies anywhere in sight. I guess Helen had seen Earl miss out on everything, and it made Kyle's rise all the more precarious. You only had to look at Earl to see what lay on the downside of success. I think even the young kids understood that. It was in the air.

Helen said, "Why don't you go on into the parlor, Kyle, and I'll bring the coffee presently." She was talking like it was the nineteenth century.

Earl stared hard at Kyle. It seemed like he was going to follow us, but I said, "I'd like to speak to Kyle alone."

I heard Helen say sharply to her two other kids, "You mind your business now, you hear?" I heard a slapping sound, and the girl let out a cry.

It took only a few moments for me to be certain that Kyle Johnson knew he'd run over the kid. He told me that right off. I didn't ask him. He wiped his nose with the back of his hand and cleared his throat.

Despite his popularity, he was civil and respectful. He wasn't your standard jock. Fame had been foisted on him and he hadn't let it go to his head. Maybe he was too full of that fearful religion of his mother. I figured there'd been an almighty fight before I got there. But of course Earl had prevailed.

It was hard talking to Kyle without alluding to the notion of a cover-up. I said, "This is all off the record. I respect you for not running from the truth, for your honesty." I was stumbling for words. "Listen, I just stopped by to make sure you are okay, you hear me?" I tried some cheap attempt at a religious undertone. "This is between you and God, Kyle."

Kyle stood against a window. It rattled in the wind. It was pitch dark outside. I couldn't see his face.

Kyle didn't turn to me, but he said quietly, "There were others in the truck."

I felt myself flinch. It took a moment to recover. I said in a flat tone, "Who?"

"My girlfriend . . . Bobby Hallard was there, too, and his girlfriend." He turned toward me for the first time. "We were doing nothing but having some fun, not drunk or anything . . ." He looked at the door and his voice lowered. "She don't know I drink."

He stopped.

I closed the distance between us. "What happened, Kyle?"

"It was just fun is all it was . . . We were zigzagging into bags of leaves. Bobby kept telling me to go faster, and I did . . . then I felt this rumbling of a sudden. I thought maybe it was a rake or something."

"You stopped?"

Kyle shook his head.

"So how do you know you ran the kid over?"

His voice grew quieter. "After I dropped off Bobby and his girlfriend, I went back." I heard Kyle's foot scrape the floor. "Cheryl was with me." He reached into his pocket and took out a key ring. "I have this penlight key ring." He shone it at me. A small, narrow beam of light lit my face. "It was like a dream. She was just lying there . . ."

I was seeing globs of yellow floating before me. "Did you check to see if the child was alive?"

He closed his eyes. "She was dead."

All I could think of right then was that Cheryl Carpenter knew everything. I was shaking my head. Did the mayor know this already? He couldn't have, could he? I wanted to call him, but while everything was going through my head, Kyle whispered, "This all happened because of what Cheryl and I were going to do, us sinning like we did."

"Sinning . . . sinning how?"

"Fornicating." Kyle came closer to me, his size disconcerting. He touched me with one of his huge hands. I felt myself tense. "There is no escaping the wages of sin, is what my mother says."

Just hearing him say something as absurd as that, to use the words "fornicating" and "wages of sin," made it seem all the more unreal. "Are you telling me your girlfriend is pregnant?"

Kyle looked toward the kitchen door. I could see the shadow of feet under the kitchen door. "That's how come I ran over the child . . . being with Cheryl, letting her make me sin like we did. That's what my mother says is how the child got put out in the road before me."

I raised my voice. "Listen to me, Kyle, that's got nothing to do with anything. It doesn't." I could see the darkness under his eye where he had been hit.

Kyle lowered his head. "I don't know."

Through the dead silence, through my own inaction, Kyle said nothing, stood still and kept looking at the kitchen door.

I could see feet under the door. They were waiting.

Kyle took a step closer to me. His breath was hot. "Cheryl don't want this baby." His hand squeezed my arm. "That's how come this all happened, what we were going to do to our baby."

I could see the look of fear in his eyes, that Old Testament religion, the religion of a vengeful God, the religion of an eye for an eye.

"Listen to me, Kyle. That woman whose child died left her door open, the child just got out of the apartment. You did nothing wrong. It was an accident. It had nothing to do with what you and Cheryl did, nothing."

Kyle looked at me. "How come it happened now?"

"I don't know."

Kyle was still holding my arm. "I want that woman to know I'm sorry. That's all I want. Say I'm sorry. It was an accident. I swear it."

I said, "You can't . . . you can't just come forward. You'd have to admit you went back to the scene of the accident. Are you going to admit that you left the scene of a crime?"

"I didn't see anything. It was just a feeling. I wasn't hiding. I went back."

"And then you drove away again . . ."

"I was scared."

"It won't work, Kyle. You saw that child when you ran her over, didn't you? You had to have."

"No, I didn't."

"But you got rid of your friends before going back. Any lawyer is going to press you on why you didn't stop the truck when you ran the child over. You saw her before you hit her. That's the only logical explanation. You must have, for just a split second."

Kyle put his hand to his head. "I don't know . . . No! I . . . I swear I . . . I don't know."

"That's just the point, you don't know. Something like that can happen in a split second. You don't know. I believe you, but all a lawyer needs is a seed of doubt, and he will tear your story apart."

I could see Kyle coming to terms with what I was saying. Had he seen the shape of the child, some fleeting image just as he ran over her?

He met the stare of my eyes, then looked away.

I said, "Kyle, listen to me. You have the potential to do some great things, you know that?" I had to say his name again to get him to look at me.

"You remember that story of Babe Ruth hitting a home run for a kid who was dying in the hospital, how Babe could just put his mind to doing things like that, not for the glory of himself, but for the solace it brought to others?"

Kyle looked at me, but didn't say anything.

"You can do the same thing, Kyle."

"How?"

"By making something of yourself in football. When you get rich

and famous, you give back something to women who have no husbands, to women who get holed up in poverty and despair. You do
something with your money to make their lives better."

It was how you had to appeal to a kid like him, that patent coaching
technique, leading him toward some life lesson.

Kyle's right eye moistened. "You think that would make up for
everything?" He squeezed my arm again.

" 'Let the right hand know not what the left hand does,' isn't that
what it says in the Bible? You can make up for what happened. Religion
is about forgiveness and redemption. It's about acts of kindness and
charity," and as I was still talking, Kyle's eyes widened. "I'm going to do
that, just what you said. I *can* make a difference."

I sensed his inner drive for a split moment. This was a kid who
responded to pep talks. I felt the way the mayor must have felt when he
got rolling, when he was selling something.

"Use your gift for the Lord. Make anonymous donations when you
get famous. Bring joy and hope to people, and let them never know
where all those riches came from. That can be your destiny. Take this as
a sign that you will commit your life to works of kindness. Remember,
this is between you and God now."

We waited a few moments before calling in Earl and Helen.

Earl stayed at the door's edge, a massive shadow. Helen came in, crying
softly. "Kyle was brought up good and proper. I want you to know that.
He was led astray." She went and stood by Kyle. I guessed that she had
vilified Cheryl Carpenter before I arrived. It was how she was going to
let herself participate in the cover-up. Her son wasn't to blame; Cheryl
was at the heart of what had happened.

And so it went. Each of us found our own way to steer Kyle away
from coming forward and admitting what had happened. We told ourselves there was so much at stake. Kyle Johnson didn't understand the
ways of the world, how you get one chance at greatness, then it recedes.
His moment was at hand.

But of course those were our rationales, not Kyle's, and he would
have to face the consequences of what we decided that night. There was
no going back, that much was clear from then on.

As I was leaving, I said, "I don't think there is anybody to blame here. Accidents . . . things like this can just happen," and though Helen nodded, her convictions didn't let her believe that life was not controlled by a higher authority, didn't let her believe that her God was not a vengeful God.

She said severely, "We reconcile with the Maker. We do his bidding as we are called to."

I didn't know what bidding she meant. I was to find out only when it was too late—the wrath the righteous can bring to bear on the damned.

I left with a Johnson rabbit, despite my protests. It was there in a wooden box, beside me on the passenger seat, sniffing through airholes as I pulled off to the side of the road and got out. I tipped the box up and the rabbit moved tentatively, scratching the sides of the box before hopping out. But it didn't move away. It stayed close, nosing the side of the road. It was raining hard, and the rabbit seemed like it hadn't made up its mind whether freedom was the thing it wanted most, whether what lay in the blackish fields of rotting cornstalks wasn't worse than captivity.

6 The euphoria of having spoken to Kyle passed, and I felt tired. I began to doubt that I had really convinced him of anything. Even if I'd gotten through to Kyle, I didn't know what guilt was worming inside Cheryl Carpenter. I had a bad feeling about all of it. I read somewhere that two could keep a secret only if one was dead.

I was still in my uniform when I stopped at a bar called The Five Corners. I put on my heavy winter coat to look less conspicuous. The bar was subdued, done in dark paneled wood. It looked like somebody's recreation room. It was nearly deserted. I ordered a beer and sat alone, drumming my fingers on the counter, staring at the back-lit amber beer signs on the wall. I checked my watch.

I wanted to call the chief, see if he knew about the other passengers in the truck. I was going to leave it open-ended, let him decide. Things were not how we had anticipated. I would let him make the call to the mayor. I didn't exactly feel comfortable undercutting the chief, taking that job he'd set aside for his nephew. I wanted to at least talk to him, get a sense of how he felt now that we were both away from the mayor. All I had to say was that there were witnesses, Cheryl at the least, and that gave us all an out. I thought if I got that said to the chief, he would call the mayor and set about undoing the agreement to cover up the accident. It was in the chief's best interest for him to call the mayor, and it got me off the hook of backing out on my word.

But for some reason, I didn't call the chief. I focused on that feeling of what it would be like to be chief, to have a pay raise, to get on the other side of debt. I downed the beer and ordered a shot, then followed it with another shot.

On the way home, I took a detour and passed my wife's house, something I shouldn't have done, but I needed a distraction. Her place was a three-story, flat-faced white house set in from the road. It had a certain fundamentalist aesthetic, the windows exaggeratedly big, with no curtains. Inside the lights were on. It looked like some stage backdrop. It was hard imagining her living there with my son.

Seth Hansen, my wife's new husband, was a Christian zealot who sold life insurance and worked with the Amish community, selling their handmade furniture through a catalog company, since the Amish community hated the modern world but somehow wanted the modern world's money. Seth also drove their communal minibus. Although the Amish had no qualms traveling in modern transportation, they didn't want to actually drive it. It was something to see them in their minibus, like a shipment of scarecrows.

I never fully got my head around Seth, how Janine picked him, although I know it was money in the end. It had to be.

Seth walked with a limp and had a slight belly, but he was a sharp dresser. He wore leisure suits from the mid-seventies, hopelessly outdated, and black shiny boots. He wasn't the kind of guy that you could just kick his ass. There was no point of comparison, no point for envy or male bravado and posturing when I finally met him at the initial divorce hearings. He showed up wearing one of those string ties Colonel Sanders made famous. The guy looked like somebody's affable aging uncle, but he was a self-made man, a guy who started a crop-dusting business, made his fortune spraying pesticides over farms. He was fifty-three years old, fifteen years older than I was.

I guess it was just one of those incongruities that was never going to sit with me, seeing Janine with Seth. We had lived through the sexual revolution, imitated the positions in *The Joy of Sex*, sought out erogenous zones and G-spots, sought out those things we thought would truly take us to another level. She had wanted all this, the groans of longing, gyrating into me, a deep physical, exhausting sex, and this is how we ended, me almost a goddamn celibate and Janine retreating to this twilight existence, half in the nineteenth century and half in the twentieth.

But our kid was a child of the latter part of the twentieth century— a child of therapy, in counseling for bed-wetting, dyslexia, and being hyperactive.

I was just short of being drunk enough to pay them a visit, to rescue my kid from his so-called inferiority complex.

When I got to my house, I called Lois and said, "Sorry."

Lois made a huffing noise. "Don't worry. I gave up on men a long time ago. So what do you want?"

"I couldn't get away." I felt like I was living an anti-soap opera, if there was such a thing.

"Where is this place where they don't have phones?"

In the background, Petey let out this shriek. I heard the rattle of his cage. Lois said sharply, "Don't rip that, Petey, just don't! Petey's a bad boy." I heard another screech, then the rattle of his cage.

I knew Lois was putting a drape over his cage, to create night for him. Life was one perpetual day for Petey, since his internal clock was solely directed by light. Lois had told me that. There were no sunrises and sunsets, no nuances in his life of captivity.

I heard Lois singing a Cole Porter number her husband liked to play, something he'd taught part of to Petey. Lois sang the refrain: "You could have a great career, and you should. Only one thing stops you, dear, you're too good."

Petey sang, "You're too good."

When Lois got Petey quiet, she said, "You still there?"

I wanted to lose myself in that moment.

"That song gives me the creeps." I made a shuddering noise. I still felt drunk. "You know, sometimes I wonder what the hell it was like for

Petey, for a species from the tropics to end up in the middle of America presiding over . . ."

"Over a suicide in some motel room?"

I breathed down the line. "I'm sorry . . . I shouldn't have said that."

Lois's voice was clipped. "What's done is done."

"Is it? Look, I'm glad I know you, Lois, I just want to tell you that. You are a better person than my wife. I mean that."

"This sounds like bad phone sex. Is that what this is? I guess you want a rain check on tonight, right?"

"Don't take it personally."

"Is there another way to take it?"

The edge from my earlier drinking had begun to wear off, so I got out my bourbon and took the drink and the bottle into the shower with me, which is something I'd not done in a great while. I had the phone cord extended so it was there in the bathroom in case the chief called to see how things had gone.

I stayed in the shower too long, until my fingertips withered. The hot water mixed with my drink. The ice cubes cracked. I was having trouble just standing up.

I looked at the phone and tried to will it to ring, but of course it didn't.

I got out of the shower and went and sat in the kitchen. Max came and licked my feet, his tongue coarse against my skin.

I turned on the local AM radio station for the sake of noise.

They were speaking about Kyle Johnson, speaking about the game Friday night. There was optimism in every caller's voice. The show was coming live from a local bar. And it suddenly struck me that, in all the confusion of the accident, I'd interviewed Kyle the night before the biggest game of his life. No wonder he was scared, heading into a game like that with the death of a child on his conscience.

I thought his wanting to make an attempt to confess could have been his way of clearing his conscience, a way of allowing him to play this game.

That was it.

That night I dreamt of the child again, a small angel sleeping amidst the leaves. I saw Kyle Johnson coming straight at me in his truck. I shouted for him to stop, until it was almost too late. I ran into the road and fell over the child, curled around her. I felt the sudden, dull impact of his truck and let out a scream, but it was only Max jumping up onto the bed.

7 I waited for the mayor in his outer office. A contagion of activity filled the hallways. The quarterfinal was that night. Betty was dressed in a nightmarish combination of poodle skirt and saddle shoes with ankle socks.

She looked at me and said, "How you feeling, Lawrence?"

I just shrugged my shoulders. "Okay," and waited out the stalemate.

The mayor came out of his office dressed in a letterman sweater, something kids wore to ice-cream parlors in the fifties.

It just floored me.

A young reporter in from out of town for the game was getting briefed by the mayor, who was telling him how our St. Joseph River flowed in the opposite direction to most rivers, its mouth to the north, emptying into Lake Michigan. "There's a metaphor there somewhere."

The mayor put his hand on the reporter's shoulder and winked, but when he saw me, his face broke into a broader smile. "Lawrence, well, this is a pleasure." He cut me off before I could say anything. "We've been waiting for this day all our lives, right?"

I said, "This is our defining moment." I didn't know what the hell I even meant, but it was the kind of thing politicians said.

"Quote him on that. 'This is our defining moment!' I like that . . . Phil, let me introduce you to the shining star in law enforcement in this town."

The reporter said, "How do you spell your name?" and in that brief moment, the mayor slipped past me, saying to Betty, "I'll be out at the high school if anybody needs me."

I followed him down the hallway. I said, "There were three other people in the truck with Kyle."

A guy from Titles and Deeds came out of his office wearing a soda jerk white shirt and bow tie, along with distinctive black-rimmed glasses. We waited until he walked down the hall out of earshot, then the mayor put his arm around me and whispered, "This is destiny pulling us forward. Do you feel it, Lawrence? Are you willing to ride the coattails of destiny? Are you?"

Before I could answer, he left me flat-footed and was gone.

In the mayor's absence, the chief materialized on the stairs, holding one of those enormous foam hands with the pointing index finger that said, "We're No. 1."

The chief looked up just long enough to make eye contact. "You got that report filed yet?"

I said, "I'm working on it."

I passed Lois's office. She was on the phone. She too had morphed into an aging soda pop debutante, wearing a Peter Pan collar with a string of fake pearls. Her hair was pulled back in a ponytail. She saw me but didn't say anything, turned away and kept talking.

It wasn't until the late afternoon that I had the report written. The building was near deserted. Lois hadn't come to see me. I called her extension, but she didn't pick up. I stopped by the dispatch office, and could tell she was gone for the weekend. Her coffee cup had been washed and turned upside down on a napkin. I saw a light on her phone flashing which I knew meant she'd forwarded emergency service requests to the county. There was no money in the budget for extra staff. I just stood there for a few moments, smelt the pine odor of pencils recently pared.

I went into the long corridor of the main hallway, then climbed the spiral stairs of carved wood back into the domed ceiling of the upper floor. I stood for a while looking at the region's geological history painted on the ceiling slats, saw how the lobes of the Great Lakes had formed against the retreat of glaciers over thousands of years.

There were other images of human settlement, the early life of first settlers, fur trappers beside fires. Another image showed a Potawatomi Indian in fur garb receiving communion from a French missionary in a small wood chapel. On a stylized scroll was a simple declaration of what we had done to the native population, something called "Red Man's Rebuke":

> Alas for us; our day is over,
> Our fires are out from shore to shore;
> No more for us the wild deer bounds,
> The plough is on our hunting ground.

There was nobody about on the third floor.

I stood at Betty's desk, watched the bubble glass of the mayor's office distorting the daylight outside. Sound filtered up from below.

A car honked, somebody laughed, the tail end of the Great Exodus for the game that evening.

The old squat radiators hissed, giving off a dry, delirious, incubating heat.

On Betty's desk sat a typewriter and a Dictaphone with a pedal mechanism, along with a box of Kleenex and an absurdly large family-size tube of hand lotion. I don't know why I felt compelled to do it, but I checked her wastebasket, saw the wads of Kleenex, saw so many unrequited, puckered lipstick kisses. And suddenly I wondered if she too knew what was unfolding, if the mayor had any secrets from her?

I still hadn't filed my report. There was time to back out, to change my account of my interview with Kyle. But of course there was no turning back.

I went back down the stairs and on through the gangway of the annex trailer to our offices. The flooring had a sort of spring to it, like gravity had just lessened its hold on things. I called that feeling moonwalking.

The chief was long gone. I opened his door and went in, leaving the door ajar. My heart felt like it was beating fast. I was forestalling the inevitable. I had the report in my hand. On his desk was a placard with his name engraved—Harlan Wright. He'd set it out during the coming and going of reporters covering the game.

I'd almost forgotten his name. He was always just Chief, though now standing there, I recalled the mayor telling me a story of how the chief had been a shop foreman at the Studebaker car plant before it ceased operations in '63, and how he'd run for chief a year later on a simple platform, "Harlan Wright, The *Right* Man for the Job." Politics could be that trivial. You could win on something like on a pun.

Over drinks the evening I was hired, almost a decade previous, I ate my one and only meal with the mayor and chief at the Elks' Club, and I learned all I was ever to really know about Harlan Wright. He was forty-three years old when the plant closed, cut loose of gainful employment at "a point of no return." He looked at me across the table and said, "You go on, but it's not the same." It was the closest I ever saw him to being human.

I remembered him pointing at me with one of those sesame bread sticks in its own individual wrapper and the way he stopped abruptly, shook his head, and said, "We should never have abandoned the gold standard. How the hell do you measure the value of something against nothing, tell me?"

Of course, I couldn't. And then I remembered him turning melancholy, and beginning to talk real loud. He felt we were being ruined by "niggers, communists, and Japs," in that order.

I never heard him talk like that again in the decade I worked with him, but I guess those were his true feelings deep down. His life had been upended when everything went bust.

I took a deep breath, shook my head, and set the report on the chief's desk. The report stated there was no physical evidence on the truck of a hit-and-run, and that furthermore, upon questioning, Kyle Johnson had made a statement to the effect that he'd seen and heard nothing that night. I'd noted that his demeanor during questioning further established his credibility. He was shocked, but forthright, answering all questions. There'd been no sense of hesitation in his voice.

I'd ended the report with the line, "This is a Dead Lead."

———

The game was held at a nearby college, since they had stadium lights and had the capacity to accommodate the masses that would be descending. I didn't have to patrol the game. The college had its own college security, and I had no jurisdiction on campus.

I knew I should go, but I was afraid of what might happen if Kyle didn't win. He wasn't just facing the image of that child he killed. He was facing the vengeance of Earl. Their fates were inextricably bound together, and I could see that the further Kyle advanced, the more Earl was going to despise him. It wasn't just about this game, it was going to be that way through the play-offs, and then on into his college career and the pros. But for right now, all that mattered was each game that was going to take us to the state championship final.

I had an image of Kyle losing it late in the game, surfacing into the absurdity of his own life, just freezing on some play. I could imagine him taking a hit hard, going down and not coming up for a long time, curled up there like that child he'd killed.

I thought about going back and getting the report off the chief's desk, to wait it out and see what happened in the game. In a way, I was hoping he'd lose. It would give me an out. Kyle could come forward in the anticlimax of defeat. The story of his involvement in the accident would have lost its sensationalism. The run at the championship would be over.

I went home, fed Max, and locked him in the basement again. I turned to go, but he whimpered and scratched the door. I let him up and took him with me, and just the excitement in his bark made me smile.

I ended up going out by the local college where the game was being held and walked Max through the throng of people tailgating, music blaring from muscle cars, everyone milling about in that huge college parking lot, the kegs pouring cheap foamy beer for a line of impatient guys in hunting coats holding plastic cups. The women were drinking schnapps and coffee to fight the cold, working makeshift grills, roasting burgers and bratwursts, laying out brownies and Rice Krispies treats on picnic tables.

Our town's greatest claim to fame up till then had been that we were one of the most stereotypical communities in America, an overweight white population of snack lovers, a test market area for major food companies. We were the collective subconscious. Each day, we shaped what our fellow Americans would find on their shelves, deciding at some time in the past, unbeknownst to ourselves, the validity of both creamy peanut butter and chunky peanut butter, for both sausage patties and links, for high-fiber cereals and low-calorie sweeteners, for nondairy creamers. We were the first to try the McRib sandwich and Filet o' Fish.

I stopped at a booth where a guy dressed as a potato chip was giving away one hundred percent fat-free potato chips. They were being test-marketed. It was the holy grail of the snack industry—the taste without the consequences, the sin without the guilt. Another guy dressed as a potato with a name tag, "Chip," was explaining how it all worked, how the fat was indigestible and passed right through the intestines.

It sounded like a hell of a snack.

The local volunteer firefighters were hosting their traditional pig roast and rib barbecue. The pig glistened on a spit, its grinning mouth stuffed with an apple. The firefighters' rubber boot toss was being hotly contested. There was a hundred dollar prize for first place.

I moved on. Across the vastness of the parking lot I saw the giant stadium lights creating a bright halo that you would think could have been seen from outer space, by some alien race.

I got back in my car and drove away. I found myself using the spare key under Lois's door to let myself into her house. She had gone to the game.

I left Max in the car, because Petey hated dogs, among other things.

Petey fluttered in his cage and squawked when he saw me. He fanned up his feathers. I put the curtain over his cage.

On a shelf that fronted the imposing leather spines of the world's great books, I found a trapdoor that revealed, not pages, but a stash of liquor.

I started with the vodka. It was going on six forty-five, and the game didn't start until eight.

By seven forty-five, I'd let Petey out of his cage. In the course of a serious discussion over why the hell he hated my guts, he took flight and landed on top of the kitchen cabinets. I took the broom to sweep him down, but he grew small and compact, tucked into the corner. I knew Lois was going to be pissed.

I kept drinking and watching the time. I guess I had been waiting to turn on the TV when the game started.

The clock crawled toward eight.

I couldn't believe it. They had a pregame show. There was pre-recorded coverage of the morning pep rally at the high school.

The reception fizzled, like it was raining. I got up and tried to adjust the set and ended up standing there, holding the rabbit ears because when I moved, the reception got so bad I couldn't see anything.

There was an aerial shot that showed the town like a toy town, two-dimensional from the air. A light sprinkling of snow had fallen. A voice-over gave the basic statistics of who we were and how we made a living some hundred miles shy of Chicago, a story of Middle America ruination, a story of our precipitous decline in the seventies, a lamen-table story of union greed, or so the voice-over announced. We just weren't competitive. The voice-over asked rhetorically, "Can a business afford to pay someone twenty bucks an hour to screw nuts into metal?" A cursory scan of the old downtown riverbanks showed an armada of factories that looked like they had run aground. All that survived were small-scale custom upholstery shops that supplied the RV plants in the next county over.

It wasn't exactly the wholesome story the mayor would have sanc-tioned, though a cropped shot showed a few local merchants sweeping their storefronts along the old part of town that held the dilapidated theater, which the voice-over said vaudevillian legends and stars from the silent movies had once graced during the war bond drives for the first and second world wars. Some of the merchants looked up and waved to some unseen passersby. The shot was obviously staged, that inher-ent tug at a former sentimentality, at what small-town America repre-sented. We were all searching for some past.

There was no shot of the mall fifteen miles south, nothing that hinted at how we'd changed. Instead, the camera focused in with a piece about the Indiana Amish community, on goat-bearded denizens in black, out in their fields fixing a fence, their breath smoking in the cold morning air. Two crows cawed like miniature foremen giving instructions.

In an Amish barn, the camera found a father and son working on a rolltop desk by oil lamp. They seemed oblivious to the camera zooming in as the voice-over talked about the Old World workmanship and detail that had been brought over from Europe and handed down. Then the camera focused on a cow curled up in the wood shavings. Nothing was wasted. The huge bovine mouth bristled with flecks of meal, the lips a spotted pink.

A child in an oatmeal-colored pinafore came into the barn to collect eggs, then turned with her basket and walked off toward a bleak-faced house set against the surrounding fields. The camera followed, cutting to an aerial shot of the land.

The camera eventually found the local high school, followed along the labyrinthine corridors, past homerooms and the cafeteria, past the principal's office and trophy cabinet, moving toward a din of sound that grew louder, until finally the doors of the gym itself opened. The TV filled with the thunderous resonance of the entire student body stomping their feet on the bleachers. The school marching band played amidst the noise as cheerleaders formed a pyramid, the wishbone of their legs showing through the accordion pleats of their skirts. The mayor was taking on the principal and teachers in a tricycle race, each absurdly big on the tricycles, pedaling in a stilted way across the auditorium.

The team was on a makeshift stage in their lettermen jackets, pumping their fists up into the air. The mayor won the race and took a bow, then went toward the stage, the crowd in a frenzy, and without saying anything, just nodding his head, like some consummate emcee, spread his arms apart and offered up the team, and the din of noise reached its pitch.

The camera focused on Kyle Johnson. He looked strong and poised, the center of everyone's attention.

When the TV cut to a commercial for the mayor's car lot, I put the rabbit ear antennae down and poured myself another drink. Jesus, it gave me goose bumps, how the segment could, at the same time, capture and not capture the lives we lived. It was not the truth we were after, but the myth.

I ended up listening to the game on the radio, because the TV reception was so bad. For almost three hours, I waited for Kyle to break down, paced nervously through four quarters of football that could have gone either way until the other team pulled away midway through the fourth quarter.

I was sure Kyle was feeling the demon of guilt crawling around inside him. I was waiting for him to crack, but Kyle had different ideas. When we took possession again, he went to the run, to a smash mouth football, handing off to our giant Amish running back, Noah Yoder, who ground out a series of first downs.

Kyle could do that, bring out the best in others. He brought us back from the brink of elimination in one of those improbable late comebacks you only dream about, and he did what no kid had done in over thirty-six years, took us to the semifinals of the state championship. After he threw a late touchdown, we gained possession again with an interception. Then with time running out, on a quarterback sneak, Kyle ran one in from thirty-two yards as the game ended.

I was on my feet screaming, my head pounding.

The small mesh speaker could hardly contain the static-filled roar of the crowd.

I felt tears in my eyes, partly because of the booze, but for so many other reasons as well. My own kid was at the game. His voice was part of that roar. I was separated from him, and I was aware of that simple fact. Seth had taken him to the game.

And at the bottom of everything, I knew I was part of the reason Kyle was playing this game, that I had whispered things into his head that a father might whisper to a son, convinced him of his own goodness, of his own humanity, convinced him that there are times when we must take our sadness and hide it away from others.

I had spoken to Kyle like I would never be able to speak to my own son. I had been the voice that gave him hope. I had whispered how he could survive and do great things.

I went outside into the silvery dark and stood under Lois's carport. The cold hit me. Kyle Johnson was our deliverance, the mark by which we would measure our lives—our lives before and after Kyle Johnson. I felt the way people might feel after shaking the hand of a president, like your life has been ennobled by their mere presence.

Max licked the foggy window. His face emerged.

I let him out and walked the block, saw into the living rooms of the few people who had stayed behind, saw them laughing and drinking, giving each other high fives.

I could see a light on in an RV across the street in Mr. Peterson's driveway. He'd planned on seeing the country, bought the RV for retirement, but he ended up senile. Now all he did was roam around inside the RV, trying to remember what it was for. I wanted to go tell him what had happened. I wanted to share this moment with someone, but he was long past understanding.

Max chased a cat into a backyard. I ended up putting him back in the car.

Back in the house, I lay out on the couch and thought of Kyle Johnson. I imagined him in his helmet, taking that final snap, saw him looking for a receiver, then, finding his offense shut down, running toward the end zone, getting within five yards of a touchdown before a guy wrapped around his legs. Then how, from somewhere deep within himself, Kyle double pumped, stretched out his arms, and found the end zone.

It was better to have heard it on the radio, to let my mind re-create the image, let it play over and over again.

Nerves had made Kyle act like he had last night. I was sure of it. The kid was superstitious. On the cusp of greatness, on the eve of the biggest game of his life, he wanted to do the right thing. He didn't want to go into it filled with self-doubt. Who could blame him?

Of course he'd been afraid, like God had put an obstacle in his path. It was almost biblical. I could see Kyle thinking in those terms, conditioned by his mother's religion.

But he had found a way to overcome his fears. There had been, in the end, no retribution, no accountability. On that final play, seeing an offense shut down, he turned from the set plan and let instinct decide his future. He had put everything aside, the horror of what he had done to that child, and made his own destiny.

We were in the semifinal.

I had nothing but good feelings for Kyle Johnson, for his resilience, for his innate sense of survival, for the way he banished the blackness of the past two days from his mind. That was the instinct of a survivor, of a guy who could come back and win games.

It was maybe also that way for the mayor, and even the chief, in those backroom dealings where they stacked the deck in their favor. They had taken the element of chance out of their lives. They had bet on Kyle Johnson's true competitiveness, knowing he would not let them down, and they had been right! It was as simple as that.

I downed three more vodka shots just toasting all three of them, and then I had another to toast myself, because I felt I had sealed my own future—and of course, in a way I had.

8 I heard Lois pulling into the driveway sometime later. I had
drunk something like eight vodka tonics by that time. The bottle
was nearly empty. I got up and pulled the curtain back with a
drunken flourish.

Lois was looking at the house. I was parked in her carport. Max
started barking and scratching the window.

The chief pulled in behind Lois and got out. Lois looked at me and
shook her head. I was standing at the window with my hand cupped so
I could see into the dark.

The chief saw my car in the drive. I think he was saying something.
I heard voices, then he saw me looking out the window.

He was holding a bottle of liquor, like he was coming to a party, still
carrying that big foam hand. I could tell by the way he was walking he'd
been drinking heavily. His car was festooned with streamers.

Lois put her hand on his arm and said something, but the chief
pulled his arm away and pointed with the big foam finger right at me.
He turned and got into his car and left.

The front of his car hit the lip of Lois's drive, and the underside
sparked against the dark.

I didn't know how the hell I came to be part of this sad spectacle,
competing with the chief for Lois. My sense of the pathetic ran deep.

There I was with my Chevy Citation in Lois's carport, only a small step up from Lois's Chevette.

The smell of alcohol hit Lois when she came through the door.

"Jesus Christ, what the hell are you doing here? Don't tell me you were at the game like that!"

Petey squawked from the cabinet, swooped down, and landed on Lois's shoulder. He hissed at me.

"What went on here?"

"I hope I didn't spoil your little party, Lois. You back to your old ways?" I went toward her, but Petey snapped and bit down on her finger.

"Damn it, Petey. No!" She grabbed at him, but he flew around the kitchen and landed on top of the kitchen cabinets again, walking sideways, back and forth in a real temper.

"What did you do to him?"

The back of Lois's hand was bleeding.

I said, "Let me," but she pulled away. "Get out, NOW! You son of a bitch!" She was holding her other hand over the cut, but the blood was seeping through her fingers. She went toward the bathroom.

I followed her with my drink. "I'm sorry."

Lois was running her hand under cold water that turned pinkish with her blood. "Damn it, Lawrence, you shouldn't have let him out of his cage." She was sniffling as she spoke. "You shouldn't even be here! What the hell do you want from me?"

I took a lurching step toward her and took her by the wrist. "Here, let me do it." I put my finger in my vodka and dabbed the back of her hand.

Lois flinched. "Stop," but her voice had eased.

"Hold still." I ended up putting a Band-Aid on her hand with some difficulty, and she winced. She took a deep breath. Her eyes were watery.

I whispered, "I'm sorry. You want to call the chief back? I'll leave right now."

Lois shook her head. "Don't . . . just don't rub my nose in it, just don't."

Petey half-flew up the stairs on his clipped wings. He couldn't fly very far. He hopped across the hallway and stood in the doorway, looking at us defiantly.

Lois put her hand to the side of her head, sniffling. "Go to hell, Petey."

Petey fanned his wings.

"You know how long parrots live, Lawrence? Eighty years or more, that's how long. You know what's going to happen? Petey is going to outlive all of us." Lois sniffled again and wiped her nose on her shoulder. "I think Lionel did it for spite. I swear to God, he got that parrot to spite me."

I smiled.

Lois kept talking. "Lionel was the kind of guy who would have known how long parrots lived. He'd have researched something like that." She sat down on the lid of the toilet seat and took a long drink from my glass.

"This is my existence. This is it. Petey courts me. You know that?"

I touched her hand again and whispered, "I'm sorry."

Lois shrugged me off. "This isn't about you, you hear me? Why is it men always think it's about them?"

I didn't answer her.

Lois took another drink. "What Petey likes to do is make a nest out of old newspaper. Then he bites my finger and draws me to his cage. He says, 'Petey is a good boy.' That's his pickup line. It's Petey this and Petey that."

Lois raised her voice, "I may be easy, but not that easy, you hear me, Petey? Jesus, where'd you get the notion that you could handle a woman like me?" She went out into the hallway, and Petey just squawked, his wings extended, moving from side to side, before trying to grab at her ankle and pull her away with him. "You're a feather duster! You hear me? A feather duster!"

We went into her bedroom and shut the door to escape Petey, though he hit the door with his beak several times before giving up. Lois stroked the Band-Aid on her hand and sat on the edge of the bed. When she'd calmed down, she opened the door, but Petey was already gone.

She called out after him. "I forgive you, okay?" then came back into the bedroom.

I watched her get undressed, saw the reddish scar the elastic of her nylons made around her middle, like she'd been sawed in half. She sat down at her vanity and began taking off her makeup. The backlight of the mirror looked like a halo.

Petey materialized.

Lois put him on the table so he was staring into the vanity mirror. She kissed the top of his head.

I felt the room wavering. I tried to stand up. "Maybe I should go . . ."

Lois turned toward me. "You're not fit to drive. Stay . . . I want you to stay." She ran a comb through her hair.

Petey's head swiveled and his eyes caught the light.

I felt cold. My head ached.

"You want aspirin? That's what you need."

"I'm leaving . . . I have to get home."

Lois ignored me and went into the kitchen, and so did Petey. I could hear her talking to him. She came back in and sat beside me, giving me the aspirin and a glass of water.

I swallowed the aspirin and drank all the water.

Petey looked small, standing on the floor looking up at me. I stood up to leave and found I couldn't.

"Just sleep, Lawrence."

I closed my eyes, heard Lois usher Petey out of the room. I heard the bed creak under her weight when she got in beside me.

When I opened my eyes again, Lois was breathing shallow. She put her finger to my lips, like I should say nothing.

"Just hold me, Lawrence."

As we lay there, Lois told me how the mother of the dead child had gone to the funeral parlor before the game that day. The child's body had been released by the coroner's office.

I had my eyes closed. I didn't know what she knew, if the chief had said anything to her, if he'd admitted to her what we'd done.

Lois whispered, "The woman wanted them to take out her daughter's baby teeth and give them to her . . . She got them to trim the child's nails and cut some of her hair. The mortician said she was like a zombie. He called us at the station. The chief ended up going down there and taking her home. Nobody came with her, nobody, no relatives, nothing."

I could feel Lois trembling. She sat up again. "Can people be that lost, that alone?"

The room was spinning. I concentrated on the ceiling fan.

I said quietly, "I waited almost a year before I told my father about my divorce."

Lois was looking down on me. Her hair was off to one side of her shoulder.

I said, "Have you heard anything about if she's going to be charged with neglect, seeing she was drunk?"

Lois shook her head. "I don't know . . . It won't bring back the dead." I saw her face come close to mine. Her finger touched my lips and I shut my eyes.

I came around sometime deep in the night. The TV was on low. I heard a guy explaining his formula for success in the real estate market, how you could buy houses with no money down. Couples were giving testimonials about how they were pulling in six-figure incomes, how their marriage was saved and their self-confidence had soared.

I looked at the TV. The guy selling the real estate tapes was sitting on the balcony of a Hawaiian beachfront hotel room. He had an island drink with a paper umbrella on the table. He was holding up the tapes and offering a money-back guarantee. Surf was breaking in the background.

Then I heard the faint bark of a dog and remembered Max was out in the car.

The hands on her clock glowed five-thirty. On the bedside table, I saw a small china cat lying on its back with its legs in the air. It was a gum catcher. Lois had set a wad of chewed gum between the cat's paws. I was suddenly conscious of the smell of spearmint.

I left without waking her.

I picked the paper up from the driveway as I left. Below the headline of our victory, in a small byline, there was just the briefest mention of the case. It listed the child, Sarah Kendall, daughter of Lisa Kendall, as having been cremated in a private ceremony.

It was a terrible thought that a child had been burned to a pile of ash. I felt responsible in some way for this inconclusive end. Standing there in the cold morning, I shivered and thought of that child's life, eclipsed like it was by our uproarious push toward a championship, and I thought how the central figure in all this was, at my bidding, hiding behind a football mask.

9 Female adolescence is a blood sport, more so than football or basketball. There is nothing to compare to the silent menstrual rivers that flow unnoticed from every female. In the cold silence of the gym, I saw the streaks that showed where Cheryl Carpenter, Kyle's girlfriend, had clawed the polished floor in pain.

Cheryl had gone for an abortion the previous day. A cop over in the next county had run a check on car licenses at the clinic. It was routine for us to monitor clinics in an unofficial capacity and exchange information. Conservative elements in the towns had never accepted the law of the land, and ever since the legalization of abortion there had been sporadic attacks on clinics and patients.

Cheryl, it appeared, had suffered complications the next day and started bleeding internally. She'd already been taken by ambulance to the hospital by the time I arrived.

Principal Stan Tanner was standing beside me. He had called the chief, a personal friend, and the chief had gotten Lois to send me down to the high school to see Kyle. Again, I was being controlled from a distance, or that's what it felt like.

Tanner had briefed me on where things stood. During the break between classes, word had spread about Kyle's girlfriend bleeding from a miscarriage. When word reached Kyle he just started screaming, hitting lockers, then he disappeared. It was only when classes started again that kids saw Kyle down on the field in helmet and pads, throwing spirals way down the field, one after another, Hail Mary passes.

By the time I got there, Kyle had been back to the locker room alone, smashed up some lockers, and gone back to class.

It was eerie as hell, standing with the principal in the gym where they held the pep rallies for the football team, where Kyle had brought the crowds to their feet before games, and now where his girlfriend had fallen to her knees.

At the principal's office my arrival was greeted with the grunting sound a pig makes. The resident lowlifes were doing detention in the outer office. Stan just glared at them, and they looked back, half-smiling, already stoned, all dressed in the uniform of the disaffected: long stringy hair, boots unlaced, RUSH concert T-shirts, and checkered flannel shirts.

The office smelt of peanut butter and jelly and pot.

Stan shut the frosted glass door of his office. "Take a seat."

I knew him from the time when Janine and I joined a bridge club. He was pretty much okay, but his attire was way out of whack. He wore leisure suits, like Janine's new husband, with either black or white stitching. He had a hairpiece dyed the same color as Roy Orbison's.

Stan flicked through his Rolodex, looking for Kyle's class schedule.

"You know, I feel like a zookeeper, that's how I feel right now!" He looked at me. "I don't know why we feel we always got to send boys to do men's jobs. That's what we always do, hide behind our own inadequacies, sending boys out to fight our wars."

Stan leaned forward in a conspiratorial way. "I hate sports. That's the God's honest truth. Nobody is getting an education right now. It's pep rallies here and there. I'll tell you, I'd like to take a stick of dynamite to that gym. You know football combines two of the worst things in American life, violence punctuated by committee meetings."

I looked at him. He had a jar of peppermint candy on his desk.

"We're a farm team for some major-league franchise. That's what high school has become."

I raised my voice slightly. "Stan?"

He looked up, the Rolodex card with Kyle's schedule in his hand.

I cleared my throat. "Cheryl . . . She a good student?"

"Top notch. Straight A." Again, Stan scanned the Rolodex. "Yeah, here's her schedule. AP Biology, English, and Math. You want it?"

"No . . . I was just asking was all," but Stan handed me her schedule anyway. I scanned the classes. "That's not exactly the profile of a cheerleader."

"In schools like this, you do what it takes to fit in."

"I guess I never looked at it that way." I let a moment's silence pass. "You know how long they been together, Stan?"

"This semester, I think. Cheryl started tutoring Kyle in English." Stan leaned forward. "Why the interest in Cheryl?"

"I just hope she recovers, I mean, emotionally."

"Oh, I don't think you got to worry. Cheryl's already proved her strength."

"How?"

"She could have had that baby and been set for life if Kyle makes it big, but I don't think staying here or with him are in her plans. She's got a future elsewhere. She's looking out of state for college."

I said, changing the tone, "At least some of them are getting out of here."

"If we can save just one, then our job is worth it."

That pretty much ended our conversation. There was a shriek from the outer office.

"Damn it!" Stan's face lost its easy look. He jumped up and ushered me out into the secretaries' pool.

A woman dressed in an ungodly outfit, a loose cowl-necked sweater, a tartan skirt, and powder blue moon boots, was covered in white spitballs. She'd been running off a test on the mimeograph machine.

"Jones!" a secretary said, pointing at a kid in a Led Zeppelin T-shirt.

Stan shouted, "In my office NOW, Jones!"

All that did was get the other kids caterwauling.

Stan spun around. "Detention: Jones, Carter, Neilson, Farber. Write that down, Miss Adams." And without looking at me, he said, "Have Kyle Johnson paged to the teachers' lounge."

I walked the long corridor of the high school alone. I remembered Stan getting ripped one night at a fund-raiser for the mayor. Before Stan's wife could drag him out of there, he told us he felt he was living in a time warp, how he aged but the kids he dealt with every day never changed. He said the name of some character I'd never heard of from Greek mythology who'd suffered a similar fate.

I waited in the teachers' lounge. There was nothing that made it a lounge, other than that's what it was called. The room was just another of those institutional spaces with vending machines and the perfunctory coffeepot—our drug of middle age, what got us out of bed and kept us going throughout the day.

Kyle arrived carrying a hall pass. He looked diminished.

I said, "Take a seat."

I didn't know if he knew Cheryl had gone off and had the abortion. I was waiting for him to tell me.

Outside in the corridor I heard footsteps, but it was mostly quiet. I could just about hear the faint noise of band practice. Classes had started.

Kyle sat down. He didn't look at me for a long time.

His voice trembled when he spoke. "You remember those plagues of Egypt, that last plague, how it took the firstborn child of the damned? That's how it feels right now. That's how my mother said it would happen."

I felt the tension ease for a moment. At least he didn't know Cheryl had gone in for the abortion.

"It happens, Kyle. Women lose babies like this all the time . . . My wife lost a baby. Miscarriages are part of nature. They happen."

Kyle looked at me, but he was having his own internal conversation. He stared down at the table in front of him, at his big hands, one on top of the other. They were worth something like a million dollars, or at least they would be in a few years. His mouth was moving like he was talking to himself. He looked lost, his eyes opening and closing slowly, signs of shock, a feeling of disbelief and bewilderment.

He whispered, "I can't do this anymore. I can't."

"Yes, you can."

"We can't escape the Lord's judgment, none of us can . . ." He took a long deep breath. "I hate her . . ."

"Don't think like that, Kyle, don't. Don't push Cheryl away. She needs you."

"She doesn't *need* anybody," and I knew right then, in that look in his eyes, that he knew what Cheryl had done. He just wasn't ready to admit it.

Somebody passed outside. Their steps echoed in the cold hollow of the corridor. I waited until the sound faded.

Kyle said, "I'm not a good person," and though it was said simply, I could tell things would never be the same again. "I don't think she even cares about me," and that scared the hell out of me.

"Nothing means anything anymore."

I said, "I think you're just learning what we all learn eventually. Nothing is ever going to really mean anything. The day you come to understand that, you become an adult. But it doesn't mean we stop trying. We move on."

Kyle was not listening to me, just holding his arm like he'd hurt it from throwing the footballs on the field earlier. He winced as he bent it.

I said, "Kyle!"

His eyes had a distant look in them.

"I'm not going to lie to you. This isn't your life anymore. I don't think it has been for a long time. There are people who have put their neck on the line for you. I hope you can see that. You remember what we talked about—you making all that money and saving people? That's what you got to focus on, what you can control, you hear me?"

He met my stare. The table was trembling. He whispered, "You know what my father does each time we win, what he's been doing for years? Come a Saturday morning, he just sits there at the table waiting, waiting to arm wrestle me."

Kyle's eyes got big when he said that. "What he says is, 'I'm waiting for the day when the boy becomes the man I am.' He says that to my mother. And you know what? I've been letting him win a long time now. But I don't know how much longer I can take it." His voice faltered.

And maybe it was the first time I got the measure of what I was dealing with, of the pressures building up inside him. I could imagine Earl pitting himself against his son, how each victory made Earl despise his son the more. But Earl needed Kyle to deliver all of them.

I said, "You want your mother to live out her life working at a Motel 6?"

His eyes closed for a moment. "No."

I stood up and put my hand on his shoulder. I said, "Go see Cheryl. This isn't her fault. It isn't anybody's fault. Tell her you love her. You can't afford to . . ."

I stopped.

Kyle had that look like he already knew what I was going to say. He said quietly, "I know," but the way he said it sent a chill down my spine.

There are times when I wonder if that was the moment everything changed, if it was Cheryl's lack of faith in him that was her greatest sin when it came down to it.

10 That evening, I arrived home to find a dish of lasagna and a garlic loaf wrapped in tinfoil on my doorstep. It felt eerie, reminding me of the weeks after my divorce. I looked toward the quiet street, but whoever had left it had long gone.

The lasagna had congealed into globs of hardened fat. I figured it was Betty and her Table of Eight.

I shivered and went inside.

Max barked and turned like a top when I let him out of the basement. I put him in the backyard, then checked the answering machine. Nothing. What I hated most was the lack of complicity. How had I been sent to follow up on Kyle, how had there been no meeting afterward, no consensus on what we should do? Of course I knew the answer. Like the mayor had said, there was no going back.

When Max came back in I fed him the lasagna and bread. He survived it.

I ate an omelet with wheat toast and coffee.

The phone rang. I thought it was going to be Lois, but it was Janine.

"Seth, Eddy, and I are driving the Amish down to Florida in the van. He won't be able to come this week." She said it like it was a threat, which was her way of talking to me always now. Then she said, "I didn't get Eddy's check."

I said, "Can I say hi to Eddy?"

"No!"

"Please?"

Janine acquiesced and called Eddy. I could hear his feet on their cold hardwood floor.

I said, "Why did Tigger stick his head in the toilet?"

"Why?"

"He was looking for Pooh!"

It took Eddy a second to get it, then, he let out this kid laughter and told Janine the joke.

She hung up.

I sat alone thinking of my kid. The *National Enquirer* was open on the table. I stared at the headline—"Victims of the Titanic Are in My Waterbed"—I read the story. I guess this was how we connected with our past, found that thread of absurdity that linked us to something great or tragic.

The deer arrived in the backyard. Max watched them, his head moving back and forth between me and what was out there.

I made eye contact with him to stop his barking. The deer had a way of setting their forelegs far apart as they licked the salt. From time to time, one turned its head toward Max, the white tail flicking, sensing him behind the glass.

I got up and went to the window. I whispered my kid's name.

The glass fogged, and the deer moved off, dissolving into darkness.

I had the TV on low. The real estate guy came on again, hawking his Wealth Kit tapes.

I called the number, and the operator asked me if I was truly committed to my own financial independence. It was like swearing an oath.

Lois called me later.

We talked for a long time about where the dead went, whether a fetus had a soul, and if Lois believed in an afterlife, if she ever thought she'd see Lionel again, and if it really mattered.

I told Lois about Kyle telling me about that plague in Egypt, how the faithful had to smear the blood of a lamb on their door fronts so the avenging angels of God didn't kill their firstborn children.

Lois took a long drink, made that sound people make after they have drunk something stiff.

I said, "You should have seen Kyle. I think he knows Cheryl had an abortion. He just hasn't faced it yet."

"Our greatest gift for survival is our own self-deception." Lois took another drink. I could hear the ice rattle in her glass.

"Maybe . . ." I changed the subject. "You didn't happen to make me lasagna, did you?"

"Is that a hint?"

"No."

"Well?"

"Remember I told you about getting those casseroles left after my divorce? It's started again."

"How was it?"

"I fed it to Max."

There was a silence for a few moments. I wanted to ask her if she knew I'd covered up for Kyle. I wanted to hear her say she did, but before I could say anything, Lois said, "Can I ask you something, Lawrence, now that we are on the subject of self-deception?"

"I thought we were off that subject."

"Well, we're back on it. This isn't drink talking, Lawrence . . . but you think we came together just to fill the void left by what each of us lost? You think we'd have found each other otherwise? How would you rate me next to your wife? You know, like if you were being sent to a desert island and you had to choose?"

It was a string of questions that she didn't really want answered.

She kept talking, pulling me away from thinking about Kyle Johnson.

She was having her own crisis.

"I'm listening here to a song called 'You Don't Got to Pick Up That Lucky Penny.' You ever hear of that? You ever feel that lucky? That's a song Lionel used to play when he got into a funk, when things weren't selling."

I said nothing. I was just an ear on the end of the line.

"Lawrence, I ever tell you about the time this woman answered the door and asked Lionel in to show her the latest vacuum cleaner he was selling? He was on his hands and knees spreading out dirt he kept in jars and used to show the effectiveness of the vacuum cleaner, when the woman opened her housecoat so she was naked . . ." Lois stopped and let out a long breath, like she was exhausted. "That was when Lionel got charged with assault. He dressed so smart. You seen the clothes, right? He said the woman jumped on his back, that she wanted him. That's what he told me anyway." Lois stopped abruptly. "Goddamn it, Lawrence, you never answered my questions."

I whispered, "I'm taking the Fifth, on the grounds I might incriminate myself."

Lois laughed, dragged herself back from her own memories. That was her greatest gift, her way of surviving. She said, "That's a wise move. Don't tell me the truth—anything but the truth. I heard too much truth for one lifetime. I think honesty is way overrated."

I said, "Good night, Lois."

She called back less than a half hour later.

"I just wanted to tell you, a preliminary report came across my desk about the accident. There may have been two cars involved. Two sets of tire prints were found."

I was stunned for a second. "When the hell did you find this out?"

I heard the phone click.

I called her back, but she didn't pick up.

I went down by the chief's office the next morning, but he was out. I went by Lois's office, but she wasn't in either.

There was a brochure on her desk for a cruise. It was called the Lonely Hearts Voyage, a cruise for singles. There was a picture of a guy with his arms around a woman, staring at a sunset off the bow of the ship. They were both middle-aged.

Lois came back into the office. I barely got the brochure put back in time. She was with the chief. They were laughing but they stopped when they saw me. We all stared at one another. The chief said my name, and then turned and left.

Lois glared at me.

I didn't know what to say, so I said, "I want to see the transcript from that caller who identified Kyle's license plate number."

"Why?"

"Just get it."

Lois made a face. "I'll have to check if it came back from the transcriber."

"Well, check then, and while you're at it, I want to see the transcript of the call the woman placed concerning her child's disappearance." My voice had heat in it.

While she was in the other room, I picked up the brochure for the cruise again.

Lois came back in. "Why don't you keep your snooping in an official capacity?" She snapped the brochure out of my hand and put the transcripts down on the table. "This doesn't leave here."

I read through the transcripts, but it was hard concentrating.

Lois stood over me and smoked.

"You want to tell me what's going on with you and the chief?"

"I don't know what you're talking about."

"He's got you keeping tabs on me, is that it?"

"You got an inferiority complex, that's your problem."

I said, "No . . . Maybe you're my biggest problem."

I kept staring at the first transcript, the one where the mother had called in the missing person report. In the top corner of the transcript report it identified the caller as her, listed her phone number and the time of the call. I just kept looking at that, because I didn't know what else to do.

I put the transcripts back on Lois's desk and left.

I drove by the mayor's lot. He saw me as I drove by, because I slowed down and looked at him. All he did was wave. It was infuriating the way he did that, no sense of recognition at what we were facing. He had to know about the second car.

He was with clients. Then again he was always with clients. There was a sale going on, but there was always a sale going on at the mayor's lot. He had music playing over loudspeakers and small American flags, and red and blue balloons fluttered in the wind.

I wanted to get out and talk to the mayor. I think he sensed that when I drove around again, but he didn't make eye contact, though I know he'd seen me.

I circled through the old warehouse district, felt a mounting sense of frustration at being stonewalled at every turn. And for the first time I wanted to know how come Lisa Kendall had never been charged with neglect or questioned as to her condition when her child died. What backroom deal had the mayor cut? Why couldn't he be honest with me, fill me in on what was going on? I hit the steering wheel, shouted, "Be honest with me, goddamn it!" I felt myself shaking.

I was going to call Lois, but didn't. I pulled to a stop across from a chain link fence, saw a building alight in the crimson bleed of a stoked furnace. It was one of the few remaining shops. I watched aluminum being pounded and shaped for RVs. I let the car idle, stared at that for a long time, the solace of working with one's hands, of making something tangible, watching something taking shape and becoming complete. I think that is what we missed most, that determinacy, knowing when something was complete, when a job was done.

I pulled away from the curb, drove into the old housing district of antiqued mansions turned apartments, and followed the only rise in the land for miles, a glacial moraine that looked beyond the brownstone shell of downtown to the cornfields. The outside world was somewhere beyond the horizon.

An hour later I went by the mayor's lot again, and a new car was pulling out of the lot. The mayor was in the passenger seat. Kyle Johnson was driving, and Earl was in the back. The mayor saw me and waved me over. They were all sucking lollipops. You got a free lollipop whenever you took a car for a test drive.

The mayor had done well. He was getting a sale out of the deal. That mightn't have been his motivation in the beginning, but that's how it was turning out. That was the mayor's particular genius—playing whatever hand he was dealt. It was surreal. I could see him asking Earl down to the lot, telling him about some deal he had going.

The mayor said, "I assume you know Earl and Kyle?" which was the understatement of the century.

We both had our windows rolled down. Kyle had his hands on the wheel. He said in this stilted way, "It's nice to make your acquaintance," and the mayor made a whooping noise. "Listen to that, Lawrence. I think Kyle here went to the Emily Post finishing school."

He turned around and looked at Earl, but Earl wasn't laughing. Earl was looking at me in a way I didn't like at all, when all I had done was save his son's ass.

I just glared at him. What I wanted was a little respect, a little courtesy. I was on the inside and outside at the same time.

That's how it felt as the mayor rolled up his window and Kyle pulled away.

I drove along the street where Sarah Kendall had died and looked up and down the length of the road. Near the spot where she'd died was a solitary plastic wreath left below a tree. The wreath already looked weatherbeaten, the cellophane misted over so the flowers inside were indistinct.

The events of that night were all receding into the past. Life went on, the game, the push for the championship, the mayor on his lot with Kyle and Earl.

I was the problem. I guess it hit me then that it was all over, that we had no souls, that there was no eternity, no redemption, but I didn't want to believe it, so I waited for some revelation, some sense that this child was in heaven, in a better place, that she was more than the ash that remained.

I wanted to say sorry to her, that's what I wanted to say right then.

I drove by the house where Lisa Kendall had her apartment and slowed down. She still hadn't been charged with anything, but then that could have been the mayor's backroom dealings, or maybe the courts weren't ready to face the fact that women like this were living alone, abandoned with children, all over the country. Her existence hinted at the fragmented state of our lives, at a society where almost one in two marriages ended in divorce.

We were living with a lost generation of kids, latchkey children, kids who found their own ways home from school, let themselves into their homes or apartments to sit and stare at the television, kids we bribed to act like grown-ups, told not to answer the door, not to speak to strangers, to lock themselves away in their homes. On the weekends we took them to malls to pick out kid things, action heroes and dolls at Toys "Я" Us. Our kids knew how to use microwave ovens and cook TV dinners. These were kids who parked themselves in front of televisions, worked the remote controls, and waited for their parents to come home.

I'd answered calls over the last few years from houses where kids had gotten into medicine cabinets and taken pills, or fallen down and called 911 in panic, kids who had their addresses and phone numbers memorized. I'd answered calls where kids had left the stove on and nearly burned the house down. And in most of those incidents, it was in single-parent homes. It was a sad and lonely world out there. I don't think any of us really wanted to face that.

I saw a movement at the curtain. I circled again and saw a woman at the window. It had to be Lisa Kendall, though the thing was, I'd never actually seen her. Her picture had been kept out of the papers.

I stayed and kept looking at her. It was strange to think of her in there with that pyre of ash, with the remains of her daughter, with the clippings of nails and locks of hair.

Almost two weeks had gone by since the child died.

I passed the house again. Lisa Kendall was still looking out. She didn't look how I imagined. She had one of those grown-out Farrah Fawcett feathered hairdos. She was attractive in a haunting way, or maybe I thought that simply because I knew what had happened to her. I felt sorry for her. She reminded me of my own situation.

I thought, how do we become so disconnected that we choose to hide away like this?

I wanted to stop, go up to her apartment and ask if there was anything she needed. I felt that was within the realm of decency, that it was something I needed to do for myself, but I didn't. I knew better. Not in my uniform anyway.

I remembered seeing *Sophie's Choice* with Janine when it first came out, both of us feeling that sense of horror, Meryl Streep being asked to choose between her two children, to make a sacrifice like that. After our separation I saw *Kramer vs. Kramer*, alone in one of those theaters that showed matinee movies for a buck fifty. I wanted to see again that image of Dustin Hoffman teaching his kid to ride a bicycle in Central Park. I just sat there in the dark watching Hoffman choking back tears, screaming his kid's name.

And it hit me in the theater, that there was Meryl Streep, again as the mother, this time choosing between her husband and child and another life. I guess there was something going on inside all of us, learning how to sacrifice and survive without our kids.

I finished my patrol. The snow turned to sleet, then back to snow, like so many wintry evenings of monotony I'd come to live with—a dying season, the quiet nightmare of suburbia.

There was a casserole set on the steps when I got home. I was tempted to throw it in the garbage.

I changed out of my uniform.

Max eyed the casserole. I was going to give it to him, but didn't. Instead, I got back in the car again and drove over to the mother of the child who'd died.

The house was divided into four apartments. The outer door to the house was busted, explaining how the child had gotten out onto the street after getting out of the apartment.

I climbed a creaking flight of stairs winding into what had once been a grand upper floor. There were numbers on the doors.

I set the casserole outside Kendall's door, waited, working up the courage to knock, when in the hallway below a guy opened his door. He kept it open just long enough to get a look at me, then he shut it. I heard the deadbolt fit into place.

In that split second I recognized the guy, Raymond Laycock, a guy I'd had a few run-ins with over the years, a petty dealer who was related in some way to the mayor. He unnerved me so much that I left.

I waited awhile in my car outside, then drove away.

When I had eaten and cleared the table and turned on the dishwasher I thought of Kendall again. I wanted to know if she got the casserole. I stood in the hallway and dialed the number I had memorized from the report.

She picked up on the first ring. Her voice was frantic. She caught me off guard before I could speak. She said, "I'm sorry . . . I shouldn't have hung up . . . I wasn't threatening you." I heard her sniffle. "I'm scared. Say something, please. Tell me you love me. Tell me you forgive me . . . Please . . ."

I said nothing.

She hesitated. "Please, I want to see you . . . I'm so sorry. Please." Then she stopped abruptly.

"Who's there?"

I set the receiver down gently, stood in the dark silence. I called back again, but nobody picked up.

11 Through a night of not sleeping, her pleading loneliness filtered through my mind. I understood that agonizing sadness. I had come to know it well enough after my divorce, that sense of alienation and displacement. It welled up inside me. The full weight of guilt over her child's death had settled around her.

I felt a sense of closeness to her. I thought about calling her again and telling her I was the one who'd found Sarah. That could have been a way to talk to her. I picked up the phone in the dead of night, called her number, but put it down before she picked up.

It was just after sunrise when I pulled up across from the mayor's lot, the day dull and overcast. A milky light showed along the old commercial strip. A motel was advertising weekly rates. There were a few beaters parked at angles to the small rooms. The old theater was out of business but the hardware store still survived, just barely. The bridal and floral stores where Janine had bought her wedding dress and wedding flowers were boarded up, as was the photography studio where we'd had baby pictures of Eddy taken. It was like a line of dominoes, one fell after another.

The mayor arrived, dressed in a heavy parka with fake fur lining. His breath smoked as he got out of the car. He stomped, huddled against the cold, a box of donuts, and his plastic bag of raw vegetables in his hands. He was on a health kick.

I watched him for a few moments, like it was a stakeout. I had my window partway down and heard the jiggle of his keys as he opened the trailer he used as an office.

The trailer suddenly glowed a pale orange. The mayor had lit the propane heater. I could see him moving about inside. He was all business, checking the answering machine.

When I climbed the steel steps up to his office, he had already morphed into a salesman, in his checkered blazer and shiny tuxedo shoes.

He said, "Lawrence, well, this is a surprise." He extended his arm. "Come in. Come in. Sit, Lawrence, sit. Welcome to the circus!" That's what he was always calling life, "The circus."

The trailer was full of the smell of aftershave, propane, and percolating coffee.

The mayor had a package opened on the desk. He took out a steel ball the size of a racket ball. "See this here, Lawrence. You know what this is?"

I shook my head.

"At the turn of the century there was a Scottish inventor who used to sleep in a chair, holding a ball like this in his hand. When the ball fell out of his hand, the sound woke him, and he wrote down whatever he'd been dreaming about. The inventions were right there, below the conscious. What do you think of that?"

I said simply, "What happens if you end up finding you dream about nothing?"

The mayor winked. "I'll take my chances." He put the ball in an ashtray so it didn't roll. "So, anyway, what can I *do* you for, Lawrence? Don't tell me you finally decided to trade in that piece of crap you're driving. I'll tell you, I got some great deals right now. We're having a winter sale." The mayor set out a multicolored sprinkled donut and poured orange juice into a small yellow Dixie cup. It looked like something you'd set out for a low-budget kid's birthday party.

"Look, for you, Lawrence, no money down. You can drive out of here today." A big poster on his wall behind his desk said, "Your Credit History IS History!" and another said, "I'm Ready to Make Your Problems Mine!"

I said, "I don't know exactly how to say this . . ."

The mayor was sitting across from me, smiling, hair slicked back. He kept looking toward the lot, like he could subliminally change my mind. He took a celery stick from his plastic bag and bit so the stick crunched. "I've given up taste for health. It's a small price, don't you think?"

The mayor was about to launch into his description of the colon and how it got clogged with toxins when I said bluntly, "What about this second car?"

The mayor lost his smile. "What about it?"

"How long have you known?"

I could see the mayor's tongue show as he pushed what he'd been eating to the side of his cheek. He swallowed and rubbed his mouth. "The day after the accident I got word another car might have struck the child."

"Why didn't you tell me?" I was looking right through him. "When this report is published, Kyle is going to hear there was a second car. Maybe his wasn't the first car."

"The fact is Kyle ran over the child and didn't get out and check and see if she was alive. It doesn't matter if his was the first or second car to run over the child." The mayor stopped for a moment, his eyes opening wide. "I'll tell you I'm tired of being second-guessed here, Lawrence. Now unless you got anything else on your mind, I got a business to run here."

It was still early morning. The mayor stood up and opened the door of the trailer, blocking my exit. Cold air poured in around our feet. He wasn't letting me just leave. He changed tone. "Look, I appreciate your concern, Lawrence. Maybe I haven't followed up with you, but what's done is done. I thought the less you knew the better. I'm saying that, not against you, but to protect you. What's that they say in the military? 'On a need-to-know basis.' That's the cornerstone of democracy, knowing when not to ask questions."

I felt him talking in circles around me. I was going to get up, but I said, "There's one final thing." I'd not planned on saying anything to him about calling Kendall, but it just came out. I said, "I called that woman . . . the mother of the child that was killed. Lisa Kendall."

The mayor didn't respond. He was looking right at me. "How'd you get her number?"

"From the transcript of the dispatch call."

I tried to say something else, but the mayor interrupted. "You took her number from a confidential report and then called her? I just want to get that straight."

He went over to his desk, took up a pen, and wrote down something.

I raised my voice. "Listen to me, Mayor, it's not over for that woman. When I called, she sounded suicidal. How's she going to handle the idea that two cars ran her child over?"

The mayor wasn't listening. "You think you can pull confidential reports on people and then just call them? You ever hear of due process, of a little nagging thing we call the Constitution?"

He made a whistling sound. "I don't know what to think right now. What's wrong with you? Why the hell would you call that woman?"

"All I did was call her."

The mayor shouted, "Stop! Just stop, Lawrence!" He shook his head. "You know, I think we need to get to the bottom of your motivations before we go any further here."

I felt belittled just sitting there.

"First you're concerned about Kyle, now this woman! Is this about the investigation or your own loneliness?" He was pointing the celery stick at me. "I'm not a psychiatrist, but you know what you need? A good old-fashioned screw, that's what I think, that's man to man."

The mayor stopped talking and made a clicking sound, like he was thinking. "Shit on it, I don't believe you would compromise us like this. What the hell am I dealing with here?"

I felt a flush of anger. "I don't see how calling her compromises anything. I'm on the police force. I found her child. What legal issue is there? I'm a goddamn cop!"

The mayor didn't answer my question. He looked right at me across the desk. "So what did she say when you called her?"

"I didn't hear much . . ."

"Well, what *did* you hear?"

"It was like she'd just been talking to someone and she thought I was them calling back. It was like she was begging for forgiveness. That was the gist of it."

"Forgiveness?"

I nodded. "Yes."

"Well, that's a natural part of the grieving process. That's what they say these days anyway, right?"

"Is it?"

"It is. So what's got you so concerned?"

"Kyle. What if that woman ends up overdosing again? She already tried it once. Maybe she'll do it again. I think Kyle's already losing it. I don't know if he could take that."

The mayor banged down on his table. "That's a lot of what-ifs. *If* my uncle had pedals and a kickstand, he'd be a bicycle . . . Now, just stop, you hear me, Lawrence? You're projecting again, flip-flopping from Kyle to this woman and back again. You got a strange take on Kyle, you know that? I think if you look hard enough you'll see your own motivations here. You're lonely. You got too much time on your hands. A woman like that holds nothing for you, Lawrence. I can see right through you. I know what you've been through, but this isn't what you need, not a woman like that. That's what this is all about, isn't it? You're lovesick . . ."

I was looking down at my feet, but I acquiesced. "I don't know."

"I don't mean to lecture you, Lawrence, but I hate to see a good-looking guy letting his life go to hell in a handbasket."

I stood up to leave.

The mayor was sitting on the edge of his desk. He put his hands up. "Okay, okay. Maybe I'm out of line here, too. I'll quit telling you how to live your life. Now sit."

He stood up and I sat down, like we were on a seesaw.

"I don't want us falling out over this." The mayor went to the windowed door and looked out on his lot, then turned. "You know, maybe it would be better if this woman went back to wherever she came from. I'm with you on that. See, we got a point of agreement, so let me take up the slack. We'll find out who she was talking to on the phone and get them to get her out of here. That sound reasonable?"

"Sure . . ."

"Not just 'Sure . . .' I'm asking for your opinion here."

I said, "What was the question again?"

"What to do about this woman . . . Look, I think your instincts are right, why take a chance with Kyle? We should get this woman back to wherever she came from. I think we have a *moral* duty to do that, if nothing else."

The mayor extended his hand. "Will you accept my apology?"

We shook hands.

"I think your humanity shines through, Lawrence. Let me get the chief on this, okay?"

"I can follow this up."

"Lawrence, stop. You're too emotionally close to everything. What I have to remember is you found the child. Somehow that fact got lost along the way."

I interrupted, "It's not that."

The mayor raised his hand again. "Maybe not, but I know what you're going through these days with your own family. I see the parallel, that sense of loss, losing a child . . ." The mayor stopped and started again. "I hope I'm not out of line mentioning your family?"

I didn't respond.

"I want you to focus on one thing in life at a time. Focus on your kid. Don't let that love fall apart. Don't."

I looked at him and nodded.

"We'll get through this together, you hear me? Both of us."

I hesitated. "What I did, calling Kendall, it doesn't change our . . . what we talked about. The promotion?" I felt my face redden.

"God, no. My word is my word. We made a deal."

A car honked outside. The mayor instinctively checked in case it was a customer. It wasn't, but he stayed standing by his door and poured himself some coffee. I could see him shifting gears, becoming the salesman he was at heart. He had his back to me, but I could see his head move as his eyes followed something.

"Look at that drive-by . . . Dollars to donuts they come in next pass. That's a sale right there. Indecision is the subconscious mind saying Yes."

I didn't leave because the mayor was following the car, his whole body turning as he watched, standing out on the steel steps of his trailer.

I looked around and saw snow boots and a shovel and a bag of rock salt just inside the door, along with an assortment of framed awards for Customer Service and Commitment to Excellence along the paneled wall of his office. The mayor had sponsored Little League teams over the years. My kid had played on one of his teams. The team photograph was on the wall.

"How come you got a Salesman of the Year trophy here if you are the only salesman on the lot, Mayor?"

I had overstepped the mark, but I felt on a level footing just then.

The mayor kept his back to me. "Some years I've not accepted the award. Sometimes it stays in the box." He turned and looked severely at me, but his look slowly changed to a broad smile, and he said again, "Sometimes it stays in the box."

The day had materialized while we were speaking, a day of clear skies and falling temperatures. The trailer had lost its burnished orange glow but it was hotter than hell. The fax machine picked up. A sheet of paper curled into a tray.

The mayor went and took the sheet and scanned it.

"Interest rates are down, Lawrence. This is the time to buy. You sure, now that you're down here, I can't get you into something nice? Let's say no down payment or interest for six months. That means you're basically stealing the car from me. I'll tell you, the car a man drives says a hell of a lot about him, and, if you are the man I think you are, you are going to be out looking to get yourself a new woman, right?"

It wasn't a question that I was expected to answer.

The mayor was pointing out into his lot. "I got what I call a Bachelor's Delight, something sporty but understated, something for a divorced guy like you, that takes into account our ever-changing social dynamics. You can take it to a drive-in movie, or to church on Sunday, or bring a kid home in a bassinet. Trust me, this has your name written all over it."

"You got Lawrence painted all over it? That's a coincidence," but the joke fell flat. There was nothing left to say.

The mayor was already distracted by a buzzer that signaled yet another round in the bout of life. "Just like I said, they've come back. I'll call you, Lawrence," and with that the mayor took a few lollipops from a bowl beside him and went out into the cold like it was game day.

12 The answering machine was blinking. Janine's voice wasn't as sharp as usual.

"You there? Pick up."

I heard Eddy laughing in the background. I couldn't even imagine his face at that moment.

Janine said again, "Call me when you get in." She waited. "We're not going to Florida. The trip is off. I'm pregnant." She said it staccato, then hung up.

I just left the house. I wanted to be anywhere but there. Max was sitting in the passenger seat—oblivious in a way I wished I could have been right then. He had his squeeze bone in his mouth.

At a storage facility on the outskirts of town, a metal fortress of barbed wire, I parked and got out. I opened the unit I rented that contained the possessions I had kept from my marriage.

I hadn't wanted to face the wholesale plunder or humiliation of a garage sale. Shit, it would have been the equivalent of signing up to be publicly stoned. It cost me thirty-three bucks a month just for the rental.

Inside was an air hockey table, a dartboard, a backgammon board-cum-chessboard-cum-checkerboard, an all-in-one weight exercise system, a stationary bicycle, a Foosball game with its stilted players impaled through their midsections, a bumper pool table, beanbag chairs, and a popcorn maker, an eight-track player, a martini kit with glasses and shaker, a broken answering machine, a first-generation big-screen TV that you had to stare at straight on or you saw nothing—all of it still unpaid for, financed over three to five years at an ungodly percent interest. We had, in my recollection, played two games of air hockey in our entire lives before our marriage imploded. At one point, I had a fantasy of admitting each piece as evidence of my commitment to the marriage.

It was after eleven o'clock when I drove by Lisa Kendall's home. I just couldn't get her out of my mind. Her apartment was dark, but there was a light on in the apartment below hers.

A shadow moved against the shaft of silvery TV light.

I should have left, and I did, but half an hour later I called her number from a pay phone. There was no answer. I let it ring a long time. I didn't care that I was breaking my agreement with the mayor. I wasn't going to say anything about the case, nothing other than that I'd been the one who found her child. There are times when want takes you under.

I circled around where Lois lived, then phoned Kendall again, and still there was no answer. I went back to her apartment house, parked, and waited. I didn't know if she was there or not. It got past eleven-thirty. Everything looked timeless, snow falling, but softly now in heavy flakes.

I don't know why Janine's pregnancy should have meant anything, but it did. I remembered Janine telling me she was pregnant with Eddy. I knew in my heart that, if I were still married, I would have been at home now, in bed, that I was out here in the dead of night running from myself, from the cold darkness of where I once lived with my family.

I stared along the street and started the car again. There'd been a subtle change over the years on this street. Now almost half the houses had been converted to apartments. The Lisa Kendalls of this world had infiltrated towns like ours. This was where I might be heading, in danger of having to sell my own house just to keep paying child support. My existence, my very survival, was that tenuous.

I felt the same sense of lingering, of not being able to move forward, that sense of estrangement and loneliness, entrapment. How do you recover from the loss of your own child?

And then I knew why I was there. I remembered seeing a late night movie about a cop who fell in love with his partner's wife. Then his partner was killed in a shootout. It was one of those two-hour movies that went three hours because of commercial interruptions, and so it seemed like I had lived through their entire life. In the end, the cop ended up with his partner's wife. Somehow I thought I could befriend Kendall. Maybe something could come of this. I had found her child's body. I understood loss, my own kid was estranged from me. I kept thinking there was common ground for us to just begin talking, that's how it would start.

Somebody arrived in a car. I watched the tailpipe smoke in the red glow of the brake lights as my eyes adjusted. A person got out of the car and disappeared inside. A light went on in the apartment Laycock rented.

I watched the shadows in the apartment merge in that night trade of longing that drew insomniacs out into the dark, where peace or numbness was exchanged in whatever form required, either injected deep in one's veins, or snorted up one's nose, or taken into one's lungs.

Over the course of an hour two more cars arrived, following the same ritual. I began to think, here was how the child had died, in this procession of the dispossessed. Maybe it had been Laycock who'd plied Kendall with the amphetamines she overdosed on?

I got out and stood in the yellow light cast by the house, then climbed the stairs, buzzed his door.

I could tell by the look in Laycock's eyes he'd been expecting someone else, but he recovered with that same wryness he had in high school.

He said, "Shit, Chef Boyardee, you make a hell of a Beef Stroganoff."

He had his foot wedged against the door. He was wearing a white tank top. His hair was cut short, military style.

"I want to talk to you, Raymond."

"I'm afraid we got a policy of no soliciting in the building. Management rules. You understand!"

From the hallway, his room gave off a hot smell of garbage.

I put my hand on the door.

"I want to ask you a few questions about your neighbor, Miss Kendall."

He tried to shut the door, but I pushed my way into the room.

I could see he was back dealing pot. He had small nickel bags on a coffee table and a set of scales.

Our eyes met.

"This is all legitimate if you work on the premise that life is a disease." He had a sneer like a rat. Laycock was one of those brilliant but disaffected types who reminded me of what that kid in *Catcher in the Rye* might have been like if he were real.

I said, "I'm not interested in whatever the hell you have going on here. I want to ask you about something else."

He looked at me. "Your ignorance of judicial process, well, frankly, it scares me. You didn't bring a search warrant, so all this doesn't exist, from a legal perspective. It's inadmissible. But I'll tell you what, I'm willing to overlook these technicalities and cooperate, solely on the grounds of our long-standing acquaintance."

Everything felt like I was moving in slow motion. I said, "Shut the hell up."

Raymond was still smiling in a wasted way.

"Were you here the night Miss Kendall's kid was run over?"

He shook his head. "No . . . I was out on business. That was a big night for me."

"All night?"

"All night." He hunched his shoulders. "I missed all of it."

"Well, what do you know about her, generally speaking?"

"Generally speaking, I keep to myself."

"Don't push me, you hear me? I don't care who the hell you're related to. I'll bust you right now."

Raymond nodded his head. "Okay . . . okay. She fights on the phone, I hear her shouting sometimes, that's all, just that." He took a long drink from a giant beer can, what they called an Oil Can. He winked and tried to deflate things between us. "Who the hell ever thought any of us would need this much beer?"

He was one of those guys with a natural ability to break down tension. It wasn't everybody who could deal drugs. It wasn't that easy.

"You ever overhear what she fights about?"

He made like he was going to belch but didn't, then shook his head. "Look, I keep to myself."

The room was littered with empty cans and fast food wrappers. I saw on the coffee table a job placement form he had been filling out. Under the heading "Things I Like About Myself" he had written some things down but then scratched them all out.

He saw me looking at it and said, "Hey, I've got another list, 'Things I Hate About Myself.' I'm bringing it out in a three-volume bound set." He took another drink and swallowed. He squeezed the can so it made that sound crumpling aluminum makes. His mood darkened. He looked at me. "You know what really blows my fucking mind? I was in the South Pacific on an aircraft carrier less than six months ago."

I was conscious of the snow falling outside. I had lost control of the conversation.

Raymond got up and showed me a picture of him in some crimson bar with a woman with chocolate-colored breasts and dark nipples. He was just shaking his head.

At that moment he looked like he was coming down from whatever he'd been on.

"You know what I do for a living right now? Pack groceries. That's what the navy's career center's come up with. Fucking packing groceries."

I looked at the pot on the table.

"That, that's my retirement fund."

I said, "Regret is like letting someone live rent-free in your head."

"Touché! Chalk one up for the peanut gallery. Maybe you aren't as dumb as you look."

I said, "No, I *am*," and I smiled back at him when I said it, and that made all the difference in the world.

I was leaving when I saw a sign above his door. It read, "None of Us Came Here on a Winning Streak."

I said, "I think you could do much better than this in life."

Raymond rubbed his arms. I could see the reddened pinprick marks where he'd been injecting himself. He saw me looking. "I see it this way, a drug addict is a sick human being trying to get well, that's all." He followed me out into the hallway and said, "Listen, for what it's worth, Kendall goes out some nights, stays out real late."

"When did she leave tonight?"

"A few hours ago."

We were standing in the hallway. Kendall's apartment was right above us.

"You want to go on up there and take a look? I know where she hides her key. One of the baseboard tiles is loose just to the left of the door."

I shook my head. Of course I wanted to see into her world, but not with him there.

"You been up there?"

"That would be an admission of breaking and entering, right?" Raymond hugged himself. He was scrawny in the way drugs could waste a body. "That woman freaks me out. I mean, she's got no husband, no connections to this town, nothing, and she's still here. She freaks a lot of people out."

We stood in the dirty yellow light of the hallway. "What people?"

Raymond shrugged. "Kids . . . kids down at the high school. There's a rumor going around that Kendall overdosed and really died the night her kid was killed, but she's come back as a ghost. She's back looking for who ran her kid over. That's weird, huh? But kids are superstitious that way. Kids come here some nights, park outside, or come up here all scared, girls tittering, their boyfriends making ghost noises."

"Anything in particular strike you?"

"It all strikes me . . . But I guess this one thing freaked me out. One night some kids from the football team came here after a game. Kyle Johnson was with them. He asked me if I ever heard her cry. I mean it was weird."

Raymond made a whirling action with his index finger. "The guy's crazy. I don't know if you ever heard, but Kyle's girlfriend had an abortion. They say it did something to his head."

I kept looking at Raymond, wanted to see if he was going to say that everybody knew Kyle had run over the child. Had the secret spread throughout the high school? Had it become lore, a town selling its soul to the Devil for a championship? But Raymond betrayed nothing, nothing that I could be sure about. He just kept shivering. He needed another fix.

I waited outside in the car for Kendall. I turned the car on just to keep warm, then killed the engine again.

Just before four o'clock, when I was at the edge of sleep, another car approached and stopped, and somebody got out. I thought it was just another of Raymond's customers. I didn't think anything of it, but then a light went on in Kendall's apartment.

The car that had dropped her off was gone. It was a few moments before I remembered where I'd seen that car before. It was the car from the mayor's lot, the car I'd seen Kyle drive off in.

I pulled out, sped toward the county road where the Johnsons lived, but I was too late. I saw nothing.

In the dead of night, alone in my car, at the edge of their property, I wondered what the hell was going on.

13 The final report from the accident investigation unit arrived in a box on Friday morning, on the eve of the semifinal game up in Gary. It was given the briefest mention in the local paper, one solitary line that revealed the sad fact that a second set of tire marks had been recovered at the scene. That was all. It was old news.

The town hall was half-deserted, since most people had taken the day off.

I went by the mayor's office. He wasn't there. I called his lot, and he didn't answer. I left a cryptic message, asking him if Earl had bought the car I'd seen him test-drive. I didn't explain why I was asking.

I stood in the chief's office. He was getting ready to leave. The report was open on his desk. The chief seemed distracted, opening and closing drawers.

"I don't know where the hell I put my game tickets." He shouted out to his secretary, who came in and showed the chief the secret place where he'd put them. The chief said, "What the hell is the point of a secret place if you can't remember it? I'm losing my mind, that's what it is." He walked right by me. "I'm running late here, Lawrence."

"You mind if I read the report, Chief?"

"Get my secretary to give you a copy."

I sat in the break room. I had the box containing the report beside me. Lois came in and pretended like she didn't see me. Her voice was full of surprise. "Lawrence?"

She put a dime in the coffee machine and waited.

I said, "Give me a chance."

"Why?"

"Because I'm asking."

She sat down across from me, took out a cigarette and tapped it on the table, and in the subdued hum of the vending machines I told Lois about seeing Kyle drop off Lisa Kendall, but all Lois did was make a smacking sound with her lips. "So it's true . . ."

"What's true?"

"You were at Kendall's house. An anonymous call was placed that you were parked outside her house. The caller said you'd been there most of Wednesday night."

I said, "They got a regular neighborhood watch going on there. How come nobody's called in a tip that Raymond Laycock is back dealing in the apartment below that woman? He called this in, right? That son of a bitch!"

Lois swallowed. "You're obsessed with that woman, is that it? You find her attractive? She a looker?"

"I won't even dignify that with an answer!"

"When the chief passed on the information about you stalking that woman, the mayor wanted to fire you right on the spot, you know that?"

"It wasn't stalking!"

"What was it then?" She was looking at me, maybe like she looked at her husband after she found out about that incident where he got charged with assault. I looked at her. "I'm sorry. It's hard sleeping at night." It was hard talking, getting it said right.

"What's that got to do with anything?" Lois made a movement like she was going to leave.

"Jesus, wait, give me a chance here. I'm struggling . . . struggling just paying child support. I'm getting further behind each month . . ."

Lois had a defiant look in her eyes.

"Just hear me out. I find myself getting up and just driving around the town. I don't want to be in my house." I picked up her cigarette and took a drag, then gave her the cigarette.

"I'm a lost soul. I can't get near my own kid . . . I can't hold my own flesh and blood. You know what that's like, to have someone take your own kid hostage?"

Lois stared at me. "You need a loan from the Bank of Lois, is that it?"

I shook my head. "I'm not asking for charity."

"It isn't charity between friends. How much do you need?"

Lois had a way of shoring up our friendship just like that.

I eased somewhat. "Just let me try and explain, please. I was patrolling one day, and I went by that woman's apartment. She was just staring out the window, and God, I knew that look. It reminded me of those weeks after my divorce, when I thought I would die of loneliness, when I thought I couldn't go on without my kid. I used to go into my kid's bedroom, just stand there and will him back to me. I thought if I could beg forgiveness, somehow that sorrow, that love I still had inside me could reach them, that they would understand and come back."

Lois's arm came up in goose bumps. "You can't do anything for her. You have to stay away."

I said quietly, "I know."

"Can I ask you something?"

"What?"

"What do you not see in me, that you see in her, that you see in a stranger?"

I didn't answer her. I waited. "I just want her gone for all our sakes."

Lois stubbed out her cigarette in the foil ashtray like things had come to an end.

"I want to ask you a favor, Lois."

Lois shook her head. "I'm out of the favor business."

"Just this once, please. That friend of yours at the telephone company . . . I want you to have her check Kendall's phone records from nine to nine-thirty Wednesday evening."

"You're jeopardizing my job."

"Please. Just do me that one favor."

"No . . . Tell me why."

"Maybe we can get to her family, get her back to wherever she came from. That's all I want to do here, give this woman back her life. I think we owe it to her, don't you?"

"I can't." Lois closed her eyes and opened them again. She looked worn. "This is none of your business or mine. Leave her alone, Lawrence, please. I'm asking you for me."

There were tears in her eyes.

I used the briefing room for town meetings, and went through the box. There were envelopes of photos labeled "Victim's Injuries," "Vehicle Trajectory," "Accident Findings."

I took the envelope marked "Vehicle Trajectory" and laid on the floor a series of shots and illustrations of the street that detailed the composite trajectory of both cars involved, established through faint tire impressions in the leaves. The paths of each vehicle, identified as Vehicle A and Vehicle B, were traced with different color markers. The paths intersected and wove across one another.

In another series of shots, the path of Vehicle A was isolated, its trajectory a straight line toward the child. That sent a chill down my spine.

The second set, isolating Vehicle B, showed an erratic, weaving pattern, in keeping with what Kyle had told me. I had them lined up alongside the shots of Vehicle A.

I picked up the report and read through it, looking from it to the photographs and back. The report analyzed a series of enlarged photographs where the tire marks of both vehicles intersected:

> State lab findings indicate that, in each instance where tires intersect, a larger tire mark (Vehicle B) is impressed over a smaller tire mark (Vehicle A). (See exhibit photographs 3.a–3.f.) These photographs establish that Vehicle A made the original impression. Although the tire models cannot be matched to any lot number, tire tread experts have concluded, by examining the diameter of the tire marks and the axle width, that Vehicle A was most likely a passenger car and Vehicle B, a pickup truck.

Kyle Johnson had not hit the child first. Someone else had. And it wasn't some kids weaving in and out of piles of leaves. Someone had driven straight over her.

That's what hit me hardest.

I went out into the hallway and passed Lois's office. She was reading a magazine. In the toilet, I splashed cold water on my face. A solitary bulb hung like a cheap earring from the peeling ceiling, its starkness betraying how I felt inside. I closed my eyes and could almost see that first car approaching, the child sleeping in the leaves. I opened my eyes and shuddered.

I passed Lois again, and this time she saw me, but I said nothing. I don't think I could have spoken.

In the briefing room, I took up the envelope marked "Victim's Injuries." I stared into the leaves, saw the twisted wire of the child's wing, saw in shocking detail what my mind had not let me see on that morning, the eyes eerily opened wide, the white marble of her face and small red lips.

I saw a close-up thread of blood that had seeped from the ear to the fringed collar of the costume. And, looking closer, I saw an earwig in the small bowl of her ear. She was already being reclaimed by nature, even then. I saw the head had been turned almost a hundred and eighty degrees, the broken neck swollen to a blackish blue. In another shot I saw the way the right foot had been twisted and crushed. Somehow that held me, the smallness of the feet.

I was staring at a dead three-year-old child.

I went to the window. The cold, bleak eye of the sun hung over the deserted town.

Lois came into the room. I turned, but she was staring down at the photographs. She closed the door behind her and put her hand to her mouth.

I said softly, "Kyle wasn't the first one to run over the child," and slowly I explained everything, walked the corridor of photographs set out in two lines, and lived the last moment of the child's existence on earth.

14 Hours later the industrial chimneystacks of Gary breathed blue fire like dragons in a lost world. I stared into the liquid blackness at the edge of the highway, saw the giant complex outlined by naked globs of light flickering against the dark. The sulfuric air was filled with the noxiousness of rotting eggs.

Our town was playing the sons of the men who worked these chemical and steel plants in the semifinal. It was like taking on mutants from some galactic prison colony.

I took the last exit off the highway, down a ramp bejeweled with broken glass. Under the pylons supporting the highway I saw a makeshift city of boxes and tarps, with a medieval armor of hubcaps gleaming in the sudden sweep of my headlights. Crowns of blue flame illuminated circles of druidic figures with hands extended like they were raising the dead.

Instinctively, I pressed down the door lock.

At the end of the ramp, a solitary red light smoldered like an imploded star.

I didn't stop, went right through it, took the turn hard, and heard one of my hubcaps rolling into the darkness.

Industrial America crouched, grand, sad, and burned out. So much of America, of what we used each day, had been created here once upon a time.

The city streets were haunted by prostitutes in short skirts slinking against the neon bleed of signs, blacks chained to the night in links of gold. Through the car window, I saw the myopic gaze of men smoking and drinking near burnt-out buildings, a line of cars up on blocks with hoods pried open, shop fronts boarded up, windows smashed.

At a big dilapidated motel, a man in a mesh undershirt checked me in. It was where everybody from our town who was up for the game was staying. Music from the *Flashdance* soundtrack was playing in one room. People were dancing on chairs and on the double bed.

The party extended into another room through an adjoining door.

The mayor and chief came out of the room and saw me opening my door. The chief teetered to a stop. He jerked his head back. "Lawrence! Jesus, I didn't expect you here . . ." He swayed when he talked and pointed to the night. "To get to heaven you must go through the gates of hell!" With that, the chief let a rolling grin break over his face, and I hated his guts.

"Why don't you go on back in, Chief?" the mayor said.

The chief seemed like he needed help just orienting himself in the right direction. Before he left, he tipped his head back and looked cockeyed at me. "We made it!" He clenched one of his fists when he said that. "We're going to be telling our grandchildren about tomorrow!"

He squeezed my arm with the other hand for balance. His breath was sweet with alcohol.

"This is Planet of the Apes, that's what this is. You know, they got niggers on that team that look like they just got off a slave ship. Honest to God. They got hands like shovels." He almost fell on me.

I waited while the mayor turned the chief toward the party.

The chief shouted, "We got the yearbook in here. Take a look at what we're up against! The Have Nots against The Have Even Less Than the Have Nots!"

A car came into the parking lot. A piled snowbank turned pink in the brake lights. Across the highway, in the switching yard, I heard the clank of carriages, the sound of trains being formed.

The mayor came back. "Let's go down to your room." He had his arm draped over my shoulder. "God, the sooner the chief retires the better. He's becoming an embarrassment."

In my room, the mayor stood by the window, backlit so it was hard seeing his face, just his outline. He didn't say anything for a few moments, just listened to the thump of music vibrating through the motel.

I waited, sitting on the bed that was one of those beds that shook if you inserted a quarter. The bedspread was covered in cigarette burns.

The mayor let out a heavy breath. "I'll get straight to the point. I got a complaint filed against you. I thought I gave you explicit orders not to go near that woman. I thought we had a deal."

"Laycock. Did he call you?"

The mayor came away from the window, his face materializing. "This isn't about him. It's about you." He sat on a chair beside a small table and ran his hand through his hair.

I didn't say anything.

"I kept up my end of the deal. I got the chief to look into that call. He traced the call. Kendall has been talking to her sister. She's having a hard time coming to terms with her child's death. That's what the calls are about, her guilt. She's afraid to go home, to face everything all over again. People do that, hide from others, hide from themselves. It's a psychological manifestation of grief, of guilt, part of a process, you hear me?"

I stayed quiet. I thought the mayor was going to launch into me, but he started talking about himself. "I've tried as best I could to help everybody out here ever since this whole mess started, and everywhere I've turned I've been shit upon. Public service is a thankless job. People are just waiting to take pot shots at you all the time."

The mayor looked at me. "You know what Earl Johnson did to me? He comes down to the lot and just picks out the best car there is. He wants to drive it. He tells me afterwards he's real low on funds. He asks me for a deal. He hands me a penny, and he drives off the lot with a new car. I'm going to have to eat that cost. You see what I'm up against? I do someone a favor, and this is how I get treated!"

I felt a sudden racing sensation in my chest. Kyle had dropped off Kendall. I wanted to say something, but the music flared. Someone opened a door down the hallway. The party was in full swing. A door shut and the walls of my room vibrated.

The mayor raised his voice. "Shit on it, I can see all of us getting busted for disorderly conduct. I can see them doing that to us here. I want to get the hell out of this nigger town." The mayor turned to leave.

I said, "Wait."

"What?"

"Kyle's been seeing that woman."

"How do you mean, *seeing her?*"

"That night I was out watching her house, a car pulled up, the same car I saw you taking Kyle and Earl out in for a test drive."

The mayor froze. "I don't believe it."

"I think maybe everybody knows what happened, what Kyle did. Laycock told me kids go to the house at night. He says there's a rumor going around the high school that Kendall is a ghost, that she died that night her child was killed, but she's back haunting the street, back looking for her child."

The mayor put his hand to his forehead. He didn't say anything.

I said, "I told Kyle that when he got famous, he could save his soul by anonymously giving away money to women like Kendall. Maybe he's trying to save his soul now, telling her he's going to make her rich."

I looked at the mayor, but he didn't seem to acknowledge my presence. I waited through a silence that persisted, save for the dull thump of music down the hall.

The mayor had his head still lowered. He said nothing, eventually going out the door, letting the cold air rush in to fill the vacuum of his absence.

At a liquor store across from the motel, I bought a bottle of Crown Royal in a blue velvet bag with golden drawstrings. I was a couple of shots away from oblivion.

By the following day, it hurt just to look out the window. The motel was deserted. It was going on three-thirty in the afternoon. I'd missed the game.

At checkout, I was charged an extra night by a fat white woman. She was watching *I Love Lucy* on a small TV. Lucy was boxing chocolates on a conveyor belt, checking chocolate candy for imperfections, discarding the bad candy and boxing the good candy, but she couldn't keep up. The belt was getting faster, and Lucy was stuffing the candy into her mouth and down her blouse, and the laugh track got louder and louder. The fat woman was smiling like it was funny, like that kind of desperation was worth laughing at.

And somewhere beyond the motel, amidst the knifing cold of that bright Saturday afternoon, somehow Kyle Johnson had already ascended from hell to another improbable victory, and I felt at that moment that what had happened to him might have been just what he'd needed all along, to drive him forward, to push him to greatness. He was finding his own way through all of it. You look back at history, and men do great things under the worst of circumstances, fighting their own personal demons. Was this to be one of those cases?

15 I followed the taillights of a truck to the exit for our town. A limp banner fluttered against the tollbooth hailing Kyle Johnson's victory. The guy in the booth looked like someone hearing confessions in the middle of nowhere.

I stopped by Lois's. She was in a housecoat. I didn't stay. She had the money she promised to lend me for the child support in an envelope.

I stood in her kitchen, not knowing what to really say. Petey was watching us from his perch.

I said, "I suppose you heard we won the game?"

Lois smiled softly. "Maybe this is the year we have all been waiting for?"

"Maybe . . ."

She touched my arm. She said, "You did the right thing, Lawrence."

I didn't ask her what she meant. She didn't mention Kyle's name. All I said as I was leaving was, "This is a loan. I'm going to pay you back with interest."

I saw her watch me leave from her kitchen window, waiting until I was out of sight.

A plow had pushed a pile of snow across my driveway. I had to get out a spade and dig myself in. The cold snared me. I felt it in my lungs.

When I was finished, I checked the mailbox, and the Wealth Tapes had come. I put them on the hall table. It seemed prophetic, them arriving that evening. Maybe Lois was right, this was going to be our year.

I snapped back from that thought, suddenly conscious of Max whimpering in the basement. He'd been down there for two days. I let him up. He whined, raised his leg, and pissed on me. I felt the spread of warmth against my knee, and the smell of ammonia filled the air. Max turned and trotted into the kitchen, then turned and looked at me defiantly.

The phone rang a while later. It was the mayor. He said, "You're getting a week's paid vacation, courtesy of the town, effective immediately."

"What for?"

"For that vacation you didn't take, for the overtime you put in." He hung up before I could even explain why I'd not made it to the game. I still didn't know if I was being reprimanded or rewarded.

Outside, Max roamed the back garden, rooting out smells, marking things, raising his tail, reclaiming this territory as his. Steam rose in the cold air. I left him outside.

I opened a can of Campbell's chicken noodle soup and sliced some cheese and boiled the kettle, doing everything slowly, then washed the dishes and put them away.

Thirty minutes of my life ticked away.

I turned on the TV and watched that kid Mikey getting a bowl of cereal served up to him by his older brother and his friends. He was maybe the same age as Eddy. Mikey's head barely came above the lip of the table. He had to stand on a chair just to eat the cereal. He had that kid smile on his face. TV was an emotional land mine. I turned it off.

I called directory assistance and got a toll-free number for cruise reservations. I wanted to see if one of those cruises Lois had been reading about was cutting any last-minute deals, but they weren't.

I said to a customer representative, "I can leave right now, get a plane out of Chicago and be there first thing tomorrow morning. The ship sails, and it sails without my money! That's no way to run a business!" I said, "Put me on to your supervisor."

But it was high season, and there were no deals, just "upgrades," or I could join the Floater's Paradise Club and have seventy-five percent off on this first cruise. But it was all money in the end. They wanted something like six hundred bucks up front just to enroll me in the cruise club. Airfare wasn't included. There was also a time share option. I was standing by the phone just listening. They had a dating service that profiled members for compatibility. It cost extra, but they had a booklet of testimonials. It was one hundred percent guaranteed. The booklet was free. All I had to pay was shipping and handling. Then the supervisor read off prices and descriptions of rooms that were currently available. I hung up.

I packed for the journey up to the cabin. My arms ached from having dug the snow. By the time I was ready, I could have sworn it was past midnight, but it was only quarter to nine.

I called Janine and told her I was heading up to the cabin. She had a way of just letting me talk until I got around to telling her what I was really calling for. I said, "I want to take Eddy up to the cabin."

Her answer was simple. "You are behind two child support payments."

I said, "You think it doesn't hurt, not being able to pay for my son? You and Seth have all the money you'll ever want. Can't you give me a break here?"

"Eddy's on new medication right now. He needs supervision."

"What medication? What the hell are you pumping him full of?"

"Don't shout at me."

"What's he been medicated for, Janine?"

"He's hyperactive."

"That's called *childhood*. Jesus, why the hell are you making him pay for our mistakes?"

"I can't have this conversation."

"You sure have become magnanimous with your newfound fortune, haven't you?"

She never even mentioned her pregnancy. When she hung up, there was a crackle on the line, like the sound of the universe beyond our small, insignificant lives. I never did get to tell her I had the back money for her.

By four-thirty, I abandoned the house. I didn't feel like sleeping. I drove around for nearly two hours, out past Janine's. I had the money in my inner coat pocket.

There was a stark light on at the house. Seth was already up. He must have seen my headlights because he came to the window and cupped his hand to the glass. They had no curtains. That was part of the religion, no secrets.

Seth came out to see who I was. I pulled into his driveway. I ended up giving him the money. He signed a receipt for the eight hundred I gave him. That was his idea. He was the businessman, not me. Like I'd always said, Seth wasn't the problem. In the upper part of the house, I saw Janine peering out at me. I didn't even ask about Eddy. All I said was, "I'll get the rest, soon."

After that I parked out at an intersection near the Johnsons'. I was waiting for Kyle to turn and head toward the high school. The football team met at the gym early each Sunday during the season. I wanted to ask Kyle what he'd said to Kendall. It was a simple question. If they had something worked out between them, that was fine with me. I just wanted to know.

Max was sitting beside me, looking toward the expanse of snow-covered fields. He sniffed the air, and made that whining sound dogs make when they want something.

A truck approached. I must have fallen asleep. It was past seven-thirty, but still darkish outside. When the truck stopped, the window rolled down and I recognized the driver, Mrs. Vanderhagen, a widow who lived on a farm beyond the Johnsons'. I could see she was dressed for church. She volunteered at the Unitarian church. "You okay?"

I said, "Sure," recovering somewhat. "I'm waiting on a friend. We're going hunting." I pointed to the stuff in the back of my car.

She pulled away.

I rewound the Wealth Tape I'd been listening to, and hit Play. A guy on the tape was telling the Parable of the Talents, how a king who had to leave his kingdom for a time allotted to one servant five talents, to another, two, and to the final servant, one, and how the first two doubled their talents through investment, but how the servant with only one talent covered it up in a cloth and hid it away. The king said on his return, "Thou wicked and slothful servant. Thou knewest that I reaped where I had sown; thou oughtest therefore to have put my talent in the bank, that I might have received mine own with interest for its use. Take therefore the talent from him, and give it unto him that hath ten; and take the unprofitable servant and cast him into the outer darkness."

All I could think of was that storage shed with all the things I had stored and hid away.

I said to Max, "I'm the guy with the one talent."

I hit the dashboard, and Max barked. I was coming in from the outer darkness.

I had not slept in over twenty-four hours. In the rearview mirror, I looked at myself, at the stubble of growth, the redness of my eyes. Pupils like pinpoints. The mayor was right. I needed to get away. I looked sick. And then I wondered what the hell had Seth thought when he saw me looking like I did?

The sun had begun to rise in a weak pinkish color across the horizon. I felt myself shiver, then yawned and hugged myself, closing my eyes for a few moments. When I opened them again, a truck had approached, and before I could see it was Earl and Helen, they had come level with me.

I saw Helen turn and say something to Earl. He said something back to her. Helen rolled her window down and stared hard at me. "You broken down?"

I couldn't think of anything to say. I said, "Where was Kyle Thursday night?"

Earl shouted, "What's this about?"

Helen looked at me. "Kyle was home."

"All night?"

Earl shouted again, "What the hell do you want?"

"Kyle was out with the mother of that child he killed."

Helen looked across at me, shaking her head. "Kyle didn't kill anyone."

"What do you want, money, is that it?" Earl was pointing a gun at me, but Helen screamed, "No!" She put one of her hands on Earl's arm, and crossed herself with the one hand. She was shaking. She said, "I'm going to pray for you. That's what I'm going to do. You don't look so good. Your wife and child were taken from you. I'm going to pray for you, pray you find peace inside." She touched her heart. "You need the Lord's guidance."

I shouted over her, "Your religion has blinded you!"

Earl had lowered his gun. He said severely, "How much do you want?"

Amidst the commotion I didn't see Kyle approach us in the new car. All Earl did was wave him on.

Kyle came by slowly, looking first at me and then at his mother, and then at Earl, who was pointing the gun at me again.

16

There are moments when I regret Earl didn't pull the trigger that morning. I didn't see a way forward. Could Wealth Tapes really change my life? Did I have that kind of faith? I couldn't see myself on some tropical island drinking cocktails, bragging about how much I'd made in the last year. I wanted to, but I couldn't, not really.

I stopped at a gas station that had a photocopier. I had Max put his forepaws up on the machine, hugged him, and hit the photocopy button. An eerie image of us emerged seconds later. I scrawled, "We love you, Eddy!" and posted it.

I drove another two hours, and felt a new faith emerge the further north I drove. The tapes for my financial success played throughout the ride, and I listened to the system, the guaranteed strategies for financial independence, topics like "How to Create Wealth, How to Buy Real Estate for Nothing Down, How to Cash In on the Barter Bonanza, How to Buy Foreclosures Without Cash, How to Make Money in Exchanging, How to Create Cash Flow."

I said to myself, "Why couldn't I be that guy in the Hawaiian shirt drinking cocktails?" as I turned off the main road. I headed along a rutted lane glistening with hard frost, crossed a wooden bridge, and passed through a canopy of trees into an opening by a lake where the light of early winter was so bright it hurt, the sky a beautiful wintry blue.

This is what I needed more than anything.

I pulled into the clearing by the cabin, something the tapes explicitly said could be leased as a time-share through a creative advertisement in a major metropolitan newspaper.

I guess I was already seeing the world in a different light.

The cabin was the one thing Janine hadn't contested in the divorce. It was basically worthless, a ramshackle fishing cabin on a lake. I'd bought it dirt cheap just after Eddy was born, since I'd had this idea that we were going to be spending summers here with me teaching him everything about nature and the wild. But I lost my own naiveté about what nature could teach us. Like I said to Eddy during the divorce, "Not all the wild animals are living in the woods anymore."

I got out of the car and sensed the stillness of the lake, barely visible, its coldness around my throat. Time pooled out there, lurking in glaciers scoured out eons ago, a bedrock of evolutionary dead ends, histories written in strata of shale. I felt myself cataloging each sensory feeling, wanting to remember this for when I wrote my advertisement, for when I tried to sell this cabin as a time-share unit.

I spent the midday airing out the cabin. I brushed off old cobwebs. Flies buzzed the windows in the last days of dying. The season was changing fast.

I chopped a cord of wood until I sweated the fear and anxiety of the past days out of me. I felt the bite of the axe on the wood, felt it catch the grain and split along seams of ancient growth. The wood smelt of spicy sap. I piled it beside the cabin. My arms were mottled with cold, but I felt on fire. I was going deep into myself, past thinking, to a contented place where I just felt the rhythm of my own body.

I went inside and set out my provisions. My breath fogged inside the cabin. The air had a bite to it. After setting things straight, I went down to the lake. I watched a loon land far out on the water. Its splash carried on the cold air, the afternoon light turning the water a shimmering quicksilver.

On the far side, a crystalline haze blurred the evergreen trees. There was a slight chop on the lake there, the rippled waves breaking in a brown scum. A flotsam of old leaves and branches had washed ashore.

In the shallow tributaries, a membrane of ice had formed, clear, like glass. I broke a piece of ice and tasted its purity.

Max wove in and out of the trees. He came to the water's edge but thought better of swimming, lapped the cold water, and ran back into the woods. I was glad he was there with me. He had a way of bounding over things, then abruptly stopping, sniffing and rutting. I threw a stick, and he broke into a loping gait along the blackish mud banks to retrieve it.

I found a place to fish, took a fly from my hat, and threaded it through the line. With my waders on, I stepped into the water, edging out until I was up to my waist. The waders made me buoyant and unbalanced. I set my legs apart. The cold tingled, and then I felt a numbing of pins and needles, like an anesthetic.

Max came to the lake's edge and barked, running along the mud bank, then turned and bolted for the woods again.

I cast a spider's thread of line in an arc that unfurled and dropped with a plop far out on the lake, then held the line steady, waiting for resistance, taking up the slack. The fly had that beautiful iridescent color of gasoline on a road after a rain. It spun against the gray of the lake.

I heard the distant putter of an outboard motor fill the silence of the afternoon. The upper part of the lake was invisible around a bend of land, and the boat never showed. Then the motor went dead.

Silence closed in on itself once more. The loon took flight over the zinc-colored water.

A while later, smoke rose against the trees. Whoever was out there was preparing against the coming dark. I heard a solitary shot fired and knew something had been killed, and that sent a shiver through me. I called Max, and he barked nearby. I could hear twigs snapping in the woods.

I fished until my hands could not work the reel anymore, until the sun began to fall low on the horizon. I felt a fish pull on my line, but let it run deep and did not fight it. I felt I was emptying myself of a great burden. The line unwound like a spool of tension.

Max watched me from the bank and barked like he knew I was in trouble. He dug in the mud in that excited dog way.

It was hard moving, keeping my balance. Max waited until I got out of the water. He licked my hands with his hot tongue. We had shored up our friendship again, and I smiled and he did that dog laugh.

I went back up toward the cabin. I felt light-headed and woozy with hunger, vulnerable in the way only nature can make you feel. Inside, I lit a huge fire and ate beans, piling them onto slabs of bread. I felt the fatigue of the day's work done, a good feeling. My back was hot and sore from cutting the wood. My legs felt sodden, rubbery from the lake water. But it was a good feeling of exhaustion, of having expended myself physically.

I thought that was the way to combat my demons, bringing myself to the point of physical exhaustion, so that I didn't lie awake thinking about things that I couldn't change. And in the back of my mind I was thinking of the tapes.

I felt I was alone with a great secret. It's what I wanted to believe.

Outside, the evening gave way to shadows. Max's barks echoed in the woods. A rind of moon hung in the clearing by the lake.

A faint twinkle of stars was just beginning to show.

I let the evening settle, watched the outside dissolve into utter darkness. I tempered the oil lamp to a yellow glow and put another log on the fire. I drank hot tea until I felt my bladder would burst, then got up and relieved myself in the night. It seemed like it had been dark forever. It was only seven-thirty in the evening. I faced the cold and shivered. Then I walked to the perimeter of trees and saw the lake reflecting the sky.

I called Max, shouted his name so the echo repeated over and over until it died. I thought I heard his bark, or maybe it was just the dying repeat of my own shouts far out in the dark.

Max did not come. I let him be. This was his true nature, unfettered from the fallout of my shambled life. He deserved to roam for just one night after an eternity of nights in the basement.

I made plans inside my head, felt myself finding a way out. Becoming chief held nothing for me except a dead-end future, watching my son grow up from a distance. I would give up everything, sell the house, and move to Chicago, start over again with the money I would make. The tapes said undervalued property in economically depressed areas was a real estate gold mine for those with the foresight to invest. It was all on a tape called "Be an Urban Pioneer."

The secret was that the federal and state governments were footing the housing bill for women on welfare and paying top dollar for apartments in the inner city. All you had to do was go bid on some inner city building zoned for apartments, some loft or abandoned warehouse, and the government had all sorts of programs to help revamp, revitalize, and rezone if necessary, to create subsidized apartments.

The government was looking for *partners* in urban renewal. "You have the vision—they have the money," is how a guy on the tape put it. I had to rewind the tapes because, when it came to specifics about what programs and what strategies to employ, the tapes always said states and cities varied in their approaches, that it was best to do background checking oneself. It listed federal agencies, starting places to get forms.

Still, it sounded promising. There was a testimonial from a guy who was pulling in over twenty grand on a property the Cleveland City Council had sold in a "fire sale." I didn't exactly know what that meant, and the guy didn't explain it, but he said he got the council to subsidize all his renovations by simply allocating twenty percent of his apartments to low-income families. The money had been earmarked from a racial integration fund mandated by federal law. All you had to do was match a federal assistance program to the property you were buying. They would leverage any deal through a bank, since banks were also obliged by law to diversify their loan portfolios.

The guy's wife chimed in and told how their marriage had been saved by the tapes.

The way things stood, I wasn't really seeing Eddy anyway. I could maybe intervene and actually protest his being medicated like he was. Of course, that took money, to get a court order against what was being done to him, but I was willing to flog money out for him. That had never been the issue. The issue had always been just having the money to flog.

And right then, I felt that was what I would do, become a real estate developer. I ran through everything in my head, the bigness of Chicago, the lakefront, eating out at real restaurants, the dating possibilities, not the monotony of where I lived now. I could do what the hell I wanted when and how. All I had to do was follow the tapes.

Before bed, I called Max one last time, but there was still no answer. The silence was absolute when my echoes died, a vegetative wilderness extending far on all sides. My body felt sore and stiff. I went back down by the lake and along the shore. Far up the lake I saw the pale yellow of a meager fire.

And still there was no sign of Max.

In the small bedroom, I curled into my sleeping bag and hit Play on one of the tapes I'd taken in from the car, and I felt that vertigo, like falling from a great height toward a chasm of darkness, and what I had been seeking for so many days—oblivion.

I awoke to choking smoke, suddenly conscious of rushing heat around me, saw flames lick across the outer room. The tape was still playing in my cassette player—like God speaking to me from a burning bush.

My lungs burned as I scrambled from my sleeping bag. There was no window in the bedroom.

I was trapped inside as the flames rose along the outer wall, the wood splintering and splitting. I heard glass shatter and a woof of hot air rushed in. A roof support beam suddenly collapsed and exploded in the outer room in a spray of embers.

The cabin groaned and creaked, wavering in a mirage of intense heat. Part of the roof in my room gave way and another beam collapsed, swaying like a pendulum.

I frantically took the sleeping bag and, wrapping it around me, ran through the wall of heat, throwing myself through the smashed window of the outer room. The sleeping bag stuck to me in a congealed gel of dripping flame. I hit the ground hard, struggled to my feet, scrambled toward the lake, and threw myself in.

The shock took away my breath.

I surfaced into the freezing night air, shaking, slipped and fell again in the water before reaching the bank and sprawling flat on the mud.

Wind swept the fire against the trees, everything glowing a golden color, the gnarled fingers of branches wavering overhead. I was freezing and dragged myself back toward the flames.

My nightshirt was plastered to my back. I huddled by the flames. My skin was scorched, tight as a funeral drum, but I didn't feel the pain yet.

Over the course of an hour, the wind rose and fell, sparks sailing skyward out over the lake, comets of ash that pulsed and disappeared, until eventually all that was left were the four foundation beams—totems, charred ruins that throbbed when the wind picked up. Then the snow started falling softly, making the fire hiss and fizzle, and the cold set back in as shock dissipated and the flames died.

I had to break the window of my car, since the keys were lost in the fire. There was an old blanket in the backseat that I used for Max. I broke through my backseat to get to the trunk and got out a pair of rubber shoes and my flashlight. I draped the blanket over me and went back and squatted against the remains of the cabin. I used a stick to unearth the reddish heat beneath the ash. It showed like a wound.

I stood up and shouted for help from time to time, heard my echoes return, but no one called back. I didn't know what time it was.

And then the cold settled hard around me, and the snow fell. I spent the night in the car, huddled under the blanket.

The morning materialized like an etching, devoid of color in the early light. No sun. Fog smoked on the lake, fire still smoldered and crackled where I kept it going, but the rest was now a pyre of ash. The upper canopy of trees had burned away to reveal sky sailing overhead.

I called Max, but he never came, so I put on my rubber boots and, huddling against the cold, made my way back along the rut of road with a cold sunrise mounting on my back.

17 I struggled out on to the main road. At a gas station a mile down the road, the guy who owned the place came out of his small office when he saw me. He touched the brim of his dirty baseball cap. "What the hell happened? You need me to call the police or a doctor or something?"

"No . . . I just need to use your phone." And just trying to speak, my lungs hurt. My windpipe was hoarse like I'd smoked a thousand cigarettes.

The guy led me into a room that stank of oil, filled with chains and car parts, then down a freezing hallway to a phone.

When Lois answered I couldn't bring myself to speak. Everything welled up inside me. I only got her name said before I felt my throat tighten.

The guy was standing at the end of the hallway listening, drinking a mug of coffee.

I looked at him. He turned and left.

"Lawrence?"

"Listen, Lois . . ."

"Where are you?"

"Just listen to me . . . I had a little trouble last night up at my cabin."

"What?"

"My cabin . . . It burned down."

"My God, are you okay?" She started to ask some more questions, and I leaned against the wall and said, "Lois."

She stopped abruptly.

"I need a big favor. I need you to go get a key from a car dealer and then come get me. I'm at a gas station just south of the turnoff for my cabin. You taking this down?"

"Wait, let me get a pen . . . I got one here somewhere." I heard her voice recede as she set the phone down.

Petey squawked into the receiver. He knew you spoke into a receiver. "No, Petey, not now. Lawrence had an accident," and just my name made him peck at the phone. "No, stop that, Petey!" She said it like you'd talk to a baby.

She got back on the line.

I gave her the model number and VIN for my car and the directions to the gas station.

She started to ask me more questions, but I said, "I can't talk . . . Max . . . he's missing."

I had to squeeze my eyes just to stop from crying.

When I came back up front, the guy said, "I got you these." He handed me a pair of overalls and a first aid kit, and led me around to the toilet.

The key was on a huge paddle.

"You figure how that fire started?"

"A spark?" I was limping as I walked.

In the cinder block coldness of the bathroom I saw my reflection in the mirror. I looked bad, shrouded in Max's blanket, my arms and legs blackened by the fire, my hair singed. But the damage was mostly superficial. I didn't feel much pain even then. I washed gently, dabbed away the blackness. I could see the extent of my injuries. I'd been lucky.

The flesh had only cracked and slightly blistered along my left arm and leg where the sleeping bag filling had congealed on my skin and stuck. I peeled off a swatch of weeping skin that smelt of chemicals.

I put zinc oxide on my blisters, got into the overalls, and went back around front.

Through the morning, the guy pored over a Chilton's car manual while working on some truck. A few cars stopped for gas, one with a deer strapped to the roof.

The guy went out and told each customer what had happened to me. I could see them looking at the garage, shaking their heads. I was the story to break the monotony of a winter day.

I ate from the vending machine, stale Twinkies and Hostess cupcakes.

It wasn't until midafternoon that Lois arrived.

We went back along the rutted road to the cabin to get my car. She gave me a running account of how hard it was to get a key cut without showing a title that she owned the car. I just let her talk. It was snowing again, but the sun was out, shining through the trees.

There was nothing left of the cabin except ash and the squat potbellied stove crouching next to the remains of the brick chimney.

I called Max. There was no response. There was the pop of gunfire somewhere in the woods.

Lois hugged herself and shivered. "You were lucky. I'm surprised you didn't freeze to death just getting to that gas station."

I worked the key in the ignition. It didn't quite catch. I had to jiggle it before it fit. The engine turned over. I revved it.

Lois had moved down toward the lake's edge and was calling Max. I went down to her.

"Maybe leave a note with that guy at the gas station. You might give a reward for anybody who finds him." Lois drew herself into me. I winced from the burns, but held her against my chest for a few moments. Snow was coming down in big drifting flakes from the trees.

I said, "Why don't we stop and get something to eat on the way back?"

Then we turned and went back up to the cars, shadows already falling across the charred ruins.

It was in the dying light, while driving along the funnel of road, just past the old log bridge, that I saw something hanging from a tree. It was like an apparition in the white haze of falling snow, like a ghost suspended in midair. I stopped, shone my spotlight into the trees, and saw Max in the cone of light. He had been hung from the branch of a tree. His eyes gleamed, but they were lifeless.

I turned to look back at Lois in her car. I think she was screaming, but I couldn't hear a sound.

18

Max was wrapped in his blanket in the trunk of my car. I didn't stop until I reached the restaurant parking lot. Lois got out of her car and came and sat in with me.

"I'm so sorry, Lawrence." Her face was half-lit by the parking lot outside.

I didn't say anything for a while.

I whispered, "He was hung up like he was executed." I felt my throat tighten.

Lois put her hand on mine. "Hunters . . . that's who got him. Maybe it was an accident, something moving fast through the trees like that . . ."

I shook my head. "His throat was slit open."

Lois put her hand to her mouth. Her eyes closed. "How can people do such terrible things?" She opened her eyes again. "No matter how it happened, Max died doing what he wanted. He died in the wild. It was no life for him in that basement." She put her hand against my face. "Think of it that way. That's how you got to look at it." She stopped and her eyes were filled with tears. "I'm glad you didn't die. I don't want to lose you, ever."

I didn't say anything. In my mind I knew it was Earl who'd tried to kill me. Maybe he really believed I would blackmail him. I had to contain myself. I wanted Lois to stop talking, but she kept talking. She squeezed my hand. "Lawrence, it's a blessing in disguise, is what it is, you'll come to understand that."

I said, "I think it was Earl Johnson that tried to kill me."

"No, Lawrence, just stop."

I pulled away from her. "You don't know the fight I had with him and Helen before coming up here."

Lois shook her head. "Why would Earl leave Max hanging like that if he burned down your cabin? It doesn't make sense. It would arouse suspicion. Think about it."

I put a hand to my forehead.

"And how would they know you came here?"

"I had the car packed. They'd have seen that."

Lois shook her head. "It was hunters, Lawrence, that's who it was."

"And the fire?"

"You had a fire going in the cabin, right?"

I didn't answer her.

Lois looked at me and whispered, "Tell me something beautiful about Max."

And for a few quiet moments I let everything subside inside me. I told Lois about Max's last day alive, what we did together, and she smiled and I smiled, and she said, "Dogs are forgivers." She put her lips to the back of my trembling hands.

In the restaurant Lois ate the nightly special, open-faced turkey sandwiches and mashed potato. I barely touched my own food.

I said, "Who do you think would have come to my funeral if I'd died?"

Lois didn't answer me. She asked me if I was eating my slab of turkey. She took it and underneath was that compressed stuffing. I felt like I was going to throw up. I had to go to the bathroom to run water on my face.

On the way back I saw the restaurant was done in the shape of a keg, with the middle of the barrel the main eating area. I hadn't noticed that on the way in.

When I sat back down, I said, "I'm thinking of resigning from the department. I'm putting my house on the market and going to Chicago."

Lois made a scoffing sound. "You don't just sell a house. If people find out you're going, they wait it out, wait until you're desperate to sell."

"I'll rent it then."

Lois made a face. "Renting is a bad proposition all around. You never get out what you put into a rental."

"Jesus Christ, what the hell do you want me to do? Burn it and collect on the insurance? What do you say to that?"

I must have been talking loudly, because people turned and looked at me. A guy in lederhosen came by with coffee refills. He told us how to say "thank you" in German. Lois smiled that way people smile when they are just humoring somebody and waited until he left us.

"You leave now, Lawrence, and you cast yourself adrift of everything, your kid, your job . . . Just don't do anything you're going to regret."

I shook my head. "I don't think I can live in my house anymore. That's the basic problem."

"Move in with me. Am I that bad?"

I looked at her. "What do you see in me?"

"It's not what I see in you so much as what I see as the alternative." She smiled. "That was a joke, Lawrence, laugh."

But I wasn't in the mood for laughing.

The guy in lederhosen shorts came around again, but this time he was playing an accordion. The back of the menu was a song sheet. You were supposed to sing along. But then he looked at my face for a moment, and I realized he was looking at the zinc oxide. I must have looked real bad because he turned quickly away.

There was a motel across from the restaurant. We spent the night there. I awoke in the middle of the night with this sudden jerk, conscious that Max was gone forever. I got up and looked out the window at my car parked in the space outside. Max was still in the trunk.

I got dressed and went out and looked at him wrapped in the blanket. His tongue hung out of his mouth, a stiff darkish color; the wound across his neck had clotted. I set him on the ground and ran my hand along his muzzle, told him I was sorry for everything. I felt my eyes fill with tears.

There was no point taking him home. The ground was too hard to dig through to bury him.

Here was a life lived in the aftermath of my divorce, now ended. There had been no change, no freedom. He'd lived out his last years a prisoner.

And then against the backdrop of the faint aqua light of the motel, I took Max and went around to a Dumpster and buried him deep under boxes.

I used the pay phone outside the front office. Someone had scrawled into the metal casing of the phone, "I don't question YOUR existence—God!"

I called Janine, but Seth answered in a sleepy voice. "Who is this?"

"Ask Janine if she remembers how we got Max as a present for Eddy. Ask her, Seth?"

Seth said in a muffled voice, "It's Lawrence, he's drunk or something."

"What time is it?"

I heard Seth say something and Janine raise her voice.

I heard the click in my ear as the line of connection died between us.

19

It was a week and a half before the state championship final in Indianapolis. Reporters were preparing sound bites on the steps of the town hall.

It was already past ten o'clock. It had snowed through the night and into the early morning, but had cleared so the world gleamed in the cold daylight, the sky a ceramic blue you only got during the winter.

There was a buzz in the air, polyester-clad secretaries near the water fountains talking in tight circles, all smoking and holding cups of coffee. Some of them stared at me as I passed.

I had zinc oxide under my left eye, and the left side of my face had come up in a rash of small water blisters. A patch of hair above my left ear had singed almost to the scalp, all from the congealed synthetic sleeping bag filling.

I smelt like burnt toast.

It looked worse than it was. That's how I was going to portray it, since it stung, but that was all. I was preparing for a long day of repetitious storytelling, but I'd told Lois to say nothing about Max. I couldn't face having to recount what had happened to him.

I just sat quietly at my desk. I didn't have to be out on rounds until the afternoon. I called Lois but she didn't pick up. I tried her house. She wasn't there. I didn't want to get coffee alone. I called her office again.

Thirty-six hours ago, I thought, I had nearly died, and here I was again, back in the sardine-can police trailer. So much for changing my life! And those Wealth Tapes—had I been conning myself? I didn't have what it took.

I scanned the Yellow Pages and found a two-page spread for a realty outfit called Admiralty Realty.

The woman on the end of the line told me her specialty was commercial, not residential properties, but she said she could discuss terms for listing my house if I wanted. She said she could fit me in between appointments. We arranged to meet at her office at the mall the next day. It was only after hanging up the phone that I saw the name. The woman I'd been talking to was the mayor's wife. I thought about calling back to cancel, but didn't.

I left my office and saw Lois talking with the chief in the hallway. They were standing close together, the chief with his hand on her shoulder. The chief turned his head for a moment and saw me. He called my name and made a whistling noise.

I said, "It's not as bad as it looks."

The chief said, "I'm sorry about your dog."

I made eye contact with Lois, and she lowered her eyes.

"Hunters!" the chief said. "A guy gets a line on something, and a dog is out there barking . . . You can't let a domesticated animal out loose like that, not up there you can't."

The mayor showed up, along with Arnold Fisher. The mayor looked at me, "What happened?" and I told him the simple fact that my cabin had caught fire.

The chief said, "His dog's throat got slit open by hunters."

The mayor stared at me. "You okay?"

"It looks worse than it is."

"It looks bad."

Arnold Fisher told a story about a hunting dog his father kept years ago that had got its muzzle caught in a hunting trap and how it pulled off its face trying to free itself.

Lois put her hands to her ears and said, "Don't tell me something like that, Arnold Fisher. I'll have nightmares."

The mayor cut in. "I need to see you, Chief, and you, Lawrence, in my office." The mayor didn't say why. He just said in a grave voice, "*Now*, if you don't mind," then turned, and the chief and I followed him up the flight of stairs.

When we entered his office, Betty looked up at the mayor and said, "They found Cheryl's body in the next town over."

There is no describing the fear that coursed through me just hearing those words. My legs felt like they'd been shot up with Novocain.

The mayor never did look at me, though the chief did for a moment. He seemed to avert his eyes toward Betty, then back toward me, like it wasn't safe to talk.

When I looked to the window my eyes hurt, it was that bright outside. I felt outside my body, like this wasn't happening.

The mayor went into his office and changed out of his plaid salesman jacket. He came out in his heavy parka with its fake fur hood. "Tell them we're on our way."

He just walked by both of us, and we followed.

We traveled in the same car out to where Cheryl's body had been discovered. The chief drove, the mayor in the backseat. CB static filled the silence that persisted between us. I didn't dare say anything.

Cheryl had been missing for two days, but her parents had only filed a report earlier this morning. Cheryl had no curfew. It was that kind of family, liberal. They had been there almost fifteen years, but were still considered newcomers—city transplants. I learned that listening to the mayor, who jockeyed himself forward and spoke with someone on the CB. He never did speak with me directly.

Cheryl's discovery in the next town over meant we had no official part in the case. We were there simply to provide information. The county was leading the investigation. Again, I learned that by overhearing a static-filled voice talking to the mayor.

I don't think the person on the other end of the CB even knew Cheryl had been Kyle's girlfriend. It was hard just trying to understand who knew what. We had become mired so in our secrets. All I made out was the chief's eyes catching a glimpse of me from time to time.

We traveled out along County Road, then east on Baker's Road. I was aware only of the flat landscape of blackish cornstalks, of the weak sun low on the horizon. We were out near Janine's house. I could see it set against the blue sky. We came up behind one Amish horse-drawn carriage, then another and another, passing each slowly. And further on, we came level with a roadblock at an intersection.

The chief spoke with a cop who let us through.

A crowd had already begun to gather, so the chief had to drive slowly as two cops cleared the way. I recognized faces from our town looking in at us.

And minutes later, on a lonesome tract of raised dirt road, not far from where Kyle Johnson lived, on the far eastern edge of the Amish holding, we finally came upon the glare of police flares, to the place where Cheryl Carpenter's car had plunged off a wooden bridge.

An ambulance had arrived, but the attendants were standing around smoking and talking to one another.

There were camera crews already on the scene, filming the police trying to get a tow truck close enough to haul out Cheryl's car. This was all flood-prone land and the road was raised, but the embankment gave way as one tow truck backed down to the water's edge.

Up on the dirt road, another tow truck hitched a line to the truck down in the embankment, then pulled away slowly until the line between them was taut.

The mayor left us and went over to a fat guy in a long black coat who was crouching with two others, pointing back at a cordoned-off area of road that followed the path the car took off the bridge.

From the rise on the embankment I watched a frogman take a heavy winch and dive into the icy water, then move like a tadpole toward the submerged car to hook it. He surfaced, raising his thumb to the driver.

Slowly the car emerged, glazed and dripping, its chrome glinting as it was dragged to the roadside, the dark shape of a body visible in the driver's seat, the head slumped forward in a wreath of tangled hair.

Police photographers took their time photographing the car. When they went to remove Cheryl's body, they had a hard time maneuvering her out of the seat. She was stiff.

She was laid out on a tarp. Her head lolled sideways, and white froth oozed from her nose and mouth. The body looked wrinkled and shrunken, aged, hair matted with silt, hands clawed.

All that indicated that Cheryl Carpenter was a teenager was what she was wearing—a cheerleading jacket, Jordache jeans, and Nike sneakers.

I turned away as she was zipped into a body bag.

It was on the ride back to town that I said, "I think Earl tried to kill me, too . . ."

The chief eased off the gas. He turned and looked at me so blankly that I looked away.

The mayor leaned forward, his voice even. "We don't know what happened here yet."

"I know what I know, what *I feel*. Don't tell me this is a coincidence, don't! The two people who knew what Kyle did . . . One dead, and . . . They nearly killed me too."

The chief raised his voice. "That abortionist committed suicide!"

The mayor put his hand on the chief's shoulder. "Let's calm down."

He set his other hand on my shoulder. I flinched. He was talking into my ear. "I called Earl this morning after I got the missing person's report on Cheryl, to see how Kyle was, and you know what he told me, Lawrence?" He waited a moment. "He told me you'd been out waiting on them the other morning. What were you doing there?"

The chief eased off the gas. I closed my eyes for a moment, swallowed, and felt my throat tighten as the mayor said, "What Earl told me was that you were trying to blackmail them."

I raised my voice. "You know that's a lie. I never asked him for a dime! He's a son-of-a-bitch liar!"

The chief shifted, looked at the mayor, then at me, and then at the road ahead. I could see his lips moving.

"You haven't answered the question, Lawrence. What were you doing out there?"

I didn't answer because we came level with the roadblock again and the chief rolled down his window and spoke with the cop keeping back a crowd of kids from our town who'd gathered. Some were crying. The mayor rolled down his window and a rush of cold air poured over our faces. He shook the hand of a girl who was holding a bunch of flowers.

The chief pulled out onto County Road, leaving behind the bite and rumble of dirt road, and the mayor came forward again so I could feel his breath in my ear. He said in a low, menacing voice, "You try and say Earl was involved in anything and you draw everything down around you and *us*."

I kept looking straight ahead. "I just want out."

"We're getting there, slowly. This isn't the time to lose your nerve." His voice was measured. "What we just saw back there at the river has all the hallmarks of a suicide. I let the lead investigator in on Cheryl having had an abortion. I know him. He says he thinks it fits . . . fits with what they've put together so far. There were no signs of her losing control. What Cheryl did was just drive off the bridge. It's a classic case of depression. It's how many people take their own lives. Guilt . . ." The mayor hesitated. "Guilt is an undertow that can pull you under. Just because abortion is legal doesn't make it right. I think Cheryl is someone to be pitied." He repeated the word "pitied."

I just lowered my head. That was going to be the general wording of the statement he was going to release to the press.

"Look, I want you to take the rest of the week off. That's an order. And I want you to promise me you're going to stay the hell away from Earl. Let me hear you say it, Lawrence," and I did.

I met Lois coming out of her office and we had coffee in the break room. Her hands were trembling. She kept looking away from me.

"They think it's a suicide, given the physical evidence, that is."

Lois closed her eyes, and whispered, "My God . . ."

I tried to touch her hand, but she moved it. When she opened her eyes they were glassy.

I wanted to ask her what she knew about what we had done. She must have known about the cover-up, but I wanted to hear her say it. I wanted to confide in someone, but instead, I said the opposite of what I wanted to say.

I said, "Tomorrow I'm meeting with the mayor's wife to put my house on the market. I'm planning on getting out of here for good."

Lois wiped her nose with the back of her hand, looked at me and then down at her coffee. There were lipstick marks around it.

She said quietly, "Do what you have to."

She got up and left me sitting there alone.

20 News of Cheryl Carpenter's death spread like wildfire, made its way into the newspaper and TV by that evening, along with rumors about her having an abortion.

In the bathroom, I took off my shirt. The hair had burned off my arms; the skin around the worst areas shone wet under the bathroom light. The crown of my head felt tight. I touched the places where the hair had singed. I dabbed my arms and the backs of my hands with warm water, then washed my face and reapplied the zinc oxide.

I thought of Lois's husband, hanging like a pendulum, marking time, out there alone on the road, a denizen of cheap motels, a vacuum salesman, selling exactly that, a vacuum, trying to fill the void in people's lives, coming with his jar of dirt and hoses, and that woman standing over him with her housecoat undone, both arriving at that appointed crisis played out against the tick-tock existence of a mantel-piece clock in her living room.

I wasn't fooling myself, I was willing to start over, to try a different life, to take that risk. I was statistically almost halfway through my life on earth. I looked at myself in the mirror. Why, in the second half of my life, couldn't I achieve both economic and emotional freedom, liberate myself through the buying and selling of real estate. Why not?

What the tapes said was that, in times of economic hardship, a keen investor could buy cheap and rent expensive. It was all there on the tapes. If they didn't work, would those commercials still be running? They came with a money-back guarantee. I had nothing to lose. I was the ideal candidate.

And at some gut level, I had another reason for leaving. I was afraid of the Johnsons, although I didn't want to admit it.

I turned to go downstairs and could have sworn I saw Max out of the corner of my eye. I knew my mind would make slips like that for weeks to come, like an amputee with a phantom limb.

The Cheryl Carpenter story dominated the evening news. A parade of classmates spoke to the camera. There was a shot of a nondescript gym shower, reminding viewers of how she had nearly hemorrhaged to death after her abortion.

Cheryl Carpenter had been severely depressed since then, and suicide seemed the inevitable conclusion. A friend of Cheryl's broke down on camera and said she knew Cheryl was depressed. She just had not known how bad it had gotten for Cheryl. When asked if she knew Cheryl had had an abortion, the girl looked into the camera and said, "It was a *secret* everybody knew."

It was a tragedy that broached so many social issues: premarital sex, contraception, teen pregnancy, abortion, depression, and suicide. The backdrop shot that defined the story was of Kyle and Cheryl at Junior Prom, Kyle putting a corsage on Cheryl's wrist. We were to witness that still shot for many days to come.

A psychologist hired to provide grief counseling spoke on behalf of the school district. She wore beads, her hair unkempt, a face devoid of makeup, one of those New Age gurus of ambiguous sexuality, a woman who kept talking of "removing the boundaries of discourse," of "the need to face our own societal dysfunction." She was leading focus groups, conducting ritualized, communal grief sessions at, where else, the goddamn center of the universe, the gym. It looked like some Pentecostal revival meeting with the faithful talking in tongues, exorcising secrets and demons. Kids were crying and hugging one another.

The media spliced and diced football footage, the Amish, the hordes descending on the high school for pep rallies, the Johnsons' miserable family holding, a telephoto shot taken from the road that caught Kyle working alongside his father in the barn, a shot of Cheryl Carpenter in a school production of *The Music Man*, juxtaposed with a shot of her car being hoisted from the river, and then the makeshift memorial next to the bridge where Cheryl had died, a grotto of flowers and cards, the stunned and grieving faces of kids and parents coming to terms with the tragedy.

Finally, the mayor spoke from his car lot, out amidst the triangular flags, dressed in his salesman's jacket. He spoke of community, of how we had lived through adversity before, that we were rallying around one another, that it was what distinguished us as a town. When asked if the game would go on, he said it was what Cheryl would have wanted.

He looked right at the camera and said, "This one's for you, Cheryl!"

I don't know how the mayor faced the camera, how he never betrayed what lay beneath everything. It was more than self-deception. It was something inherent within him—the political animal.

He had been party in some ways to her death. We all had been.

And for the first time I imagined Cheryl veering off the road, the horror of what she'd done catching up with her, that sudden moment of self-doubt, alone with her secrets, her sadness, second-guessing herself, the absurdity of everything going on around her: the pomp and ceremony, the high school floats for homecoming, the pep rallies, the games, the push for glory, the swirl of color guard. How had she put all that out of her mind, walking into the cold sterility of an abortion clinic? Of course, the answer was she hadn't put it out of her mind.

Amidst the swirl of activity, Kyle never appeared on camera, never made a statement. I could almost hear Helen Johnson telling Kyle that Cheryl had succumbed to her sin, taken from this world for what she did to the child inside her, the glib righteousness of the Saved passing judgment on the Damned.

I woke cold and lonely. I didn't feel much like doing anything. I was on a so-called vacation. I turned and faced the window. It had rained through the night, but now the day had lightened.

Getting out of bed, I stepped on Max's squeeze-rubber newspaper. The shadow of death had fallen over all of us, or that's how it felt, like we had all been cursed.

I was going to cancel the meeting with the mayor's wife simply because I felt awkward dealing with her, but when I called to cancel, she talked in such an upbeat way about fair market value for my house that I caved in and said I'd just called to confirm the time of the appointment.

I spent almost forty-five minutes in the shower trying to get that cold feeling out of my body. As I was leaving, the phone rang.

It was Janine's lawyer. "I'm advising you that, pending all back payments of child support, your visitation rights are stopped."

"You need a court injunction to do that."

"I've drawn up documents. You got a lawyer I can send them to? We're filing at the courthouse today."

"No, I don't."

"Well, get one."

I shouted, "I just gave her eight hundred bucks! What the hell does she want from me?"

Janine's lawyer said flatly, "There's an outstanding balance of seventeen hundred owed. Just call me with your lawyer's name," and hung up.

And of course that was an added expense, getting a lawyer involved. The link of my parentage loosened yet again, and I knew my decision to move away was the right one.

Outside, the rain had melted the snow and the word "PIG" was visible again on my lawn.

I passed a cart in the middle of the mall advertising chiropractic services, offering a deal where you got a free X ray so they could see if you were aligned. The scam was, when you went to the office for the consultation, the chiropractor told you he needed to X ray the other side of your body. The free X ray was only for one half of your body. You had to pay for the other side. I knew this, because I'd been screwed by the scam. It was one of the things still on one of my Visa cards. I felt like smashing the cart.

The mayor's wife, Jean—that's what she insisted on being called— was set up in the mall next to a bank. I knew right off I'd made a mistake coming to talk to her.

The only thing I knew about the mayor's wife was that she was a breast cancer survivor, that she'd had a radical mastectomy. She'd sponsored a Breast Cancer Run in a neighboring town for the past few years.

As soon as I saw her, she reminded me of that rich wife of the millionaire on *Gilligan's Island*, a birdlike flake, decked out in an embroidered gold-crested blazer, sporting that overdone nautical look, with the typical realtor's oven-baked tan.

However, the flake facade was short-lived and she quickly got down to business, asking me for details of square footage, number of bedrooms, whether the basement was finished or unfinished; then she pulled out some listings of houses that had sold in the area in the past year, and I arrived fairly quickly at the conclusion that I was going to take a bath selling the house. The market had tanked.

So Jean moved on to a discussion of renting out the house, which I gathered was her specialty. She discussed what structural changes might be necessary to divide the house into two separate units, gave me an overview of the process for gaining building permits, the zoning rules covering multiple dwellings for my zip code, referencing volumes of official state and local binders on esoteric issues I didn't even pretend to follow, and when she got to doing the numbers, I can only liken her proficiency with an adding machine to a chicken feeding, a frenetic pecking.

Over the course of twenty minutes, she assessed and calculated how much I would have to invest, and how long it would take me to realize a profit from renting a portion of my house.

By all estimates, she felt I was about eighteen months out from seeing a realistic return on converting my house into a rental property, even with the financing and payment schedules she felt she could negotiate with the bank on my behalf. And this wasn't to mention that I would be homeless.

With the figures laid out before us, she was inches from me. Her press-on nails tapped the lacquered tabletop like an agitated insect. I could smell her coffee breath and the chemical smell of her perm, overlaid with a rose perfume.

When she went to her filing cabinet, I could see her panty lines, but it wasn't sexy. She and the mayor never had children, and somehow, just looking at her, I thought of the plastic anatomy of a Barbie doll's nether regions. I don't think I had ever hated and respected someone simultaneously at one time in all my life. I thought, here was a woman who needed to make her own Wealth Tapes.

She sat back down again and showed me the listing of properties she managed, both commercial and residential. Most of her residential properties were clustered in the old historic district where, with each passing year, the big mansions were being converted into one-room apartments.

At the end of our conversation, Jean asked me about my personal finances, if I had any savings, and as she was photocopying the property listings she managed in the area, I said flatly that I was expecting to collect on a fire insurance policy, that I was expecting a settlement any day. It seemed like the only way out of my financial ruin.

As I was leaving, Jean said candidly, "How come you decided to move?"

It stopped me for a moment, the candid way she asked the question. Did she know about what we'd done? But she just looked at me straight in the eyes, betraying nothing. Maybe it was just small talk, so I said simply, "No real reason," shrugging my shoulders. "I felt like I needed to start over was all."

And then she said something which changed my opinion of what she knew. She said, "You were the one who found Sarah?"

It caught me off guard for a moment, her using the child's name.

Jean said, "Sorry, I shouldn't have asked you that." She was holding the listing in her hands and gave it to me.

The pages were warm from the photocopier.

I said, "The truth is I was thinking about leaving a long time before that happened. I had a marriage that didn't work out."

She was looking right at me. "We only live once. I don't think we ever really confront that until it's too late."

I knew she was referring to her own cancer. Somehow we had bridged the differences between us. I forced myself to smile. "I'm hoping it's not *too* late for me."

"You're taking the first step. That's what counts. If I can help you, call me."

I felt this flush of warmth on my face. "I appreciate you meeting me. I think I'm making the right decision." And at that moment I felt I was.

On the wall, as I was leaving, I saw a photograph of Jean at one of her runs in a T-shirt and sweatpants, looking defiantly at the camera. Jean's shirt said simply "Survivor," and just maybe I had been wrong about her humanity. I was willing to admit that.

I put a call into my insurance agent—Friendly Bob Adams, or that's what the commercial called him. Bob didn't sound too friendly when I explained what happened. He gave me the runaround and said I should have reported the fire immediately, since claim adjusters usually like to arrive while a fire is still smoldering.

I said, "Come on, Bob, don't pull my chain here. I've paid my premiums. You want me to come over and show you what I look like? I was nearly burned to death."

I imagined him trying to figure out how the hell he could dismiss my claim. But he said diplomatically, "Let me discuss the issue with my field office, given you probably couldn't get to a phone to file this claim, right?"

It was a leading question, and I said, "Right, I didn't have access to a phone."

I didn't know if Bob was feeling magnanimous or what, or if the claim was so paltry that he felt it could be shoved through. Guys like him lived on word-of-mouth recommendations.

He said, "The field office might have a claim adjuster up that way who can go on out and investigate the cause of the fire," then he back-ended one deal with another, and I wanted to tell him to forget it, but Bob said, "Now that I got you on the phone, I have a hell of a deal here on life insurance. It's something you shouldn't pass up. I see here in your file you're covered for less than thirty thousand right now."

I said, "I'm divorced, Bob. What's thirty grand going to do for me if I'm dead?"

21 I spent Friday driving around listening to the Wealth Tapes. I stopped off at a Walgreen's and bought a flash for my Polaroid. I wanted to document my injuries. I didn't trust Friendly Bob.

That evening, I went by Lois's house and saw her porch light on. Her car was in the drive. I wanted to make up with her. I got out and knocked on the door, but there was no answer.

I went around to the living room window. Petey was sitting inside his cage, moving his head in a bobbing manner, trying to make out who'd knocked at the door.

I knew Lois was out with the chief. I felt like I'd been sucker-punched.

I couldn't bring myself to go home and instead stopped off at a diner, bought the *Chicago Tribune*, ordered a coffee and a slice of banana silk pie with that godawful fake whipped cream.

There was a picture of Kyle and Cheryl in the lower right-hand section and a summary account of the tragedy. On the following page, there was a shot of the car being hoisted from the river. The image brought home the depression Cheryl Carpenter must have felt to drive off a bridge like that.

And sitting alone, staring at the paper, reading about how Cheryl had committed suicide, I knew I had been wrong about so many things.

Because of my own paranoia, I had jumped to conclusions that had turned out to be false. I had been wrong about everything, about Kyle's fortitude and will to succeed. He had not broken down.

As I leveled with myself, I began to doubt whether I'd really seen Kyle drop off Kendall that night, or whether I was influenced by what Laycock had said about Kyle. I'd raced after the car a minute or so after it left. In the six miles out to the Johnsons' farm, I would surely have caught up with Kyle if it had been him.

That was the cold reality—it was my own paranoia, all of it.

A waitress refilled my coffee. It tasted strong. In the dark circle of the cup, I could see myself looking back, and I didn't like admitting it, but I felt a sense of security, felt safe for the first time since this had all started.

Cheryl Carpenter was dead. Kyle Johnson's secret was buried once and for all.

In the quiet diner, I spent another hour scanning the For Sale and Legal Notice listings in the paper, marking off blue-collar specials along the border of Indiana and Illinois, small ranch-style homes on streets with Polish and Russian names, houses in foreclosure or going cheap since the steel industry had bottomed out. I set my sights on these properties as potential rentals. Of course, I needed the money from the insurance on the cabin as a down payment, but it would come.

I took off my shirt in the bathroom and pointed the Polaroid Instamatic at the mirror, taking a series of shots of my reflection, documenting my injuries, then took the shots and spent frosted flash cubes into my living room.

I let the shots materialize on the coffee table, then I set about getting drunk.

Later that night, I thought, even if Earl Johnson had tried to kill me, the irony was, he'd bought my freedom, and somehow I couldn't resist calling their house when I got stinking drunk. I shouted, "You son of a bitch. I know you tried to kill me, but I got one up on you!"

Lois called Saturday morning. "You awake?" I could hear a coughing noise in the background. I looked at the clock. It wasn't even seven o'clock. I still felt drunk.

"Wait, Lawrence, wait a minute . . ."

Lois put her hand over the phone, muffling the sound. When she started talking again, it was in a whisper. "How do you get somebody out of your house?"

"Let me guess, the chief?"

"Don't, please."

"Where is he?"

"In the shower."

I said, "Cook him the worst breakfast you have ever cooked in your life."

"This isn't a joke," but her voice eased a bit. "How come I keep making the same mistakes?"

I didn't say anything.

"You know Lionel used to have me eat naked sometimes when he got mad. He said that's how you watch calories . . . I was never good enough for him." I heard her voice quake. "Please, Lawrence, I want you to take me with you. We can start over. I got money . . . Please, it's not what you think, Lawrence. He's . . . he's impotent. All we do is hold hands, that's all, I swear to you."

I closed my eyes. "Lois! Stop! I don't want to hear . . ." But before I could finish, she said, "He's out of the shower. I have to go. Maybe tonight you can come by for tuna casserole, if you think you can still stand me."

Two hours later I saw Chicago as a mirage in the distance over the lake. The Sears Tower, the tallest building in the world, rose out of one of the flattest landscapes in the world. Here was a city twice born, reduced to rubble by a cow kicking an oil lantern, if that was to be believed, if such small events could change history, but the truth is they probably did. This was the city where the first atom was split, in a laboratory tucked under, of all places, a football stand.

I passed the vocational school in Gary we had defeated in the semi-final. It was set off to the side of the skyway, in the shadow of the plants, the hot foundry cooling pools steaming. Mutated fish swam in the warm-water runoff swamp surrounding the plants, and yet people still fished there.

The smell of sulfur made the air taste bitter, a haze of pollution hanging in the wintry light, the chimney stacks breathing fire. I watched it all rise along the skyway, and it seemed longer than a week ago that Kyle led us through this netherworld to the final.

I exited the skyway along a tongue of asphalt and parked in the parking lot of a discount liquor and smoke outlet, watched a black guy in a Member's Only jacket dealing drugs, his hair greased and plastered to his head with Jeri Curl. He had a flat-handled comb sticking out of his designer jeans. He turned and saw me looking, maybe saw that cop look about me, and went inside the liquor store.

I knew I should have just turned around, that the easiest thing in the world would have been to go back to Lois, to take her money, to move in with her. I don't know why I fought the idea of being with Lois. It wasn't that she was bad-looking, or that there was anything wrong with her. I guess the problem was I would never have given her a second look before my divorce. Just thinking of her, I thought of the chief, saw him holding one of his fishing rods, staring at it. It was pathetic given what I knew about him, one of those indelible images that I was always going to associate with him from then on. A shudder ran down my spine.

I had a Chicago map with me and checked the addresses of the houses listed in the *Chicago Tribune* just to blank that image of him out, then put the car in gear and set off along the road under the skyway.

At a blinking traffic light, I took a right and drove into a subdivision of identical squat, ranch-style houses of postwar vintage, small utilitarian dreams poured literally feet apart into postage-stamp lots, rows and rows of them. Some lawns were decorated with those gaudy pink plastic flamingos, others going for improbably happy gnomes pushing wheelbarrows, all imprisoned behind cyclone fencing.

It felt like I was watching foreigners struggling to speak a new language, that inexact mixing of tense and verb agreement, stuttering, missing the nuances of language. Each year Nazi prison guards, murderers of thousands, were found hiding out in the obscurity of an autoplant assembly, tracked down by the Jewish League to blue-collar areas like this around Chicago and Detroit. It was strange how hatred could morph into autoworker, how evil could transform itself. I thought of John Wayne Gacy and his suburban mass grave, over thirty young boys in a crawl space.

Skirting the periphery of these houses, I stared across the no-man's-land between the factories and the city, stared at the foundry pools and spines of freight railway tracks.

I could tell I'd walked into an emotional land mine at the first house on my list. The door was opened by a middle-aged Slav woman in a loose-fitting roll-neck sweater. Her arms were folded in that foreign way, her oversized breasts resting on her arms. The woman had been arguing, her face red, but she smiled despite whatever was going on and led me into an absurdly small and oppressively hot living room, where an older woman sat staring out the window, purposely ignoring me.

I wanted to get the hell out of there. *Wide World of Sports* was on the TV. A guy with the worst toupee in the world was preparing to bowl.

The daughter turned and saw me looking and said, "This man, they give fifty thousand dollars for that?" She said it with such disgust. The asking price on her house was forty-two thousand five hundred dollars.

I spent a few more excruciating minutes taking the so-called tour of the house. The daughter told me she worked in the cosmetics department of Lord & Taylor in downtown Chicago. That was where she lived now. She said her mother was going to Ohio to live with her younger sister.

I moved along a narrow shag-carpeted hallway, past a bathroom, to two small bedrooms, one with a double bed that took up most of the room, the other obviously the childhood shrine of the daughter, done in pinks and lace with a princess's canopy bed. The porcelain faces of dolls stared back at me from a small table with one of those backlit vanity mirrors. This was the dream of a proletarian Alice in Wonderland, of an émigré peasant.

The house next door was so close I could have climbed into it.

I decided not to visit the next two houses on the list when I got to them. One of them was overshadowed by a series of giant electrical transmission poles that sizzled. There was a Doberman at the window of the other.

At the last house, I was confronted by a smell of cabbage soup, a smell so strong I could almost feel it coat my tongue. A small transistor radio was tuned to a Polish station. I heard someone say "Solidarnosc" and "Lech Walesa."

A skeletal man of retirement age sat at his kitchen table, playing solitaire, licking his thumb, peeling each card from the deck, laying them down one at a time, as though he were reading a fortune. A cigarette smoldered on a saucer.

The man looked up when I opened the screen door. It was freezing inside, but he was wearing only a short-sleeved shirt. He had one of those Holocaust tattoos on his arm. We had all seen them on TV, but seeing it in real life stopped me cold. He looked like what one of the Horsemen of the Apocalypse might have looked like with his robe off, when he was at home.

The house was sparsely furnished, just the bare essentials. I walked along an identical hallway to the Slavic woman's house I'd gone into, but only one bedroom was furnished, with a single bed and a small dresser. There was a sepia shot of a woman and children that looked like it had been taken years ago, in his homeland maybe, but since there was no sign of a wife or children in the house, I wondered if they had perished. The other bedroom was an empty box, like a cell.

Off in the distance I could hear the railway, and I thought of trainloads of Jews destined for ovens. That is how it all affected me.

The old man shuffled down the hallway, wheezing when he breathed. He had emphysema. He told me he was going back to Poland to die. His asking price for the house was a mere thirty-three thousand five hundred dollars. He was even open to a renting option, where he'd put a percentage of my rent toward a down payment.

It was maybe the only thing I could afford, but it was a house filled with ghosts. It gave me the creeps. I could see the sepia shot of his family beside his bed, staring out into this foreign land.

I said, "Let me think about it," and took a copy of the house listing, but I knew I would never go back there again.

22 I felt sick to my stomach. The morning seemed years ago, as though I had been away for a long time. It was dark when I pulled off the highway into the glare of the gas island and filled up. The beginnings of lake effect snow swirled and showed against the light, but none of it was sticking yet. A strong wind pulled at my trouser legs. I felt cold in the pit of my stomach. I'd not eaten all day.

I sat down and had a cup of coffee and a donut at Hardee's. The bright fluorescent light obliterated the fact that there was a world outside, though I could hear the slur of trucks passing out on the highway. Everyone who came through the door was adjusting to the brightness, blinking like they were testing new eyes.

It was when I was getting up to leave that my eye caught sight of a TV screen mounted in a far corner of the room. I looked over just as a camera was panning to the river from which Cheryl Carpenter's body had been recovered. I thought it was a recap of the previous events, but the camera shifted live to a shot of Cheryl Carpenter's parents, both weeping, outside their house. Mrs. Carpenter half-collapsed on her husband's shoulder.

I got up and moved closer to the TV. The volume was on low. A detective stood before a podium. I suddenly recognized him as the fat detective the mayor had been talking to when Cheryl was taken from the water. He began reading a prepared statement. In the lower corner of the screen, it read, "Recorded Earlier." "Based on the coroner's findings, Cheryl Carpenter's death is now being treated as a homicide. It has been determined that Cheryl Carpenter was already dead before her car went off the bridge. At this time we cannot release specifics, given the sensitive nature of the ongoing investigation. Tomorrow morning the coroner's office will make a further statement. For now, we ask for patience and cooperation as we move forward with this part of the investigation. We are appealing to anybody who might have information related to the case to come forward. A toll-free number has been established to take calls."

I just stood there, feeling myself float. I couldn't think straight. From a bank of phones in the outer hall, I called the operator and asked to be connected to the mayor's house. Jean answered.

I was shivering in the cold as people came through the doors.

I told her who I was.

She seemed distracted. "Who?" hesitated, then whispered, "Oh God, what's going on?"

"Jean!" I said my name again. "We met at the mall. Remember? I need to speak with the mayor. Where is he?"

Her voice was suddenly rushed. "At the town hall."

I drove through heavy wet snow, finally exiting into the old part of town, passing the perpetual glow of the mayor's car lot and, further on, the abandoned Woolworth's, still illuminated by security lights. Through the window of a derelict building I saw broken mannequins heaped up like a factory of human parts.

At the town hall, the TV crews were already camped in the parking lot. There were walls of TV screens inside the vans showing those multicolored test strips. The generators made the world throb, gave it heart and pulse. I got out, followed the tentacles of wire into the town hall.

I used my key and went in by the annex. The building was deserted, the long polished hallway decorated with banners for the final. I climbed the spiral staircase. I could hear the mayor's voice echo along the curved ceiling. He was in there, making a deal for himself.

I got to his office and saw him sitting behind his desk. He was dressed in a golf shirt and red pants, what he must have been wearing when he got the news about Cheryl.

And just as on that terrible night when the child died, Betty was at her desk, one of those lonely hearts, waiting to spread rumors. She buzzed the mayor, and his voice came over the intercom, "Lawrence! My God, send him in."

The fat guy from TV who was leading the county investigation was in the office.

The mayor came toward me immediately and squeezed my arm. His eyes locked on mine. He said solemnly, "You heard the news?"

I nodded.

The mayor introduced me to the fat guy, who had to swivel his whole torso around just to look at me. His name was Ronald Bains.

I shook his hand. It was clammy. He had one of those youthful faces, lost in folds of fat. It was hard to judge his age.

It took me another moment to realize the chief was in the room. He sort of materialized on a chair. I'd not seen him. When he saw me looking, he said, "Lawrence," and tipped his head.

I felt light-headed. I was waiting to see how things stood, how they were confronting the fact that Cheryl had been murdered.

I saw there was a chalkboard on wheels next to the mayor's desk. The mayor was holding a piece of chalk between his thumb and index finger. On the board he had written the word "Suspects." There was nobody listed beneath the heading. The mayor said, "We've been trying to put things together, looking at everything here except what some might think the obvious—Kyle—because I think that's too easy a conclusion to jump to. It doesn't make logical sense. Kyle is on the verge of a state championship." The mayor rubbed the side of his head with the piece of chalk and trailed off. "It makes no sense." He looked at Bains and then at me. "Maybe we should recap what we know, for all our benefit at this stage?"

Bains's fat head moved up and down. "Okay." His breathing was heavy—a slow leaking sound between words, like he was deflating. He went over to the mayor's desk. His back was to us.

The mayor stared at me and raised his index finger ever so slightly, his eyes narrowing.

Bains fumbled through a series of manila envelopes, opened one, laid it out on the mayor's desk, and pointed at the first series of shots. He said, "Let's start here."

I could hear Bains's voice behind the sound of blood rushing through my head. It was like he was talking someplace far off. His professional detachment belied what we were seeing—the photos of Cheryl's head and neck.

Cheryl's neck was tipped back in each shot, exposing discoloration marks around her throat. "Death by asphyxiation . . . manual strangulation . . ." His voice came and went inside my head. He pointed at the marks, indicated how they pointed upward.

"We believe the perpetrator faced the victim, forced her back, pressing her up against the inside driver's side window."

I followed Bains's squat index finger to a circled area at the back of Cheryl's head. "The victim suffered a blunt trauma." Bains put his own hand under his fat throat and tipped his head back so the double chin smoothed out, a simple exertion that made him wheeze.

"What is significant is the force involved in the attack—the physical strength of the attacker. The autopsy revealed bruising deep in the neck. Whoever strangled her never had to reestablish a grip, even though the victim must have struggled frantically as she was dying." Bains swiveled around, picking up another envelope with shots showing Cheryl's hands. "You see here, her fingernails were broken during the attack."

Bains kept talking, shuffling photographs.

The mayor came and stood beside me and said something to Bains, but I didn't hear what he said. All I thought about was Kyle and Cheryl, out there on the road, the car parked off to the side, two kids arguing as evening settled, that sudden sense of claustrophobia, life reduced to just the two of them, intimately bound forever, not by love or marriage but by the terrible secret they shared. And in having the abortion, hadn't Cheryl turned away from Kyle, sought another life? Was that the plain truth Kyle confronted—what he'd told me at the high school—that she didn't love him? Who could have hoped for loyalty between adolescents when adults walked away from their vows, from their own offspring, with such regularity? Could it have ended any other way for Cheryl, except in her death?

"Lawrence?"

The mayor put his hand on my shoulder. "You want a glass of water?" I said softly, "No." I felt my face drained of blood.

Bains maintained his officious manner, shuffling through the pile of photographs, laying them out, oblivious to the look the mayor gave me.

But what Bains showed me next was to change everything for all of us forever. It was like nothing I could ever have imagined.

He picked up another envelope and laid out a series of shots that showed Cheryl's torso. For the first time I saw what else had happened—her torso repeatedly stabbed, raised welts under the heart, lungs, and midsection. Her flesh had the look of something I'd seen in high school biology classes, bloated and blanched like a specimen suspended in formaldehyde. It didn't seem real.

Bains kept talking. "There are twenty distinct stab wounds." He shuffled through some more shots. "We've determined the victim was unconscious or dead when she was stabbed. There is no indication of a struggle, no slash marks on her arms. This wasn't a frantic attack . . ."

Bains leaned against the mayor's desk. "And it gets even more bizarre. One knife was used, but the depth and entry angle seem to differ for various wounds. The coroner is investigating if there might have been more than one individual involved."

The mayor lowered his head as if in solemn prayer and said simply, "What kind of world are we living in?" His eyes caught mine and he squinted slightly.

Bains had his back to the mayor. "I don't know." He began gathering the photographs, putting them back in order.

In the sudden silence, I could see our reflection in the big glass window, a small-town portrait in stale yellow light. It was like we were inside the window, trapped or preserved. What I'd seen seemed unreal. I felt disconnected from it.

I watched the mayor's reflection fill a Dixie cup of water from the cooler by the door, conscious too of his secretary's typewriter keys clicking in rapid-fire, saw the distorted shape of Betty at her desk through the bubbled glass.

How could one tragic death have led to this, to Cheryl Carpenter being strangled and butchered and dredged from a river? How could we have known it would turn out this way, that it was the end for all of us?

Overhead, two ceiling fans wobbled and turned, like the room was being held aloft, hovering, like we might all be carried off somewhere. It's what I wanted, to be transported, anywhere but here.

Bains had sat down again, his face shining with perspiration, his trousers bunched at the crotch. He'd run out of things to say. We all had.

It was in this surreal silence, with all of us facing the grim facts of what had happened to Cheryl Carpenter, that the chief spoke for the first time.

"We might have a suspect, or suspects . . . Owensboro."

I cleared my voice. "Owensboro?"

"The team we're meeting in the final. You've heard of a team stealing another team's playbook, maybe, in this instance . . . something more." The chief's eyes got big. He turned toward Bains. "Like I was telling Ronald here, memories of defeat run deep in these parts. People got a whole winter to brood."

Bains's tongue flickered out then disappeared. "How much is the point spread on the final?"

"Us, by twenty-one points."

"Three touchdowns."

The chief nodded. "And that's being generous."

"Real life is stranger than fiction sometimes." Bains's double chin obscured the noose of his tie. He looked at the chief. "I think Carpenter's car was meant to be found now. The bridge railing broken like it was, that was a dead giveaway, too easy. There are ponds and lakes out there deep enough for her car not to have been found for weeks or longer. Someone wanted her found now."

Under his breath, the mayor said, "My God." He brought his hands together in a spire under his chin. "Kyle was set up."

Bains said, "How?"

"You just said the car was *meant* to be found, right? Say, over in Owensboro they learned about Cheryl's abortion, what if they . . . if they killed her to unnerve Kyle?"

"I don't know. Killing a girl over a game." Bains's eyes blinked, a slow exposure, like he was processing each moment. He said quietly, "Why not kidnap her, cast suspicion on Kyle? Why murder her?"

"Maybe that was the plan. They came to kidnap her, but it went wrong, and in the struggle she was strangled."

"And her being stabbed like she was?"

"We're dealing with kids here, Ronald. Sometimes there is no logic. You get a group of them together, and something goes wrong, and everybody is pulled into the moment. I can see that knife being passed from hand to hand, ritualistically, like a rite of initiation, like kids pledging a fraternity. This isn't just some game that's being contested here. People hold onto whatever they can in places like this. You drive through any town, and what do you see as you enter? Placards citing each town's victories: State Champions double A, triple A Football, Baseball, Basketball. It doesn't matter if that championship came ten years ago. The sign remains. They hold onto what history they got. Out here, it's what the children do that counts. Children live their parents' dreams.

"I remember in '74 a kid named Nelson Parker paralyzed a kid with a hit on a Hail Mary pass. The kid was hanging in the air waiting for the ball when Parker drove his helmet right into the kid's lower back, snapping his spine. People swore they actually heard it snap. Turns out, earlier that same week, Parker's family farm had been foreclosed on. Right there on the field, Parker just broke down, crying. The kid he hit never walked again."

Bains's head shook.

The chief said, "I remember being at a game a few years ago where some kids under the bleachers doused a cat in gasoline and set fire to it. The cat ran right out onto the field. It died of its burns, but you should have heard the fans in the stands when the cat was running around like a firecracker. Everybody thought it was hilarious. The opposing team was called The Wild Cats."

Bains made a smacking sound with his lips. Fat hung over his fat-man trousers.

The mayor said, "You know, fifteen years ago, Owensboro was given a choice, either a new state college or a new state penitentiary. They went with the penitentiary. I think that says something."

With that, the mayor pulled a bewildered face from his repertoire of expressions, turned and said, "Let's start there for now." He wrote on the board, "Owensboro."

When he turned, he had a chalk smear on his nose. Dressed in his golf shirt and red pants, he reminded me of Bing Crosby, in one of those Christmas specials.

He put down the chalk.

"I appreciate you coming over to see us, Ronald. I'm not here to defend Kyle. What I'm asking is for you to not jump to conclusions, but to look past . . ." The mayor's voice faltered. "To look past *the obvious*. We've got a kid's future in our hands, *lest* we forget it. If he's guilty, so be it, but let's get the facts first—that's all I'm saying—for *all* our sakes." He'd spoken like a guy giving a sermon.

Bains nodded.

The mayor said, "Frankly, I feel like we owe you dinner, Ronald, getting you in here like this. You hungry? Let us take you out, our dime!"

Bains's whole body rippled when he moved. A smile showed on his face. "I just might take you up on that."

He set his legs apart before rising, leveraging his weight in just the right direction, then moved with a lightness some fat people have about them, reminding me of one of those hippos dressed like ballerinas in cartoons.

As I stood there, about to leave, I actually found myself believing that players from Owensboro could have been implicated in Cheryl's murder. The mayor had that much power of suggestion.

And in my mind I saw a circle of kids passing the knife from one to another, earnest faces full of fear and terror, each doing what had to be done, absolving any one individual of her death, each stabbing Cheryl Carpenter in macabre fraternity. I believed that we were capable of acts like that.

23 I sat in my kitchen through the night. I left a message on Lois's machine. She never picked up. When I closed my eyes, I kept seeing those images of Cheryl Carpenter, the gray of the bloated torso, the strange blanched color of the wounds. It hadn't seemed like human flesh, not really. I'd seen pickled whole fish in jars at the supermarket; the flesh always seemed compromised, barely held together, like it might flake apart. That's how I saw her in my mind.

I got up and made a pot of coffee, then stood in the cold at the back door, wanting to stay awake, to stave off those images. I kept wondering if the mayor had really convinced Bains. Wasn't Bains going to get to Kyle eventually anyway? But then, maybe I never had understood Kyle, or the mayor, or the resolve people like that had within them.

The phone rang next to the table in the living room. I thought it was going to be Lois.

It was the mayor. I knew from his voice he was checking up on me. He said with a fake laugh, "God, that Bains can pack the food away. I just got through with him. You saved yourself heartburn. I'm going to be eating celery sticks for a month just to make up for that meal."

I said flatly, "Where's it going to end, Mayor?"

"I think it *has* ended."

I took a deep breath. "How do you survive these nights, Mayor?

Where does that intuition for survival come from? How do you see into people's souls?"

I heard the mayor half-laugh. "I think you give me too much credit, Lawrence." Then his voice settled. "I'm just a car salesman is all, Lawrence, *just* a car salesman trying to get by."

I said, "Can I ask you a question, Mayor?"

"What?"

"Who do you think killed Cheryl Carpenter?"

"I'm sticking with Owensboro until someone proves otherwise."

The live footage began at 6:15 A.M., while it was still dark, with a Vietnam-style night-vision image of the Johnson property, the shadowy figures moving inside the house. By sunrise, the TV crews had their telescopic lenses trained on the property, and the Johnsons' life was slowly emerging like a Polaroid.

Live on TV, I watched Kyle emerge, hidden under his varsity jacket so that his face was unseen, and get into Earl's car. Right then I knew Kyle had taken on the aura of myth, become one of those figures shunning the camera, one of those politicians or gangsters, movie stars or murderers, the famous or the infamous. We did not discriminate when it came to celebrity. The particulars of the circumstance, of guilt or innocence, were less important than the archetypical image, for in months and years to come, the names would recede but the image would remain.

Of course, they were setting Kyle up as the main suspect. Who else could it have been? His silence through the early hours of the investigation made him all the more enigmatic, made him and his family seem even more of an anachronism than they were. We had become so accustomed to parents making pleas for the return of a child, watching horrified and then relieved parents break down and cry as their child was pulled from some well. We were conscious of how to act, of what to say in those circumstances—but Kyle had said nothing.

A voice was talking about Kyle's meteoric rise to fame, splicing in footage of the game outside industrial Gary with the footage of the Amish yet again, the crude juxtaposition of different lives lived along this same lake. Then they cut to that piece I'd watched about the pep rally, that long, searching shot through the high school hallways that suddenly exploded inside the auditorium with the cheerleaders and the painted tribal faces, the stomp of feet on the bleachers, and Cheryl Carpenter, there amidst the pyramid of cheerleader flesh, Cheryl halfway up the pyramid holding her long, slender, flexible leg out so you could see her bloomers, and the band playing over it all.

I felt as though I'd lived through all this before.

They covered every angle, how much Kyle could bench, his broad jump and his speed in the forty. The high school coach said he never coached a kid with so much discipline and willingness to learn. He said, "The guy is a team player."

There was an oblique reference to Cheryl's abortion, and to the religiosity of Kyle's family, a first hint at the trail the media, if not Bains, was following. Someone had leaked that Cheryl had been strangled. A reporter broke that early in the newscast.

A camera cut to the small, white, single-roomed Reformist church where Helen Johnson gave praise to the Lord, the church's austerity as bleak and unforgiving as the putrefying black cornstalks in the surrounding fields. Then the camera left that oblique and sad faith for the heady realism of the coroner's office, where the medical examiner was preparing to give a press conference.

You could hear the muffled breath of the medical examiner in the makeshift press room, crumpling his papers as he prepared to make his statement, and the constant click of cameras.

In a brief statement, the medical examiner described Cheryl Carpenter's death from manual asphyxiation, from a massive force applied to the neck and throat. The windpipe and larynx had been crushed. In his opinion, he said in reply to a question, the victim had likely known her attacker. He noted how the angle of the discoloration around the neck indicated the perpetrator had faced the victim.

The medical examiner never mentioned that Cheryl had been repeatedly stabbed.

I knew they were onto Kyle, but somehow I felt drained of emotion. Or maybe I was still in a daze, a state of shock from already knowing what had happened to Cheryl.

24 It was past nine in the morning by the time I left for work. In the car I turned on the local radio and heard the breaking story at the high school. If I hadn't turned on the radio, I would have shown up, like a fool, at the town hall.

The reporter, live on the scene, spoke in that heady way reporters do, as he recapped what he called, "the extraordinary and tragic events unfolding at the high school."

In the background, I heard a fire alarm ringing incessantly.

I kept driving. Adrenaline shot down my legs. The reporter's voice was muffled, like he was moving away from the fire alarm. Then his transmission went dead.

The news cut back to the studio, where a stylized studio voice said, "It seems we are having audio transmission problems, but what we can tell you so far is that, during first period this morning, at about eight-fifteen, authorities arrived at the high school to interview local football sensation Kyle Johnson after the release of the coroner's report indicating that Cheryl Carpenter, Kyle's girlfriend, whose body was retrieved from her sunken car, was apparently strangled to death.

"According to sources at the scene, Kyle Johnson was called over the PA to the principal's office. A few moments later, gunshots were heard. Eyewitnesses say the school principal, walking toward Johnson's classroom, turned a corner, and encountered Johnson in the hallway. In the ensuing struggle, two shots were fired, and the principal collapsed. Kyle was seen fleeing toward the men's locker room, holding the gun he'd discharged. At this point, we have no further details. Currently, we are awaiting corroboration of events from police sources. As yet, no statement has been issued."

I knew it was over for all of us if Kyle ever emerged from the locker room. The question was simple—would Kyle live to tell or put a bullet in his head? Would he follow his girlfriend and unborn child to the Other Side?

The shooting had taken place an hour ago, and already there was a surreal air about the school as I arrived. Three sheriff's patrol cars, two fire engines, and an ominous black truck had arrived. An ambulance had pulled right up to the main entrance. Its door was wide open, but there was nobody in it.

I was there in my Citation, a ludicrous figure on the edge of this unfolding drama. I parked well back from everything. The radio kept jumping back and forth from the studio to the reporter at the scene, then back to the studio, where they began filling in the background on Kyle Johnson, who he was and what he meant. This was being fed to the major affiliates. We had attained national notoriety.

The sheriff's department had taken over the situation. I had not even been called to the scene. Our department had been eclipsed. A rim of police tape cordoned off the front of the school.

Students were standing around the parking lots. Most weren't even wearing coats, shivering or stomping from one foot to another, but they weren't leaving. A row of school buses stood nose-to-nose against the chain-link fence, all with their exhaust pipes smoking in the cold air, but nobody boarded them.

The radio newscast broke live again to the same reporter who'd been covering the story. I could see the guy speaking from just beyond the rim of police tape. He was interviewing some kids. Eyewitnesses were suddenly celebrities. They spoke in that frantic way kids speak when they want to get everything said. Beyond them, the TV reporters were interviewing other students.

I pushed through the throng of kids, saw a wreath of secretaries furtively talking among themselves. They looked stunned. They had, of course, run from the building, as had the teachers, who stood alone in their drab, short-sleeved shirts, some with pocket protectors and glasses, stereotypical targets of teen pranks, bewildered, just looking around at everything.

Some had scrawled their homeroom number on pieces of paper and were holding up the signs. The simple rule in cases of natural disasters, usually tornadoes, was to find your homeroom teacher, to let the living be counted.

On the school roof, I saw two figures stand up and raise their visors, showing their faces, and then another and yet another materialized. One was talking into a portable radio, and I guessed whatever had happened had already passed. Kyle Johnson's fate had been sealed.

I went toward the main entrance. The mayor was in his car, talking into his CB radio. He was sitting sideways, his legs facing out of the car. I went toward him.

He looked up at me and said, "Kyle committed suicide," and I say it with a measure of shame that I felt a sense of relief in just hearing those words.

The mayor set his feet back into the car and started talking to whoever it was he was talking to on the CB radio. He shut the door.

The reporters covering the story didn't know it was all over. One approached me as I went toward the main entrance and asked me my name. A sheriff's deputy pushed him back, but I had to tell the deputy who I was before he let me through, even though I was in uniform. I heard the reporter say who I was into his microphone. He called me a member of the local law enforcement.

Inside the desolate corridor off the main hallway was where the school principal, Tanner, had died. I met Fisher standing near Tanner's body. Fisher told me that after having second thoughts about paging Kyle over the PA system, Tanner had gone to meet Kyle as he came up toward his office. Fisher said he was walking right behind the principal, when he turned a corner and suddenly collided with Kyle, who just fired out of instinct, out of fear.

Fisher said it could have just as easily have been him that took the bullet. Tanner hadn't stood a chance—the force of the first shot blew the hairpiece off his head.

Fisher didn't know yet that Kyle was dead. He was still talking about himself, about how close he came to dying. You could see the fear in his eyes.

Tanner was on a gurney, his body draped with a white sheet. He had died outside the science lab. I looked into the lab. Everything smelt of formaldehyde. There was a plastic bin of fetal pigs beside the door, and at the front of the room, a medical chart of a pig's anatomy.

I waited by the lab. The quiet belied the horror of what had happened. Bars of morning light showed through windows, and beyond I could see the football field. It seemed almost peaceful.

Minutes later, the chief and Bains emerged, solemn-faced, along the corridor, followed by some other cops I didn't recognize.

Fisher approached the chief who said quietly, "Kyle's dead. He blew his own head off."

25 In the hours following Kyle's removal from the school to the county morgue, the savage chronology of Cheryl's death—of first, her strangulation, then the subsequent ritualistic stabbings—flooded the airwaves. The mystery deepened. Had there been other persons involved in Cheryl's death? The coroner's office was still reviewing the evidence.

Cheryl Carpenter had been stabbed twenty times.

Allegations and questions began to fly on AM Talk Radio. People wanted to know how the police could have been so negligent in not picking up Kyle at his house. Hadn't the evidence from the coroner's office all pointed to Kyle as the likeliest suspect? Cheryl had faced her attacker. She most probably knew her attacker. The physical force involved in the strangulation was overwhelming, suggesting a figure such as Kyle Johnson. Didn't that at least arouse suspicion around Kyle? And why had the details of the death been withheld for so long, why had people been misled that Cheryl had committed suicide?

I listened to all of it on the radio at the office. I was waiting for the chief or mayor to show. They didn't.

I sat within the deadness of the office, no calls, nothing. The mere fact of Cheryl being murdered in the next town over had removed us from really being involved in the case. The investigation had been handed over to the county. They were the ones facing the crisis over the revelations concerning Cheryl's death and the handling of Kyle.

Bains went on the offensive, and kept trying to link Cheryl's death with a conspiracy among members of our football team, pointing to the ritualistic nature of Cheryl's murder. He insisted he and his department had proceeded with caution, awaiting the coroner's report, before picking up Kyle, though Kyle had been put under surveillance, his comings and goings monitored, in an effort to establish who else might have been party to Cheryl's murder.

By early afternoon, another bombshell had dropped, further evidence linking Kyle to Cheryl's murder. Pieces of Cheryl's fingernails were found embedded in the leather arms of Kyle's letterman jacket. A janitor had found the coat in Kyle's homeroom.

Of course it was too little, too late, but again, the airwaves were filled with questions concerning how the case had been handled, how the physical evidence could have gone unnoticed. If Kyle had been questioned earlier, the evidence would have been found earlier.

The janitor described to the media a tear on the left arm of Kyle's jacket.

Lois stopped by the office, dressed in pink moon boots and matching down coat. She said in a sarcastic voice, "I didn't think I'd find you here. I thought you were gone to Chicago for good."

I knew she'd come to see me, or at least I was hoping so, but I said abruptly, "If you're looking for the chief, he's not here."

The radio was playing on my desk, and in the moment's silence between us, the host was recapping the news about Kyle's letterman jacket.

I looked up from my seat at Lois. "You think it was all worth it?"

Lois lowered her eyes. "Don't say anything." She shook her head. "The less I know the better."

I shifted forward in my chair. "What do you know, Lois? What's the chief told you?"

Lois looked around like there might be somebody in the office.

I took hold of her arm, and she pulled it away. "Don't worry, Lois. They're all out. So, what do you know?"

Lois glared at me. "I know you're not the man I thought you were."

"I wasn't asking about me."

"I know everybody tried to help Kyle."

"Did they? I think we were helping ourselves, is what I think. Kyle had wanted to come forward and admit to running over the child. He'd been willing to face the consequences, but he was stopped by all of us."

"No . . . The only reason he went back was because his girlfriend saw what he'd done . . . He played you for a fool, twisted it so you felt like you were manipulating him, when all along it was the other way around. That's the secret of a great quarterback . . . reading a play, reading the defense, making adjustments. He draws you one way, then he goes another way."

I said, "You sound like the mayor."

Lois ignored the comment. "How long before you leave for good?"

Kyle Johnson was laid to rest in a private ceremony during the same week the state football championship should have been contested. Cheryl Carpenter remained locked in an icy vault at the morgue, and it added to the lore, the myth, this surreal sleeping beauty, or—as some called her—that abortionist, now state's evidence.

We forfeited the title, though the Owensboro team had to dress for a game where nobody showed. Those were the state athletic rules. You had to show up and have the opposing team not show. You had to run out onto the field. In Owensboro's paper, they described the victory as "clapping with one hand."

Suspicion regarding those who'd abetted Kyle rested firmly with our football team, and so began an ongoing series of interviews, establishing and verifying alibis. Bains set up offices at the town hall and at the high school, a long process of interrogation unfolding behind closed doors.

I was privy to none of it, nor were the mayor or chief.

The town pushed back against the interrogations, feeling under siege by both the media and the police. That's how it was portrayed as parents of kids on the football team rallied and met at the school gym, in a show of solidarity. Already, the coroner's findings were coming under scrutiny, doubt cast on the validity of his suggestion that more than one person had been involved in the stabbing. The coroner was beginning to backtrack and began qualifying his statements, referring to the ongoing nature of his investigation, referring to preliminary find-ings, giving himself that hedge room. It was a backslide that developed as nobody on the team came forward, or cracked under pressure.

And with each passing day, the question surfaced again and again on radio and TV: Was it probable that a group of kids would stand around while Kyle strangled Cheryl to death inside her car, and then partici-pate in a ritualistic butchering of her corpse?

Put that way, the tide turned against Bains. The community railed against the way they felt their children's lives were being disrupted, the unconstitutional nature of what amounted to interrogation and scare tactics. How long was the community going to be held hostage on account of the police force's inept handling of the tragedy? How long was the interrogation of students going to continue?

Of course, the mayor let everything play out in the court of public opinion.

The version of the truth that came out in the community about Kyle and Cheryl was that, in the grip of guilt over his mother finding out that he got his girlfriend pregnant, Kyle had lost it, that his mother's perversion of spirituality had driven him over the edge. He'd felt each victory was the Devil testing him, leading him to the wages of sin, to a false reward. Fellow players spoke of their growing feeling of distance from Kyle. He had played with an intensity they'd never seen, even in him, as they'd advanced through each game. But after each game, Kyle had been like a zombie.

Kyle's coach admitted seeing the difference in him, but said it was the look of a guy who'd given "one hundred and ten percent for his team. He was a guy carrying the dreams of a town on his back." The coach looked at the camera, a whistle around his neck. His eyes watered as he swallowed and said, "The kid was only eighteen years old."

Students came forward talking about a fight that had taken place between Kyle and Cheryl after he'd found out she'd aborted the child. Kyle had been seen forcing Cheryl up against her school locker in the days prior to her murder.

Everybody knew Kyle and Cheryl had broken up.

Principal Tanner's funeral was also held the week of the final. The mayor spoke at the graveside and said he was going to bring a resolu-tion before the town hall members to consider renaming the high school football field Tanner Field. It, too, was a subdued service. It seemed we just wanted to get all the bodies buried.

In the cafeteria, a few days after Tanner was buried, I overheard a secretary say Cheryl Carpenter had gotten what was coming to her.

It was a sentiment that found its way onto the radio, oblique references to Cheryl's past relationships. She'd dated a guy in college during her sophomore year in high school. She'd been an A student, always looking to getting out of the town, had aspirations to an out-of-state college, precocious in a way boys her age weren't. She'd known what she wanted for a long time. Rumor had it that inside Cheryl's locker, she had a sticker that read "Eve was Framed." She also wrote feminist poetry. In the context of the discussion, that was a bad thing.

There were suggestions that this hadn't been her first abortion, and through the night the discussion meandered across so many issues, from male versus female sexual maturity, to debates on contraception—if condoms and the pill should be made available to teenagers and whether or not it would contribute to sexual promiscuity—to discussions on abortion—whether the father of a child should be informed, whether a woman had the right to abort a fetus without the father's consent.

Bains stayed through Tanner's funeral, but he didn't attend it. He was still working the case out at the high school, though the more he persisted in his investigation, the more the community pushed back against him.

Bains was the scapegoat we needed. If Kyle had been taken into custody, Tanner would not be dead and we would have known what actually went on the night Cheryl Carpenter was murdered.

Again, questions were asked regarding the theory that more than one person had stabbed Cheryl. Couldn't Kyle have angled the knife differently, couldn't his plan have been to confuse the authorities, to use reverse psychology to shift the blame on Owensboro, to unsettle them and cast doubt on their team?

Then one night, in what I thought were the dying days of the investigation, a caller called a late-night show and related a disquieting story of our propensity for conspiracy and silence, arguing a whole town could keep its mouth shut. He went on about Indiana's clandestine Ku Klux Klan past, what he called, the *invisible empire*, noting that, in the resurgence of the KKK in the Depression, Indiana had the highest number of klansmen, and that there'd even been a female equivalent, called Queens of the Golden Mask.

I hadn't seen Lois for over a week, and she didn't call. I avoided passing her office. I didn't talk to the chief or mayor either, though we saw each other in the hallway. We just nodded and kept walking our separate ways. We had all retreated into ourselves, not really believing that it was over, that we had survived intact, that the sad truth of how all this began had not emerged.

For days, I waited for Earl Johnson to say something, to make a statement, to rail against what he'd lost. I felt it, that sense of rage that everything he'd put his stock in was gone. I was waiting for him to take all of us down, but he never said a word.

The only change was that Arnold Fisher was taken on full-time. I read that in the town hall *Minutes*. His position was vaguely defined as administrative. There was, of course, no mention of the chief retiring.

We had arrived at a stalemate.

26 Thanksgiving loomed that Thursday, lopping off the continued national interest in the story, a week cut short with people going home early, planning to travel or receive relatives over the long weekend.

On Wednesday, I was facing the prospect of eating some microwave turkey dinner alone the next day. I had a brother in Iowa whom I contemplated calling, but it had been something like two years since we'd spoken.

I was about to leave for the day when my insurance agent Friendly Bob Adams called. He didn't sound too friendly.

He said, "I got bad news. That claim you put in against your cabin has been denied."

"Denied?"

"That's right. Seems some type of fire accelerant was used to start the fire. You know anything about that, what might have started the fire?"

I said, "No . . . no I don't, Bob."

"Did you have any flammables at the cabin that might have ignited, gas canisters or gasoline lying around? They found some kind of scorch pattern that makes them think an accelerant was used."

I said, "Gasoline, let me think. No . . . I didn't have gasoline with me. Maybe that expert got it wrong."

"Maybe . . ." But Bob didn't sound like he meant it. I heard him clipping his fingernails on the end of the line. That was something Bob was notorious for doing.

"Listen, Bob, how about we forget the claim? You know . . . if that agent or whatever feels you shouldn't pay out, then fine with me. All I'm saying is, I don't know what the hell could have happened up there, but, you know, if he says somebody tried to kill me, then why the hell should you have to pay out, right?"

"Somebody tried to kill you?"

"What I'm saying is . . . Shit, I don't know what I'm saying. All I'm saying is, I nearly died up there in my sleep, and I don't know how the hell the fire started, but you know what? I'm glad to be alive. That's what I'm saying. The claim doesn't matter . . ."

"Hey, relax, Lawrence. I just had to ask. Simple procedure is all. Look, I got to go, but you'll be getting a call from our internal division related to your claim. You can deal with them. This is basically out of my court now. I just called to advise you that your claim has been denied."

I didn't say anything, but was left again facing the cold coincidence that I had almost died the same weekend Cheryl was murdered.

That evening, going home alone, I passed the mayor's parking lot. He was under a blaze of spotlights shooting a commercial. He was dressed as a pilgrim, talking right into a camera, talking car deals. He had turkeys in a wire cage out in front of his lot.

I assumed you got a turkey if you bought a car.

Late that night, I saw the car commercial.

The turkeys were going, "Gobble, gobble, gobble," and the mayor said, "That's right, let's all talk turkey, let's talk deals!"

The camera panned down the lot, and in each car there was a turkey in the passenger seat.

I woke to a Thanksgiving morning that yawned like a chasm, and decided to volunteer at a food shelter in the rundown part of town. I went by the local store, picked up two pumpkin pies, some condensed milk, beans, and other assorted canned goods. Not that I had the money to waste, but I did it anyway, just to hide from the day's loneliness.

And for the first time in ages, I thought about Kendall. From a phone booth inside the store, I called her number, but hung up quick. What the hell was I doing? Then I called Janine, and Eddy answered, and that hurt, hanging up on him, but I did.

Half an hour later I parked outside Kendall's apartment. I'd bought an extra pumpkin pie as a gift. It was the first Thanksgiving, the first holiday without her child.

I slipped through the outer door, measuring each step up the stairs. I could hear music in Laycock's apartment.

I knocked quietly at her door. Nothing.

I could see light around the edge of the door. I knocked again and waited. I had the pumpkin pie in the other hand. It was still warm.

I found the loose board where Laycock had said it was, and felt the key. I slipped it into the lock, and it turned.

I eased the door open, holding my breath.

It was freezing inside the room like it hadn't been occupied for a long time. A curtain billowed in the sudden draft, a light bulb hanging from the ceiling swayed. A window was open.

I closed the door behind me and shivered, and stood in a big open one-room apartment with tall ceilings, ornate cornices painted over with a stark utility white like so many rentals. A fireplace had been boarded up. A makeshift toilet and shower had been installed in the far corner. There was water damage on the floor.

A wooden futon was unfolded near a bay window. That and a small table and a set of drawers comprised the extent of the room's furnishings. I scanned all of it, somehow waiting for Kendall to materialize, still standing with my back against the door, but there was no place for her to materialize from. She was not there.

I could still hear Laycock's music.

The cold was bone-chilling, my breath smoking each time I exhaled.

I went toward the bay window and checked the street. This was where I'd seen Kendall standing behind the curtain, waiting, staring down onto the street. But ice had formed on the inside of the windows.

I got the feeling Kendall had left days ago, probably gone home to relatives for the holidays. Maybe she was crawling back toward life, and that thought brought a certain comfort, or eased the guilt.

I was leaving, when beside the futon, on a small coffee table, I saw plastic freezer bags. I stopped and leaned down. One of the plastic bags held newspaper clippings about the child's death. Then my eye was drawn to the other bag, and for a moment I couldn't make out what it contained. I picked it up and held it up to the light. It looked like a shriveled, molted skin, and then I realized what I was holding—part of an umbilical cord.

In the hallway, I set the key back. My hands were trembling. I walked down the stairs.

Laycock's feet showed under the lip of his door. He had his eye pressed to the door's fisheye lens. I said nothing.

A neon cross sizzled above the homeless shelter as I pulled up. Across the street were some strip bars open twenty-four hours a day. I saw somebody coming out.

It wasn't even ten-thirty in the morning.

On one wall of the shelter was a mural of a boat run aground on rocks during a tempest of black swelling waters. There was a lighthouse in the distance, shining bright. Under the boat it said, "This is your soul," and under the lighthouse, "God." It was done in such dark, ominous colors, done so unambiguously, that you wanted to go toward the light. You wondered how we weren't all looking for that kind of salvation.

Inside, I put down my bags of groceries on a table that said, "Donations."

The simple rules were posted. Anybody who hadn't showered had to go down to a communal shower to soap up and get hosed down, then they got a new set of clothes, attended church, and then were given a Thanksgiving meal.

The churchgoing folk, those redeemers of souls, were milling about in their polyester brown suits, dividing the men from the women, the single people from the families, dividing the drunks from the sober, directing those who smelt down to the communal showers.

The righteous lived outside of irony, and could demean you even while they were telling you how special you were, even as they were trying to save your soul. I saw a guy who needed a meal real bad arrive drunk. He was pushed out the door. He cursed and banged the reinforced glass.

I ended up getting mistaken, despite my suit, for one of the hapless souls in search of a meal. Somebody asked me if I'd been drinking, like that might be my reason for being there.

I had to tell them I was a volunteer. I was sent in to the wives to help set out the buffet-style Thanksgiving dinner.

The fat wives in floral dresses stirred huge pots of soup and boiling yams and sweet potatoes, their hair tightly tied back, some wearing aprons, their faces gleaming from the hot steam. I saw this monstrous institutional oven. A turkey leg was up against the glass oven window. I swear it looked like a kid's thigh.

I got the job of arranging paper plates, napkins, and Dixie cups on picnic tables and putting out the lawn chairs. Donated toys, aged dolls, ABC blocks, and decks of cards were laid out in a play area for the kids.

A little girl came over to me riding a toy horse that was just a stick with a horse's head attached. She wanted some food for the horse, so I took a sugar lump and pretended to feed the horse the sugar lump when really it went up my shirtsleeve. She smiled at me like she knew what I'd done but didn't want to believe it was a trick.

Her mother called the girl. "You don't be disturbing that man now, you hear?" She came over. She was young and good-looking in a drawn and weary way. The kid's face was just a baby image of what the mother looked like, and it was sad to see how things could turn out for somebody like that. The mother smiled. "You're good with kids. You got any of your own?"

I lied and said, "No."

"You single?"

"Divorced."

"You say that like there's shame in it."

I said, "It's hard to give up on things."

The mother smiled again. "I like a man with compassion. So, you here to redeem your own soul, or mine?"

"I'm just running from myself, if the truth be told."

"You're not very uplifting." She winked when she said that.

The mother was smoking a cigarette, which was against the rules, but I didn't say anything. She scratched her thigh with her other hand, so the dress she wore bunched above her knee. She saw me looking at that, and her lips curled.

She said, "You don't exactly look like a believer."

"I believe I like what I see."

I felt a sense of euphoria; out of the darkest days, something like this had landed before me. I was about to ask her if she wanted to get the hell out of there, when who of all people was standing off to the side but Betty from the mayor's office. Her goddamn Table of Eight was sponsoring the Thanksgiving dinner.

She said to me, "Praise the Lord, you coming back to Jesus, Lawrence?"

Before I could answer she asked, "Those tables need setting up over there. You mind handling that?" Then she turned her wrath on the mother, and a fight broke out about the smoking.

I just moved away. I don't think I have ever seen anyone demeaned like that for the sake of a meal. I was a heartbeat away from taking her out of there, but I didn't. I said nothing. I went out to where services were held, to the religious zealots, cricket-thin, in their ill-fitting suits with their wrists and ankles sticking out, wearing ties that had thrift store written all over them.

They were talking to unmarried women with children, taking them aside for a morality lesson. The women were obliged to hear the word of God, to acknowledge their own sin, or at least contemplate where they had gone wrong. They used words like "fornicator" and "harlot" like Helen Johnson. I just stood amidst them, saw how the zealots all laid their hands across their crotches the way preachers did, holding the Good Word. They looked like they were all hiding hard-ons.

Humiliation and self-deprecation were simply the price of admission.

The woman left with her kid and two other kids I'd not seen with her earlier. Her eyes were wet. She looked right at me and said, "What the hell are you looking at? I wouldn't fuck you if you were the last man alive on earth!"

She left in a station wagon that had no front bumper.

By noon, I was watching the matinee at the strip club just across from the shelter.

A middle-aged woman in a G-string danced before me and three other guys who were drinking cheap hard liquor, each of us at our own table.

I put dollar bills into the woman's G-string, and I felt more humanity in that single act than in anything I had done in a long time. Each time she got a dollar she danced around a pole and touched her toes, then she spread her feet apart and slowly did the splits. I figured she'd been doing that for a long time, doing that same act always for a buck. She worked outside of inflation. Desire would always cost a buck.

At the end of her shift, I watched her count her money. She was smoking a cigarette and talking on the phone at the same time. She had a drink poured for her by the bartender. I heard her say, "sweetie." It sounded like she was talking to her kid. She was telling whoever it was how to make gravy so it didn't get lumps in it. She was heading home for Thanksgiving dinner, her work done for the day.

I guess if you knew the rules, life was negotiable.

27 By three o'clock I ended up with Lois. She was waiting in my driveway when I got home. I nearly rear-ended her.

Petey was on the backseat moving from foot to foot. He fanned himself when he saw me through the back window. Then he hit the window hard with his beak.

Lois rolled her window down all the way. She was listening to a song called "A Kiss to Build a Dream On" by Louis Armstrong. She reached out and took me by the collar and kissed me on the cheek. When I tried to say something, she put her finger to her lips and shook her head. She was, of course, drunk, and so was I, and sometimes that was what was needed, to find a way back from the edge.

Lois got out of her car with Petey, and we drove over in my car to her house. Petey was acting up.

Lois said, "Let me just put him back inside."

Mr. Peterson was sitting in his RV along with milling relatives. Someone was cooking a turkey outside on a grill. It smelt wonderful. I stared over at the RV. I said, "I've imagined a life like that for a long time."

"Senility?"

I said, "If you could just stay drunk, I think we got the beginnings of a working relationship."

Lois turned and nearly fell over. Petey hissed inside his cage.

Inside the living room, Lois stuck a video in the VCR. "You want to see Jane, Petey?"

And suddenly, Jane Fonda materialized in a leotard in one of her exercise videos. The workout was already started.

I said, "What the hell is that?"

Jane was sweating. She said, "Go for the burn!" and Petey just started rocking from side to side.

I said, "Am I *that* drunk, or *is* Petey doing aerobics?"

Lois went and linked her arm in mine, like women did in the thirties. "He likes all the colorful leotards, the way Jane and all of them jump up and down and side to side. It's like a mating ritual. Jane Fonda is Petey's new girlfriend, right, Petey?"

I looked from the VCR to Petey. He was rolling his head, stepping from claw to claw, like he was in rhythm with the music.

I said, "Let's get the hell out of here."

I turned my back, and Jane shouted, "Go for the burn! Go for the burn," and then I heard Petey in that parrot screech say, "Go for the burn! Go for the burn!"

We went driving out by Janine's new home near the Amish. The sun was falling, casting a long wintry light across the land.

I could see the shadow of my car running alongside.

Petey had sobered me up. How far had I come from Thanksgivings past that I ended up with a boozed-up woman and a parrot into acrobics? I took Petey as a sign, a harbinger of bad things to come.

When I parked near Janine's, I heard this buzzing noise overhead. I got out, and up there in the sky was Seth's crop-dusting plane.

It was a kind of old-style plane, a two-seater where the passengers were practically sitting outside.

Seth must have picked me out coming along the road.

The plane banked off to the north and turned to face me. I was just standing there in the road. The plane swooped down to maybe fifteen feet above the ground and came right toward me.

I could see Seth in his leather cap and goggles. He got so close to me that I ducked and had to cover my eyes. The ground boiled around me. Then the plane pulled up, and in the rear I saw a hand waving.

I knew it was Eddy.

Lois had recovered enough to shout, "What is that?"

I said, "That's my kid up there."

I was staring at the sky.

The plane banked again, almost suspended for a brief moment. I could see them against the pale disk of the sun.

The plane dropped down low and came along slow and parallel to me. Seth pointed back to Eddy, who had on goggles.

Eddy looked like a bug. He was waving frantically.

I think I forgave Seth a lot of things just then. I thought, what a hell of a gift to give a kid, to take him high above the world like that, to let him experience that freedom.

The plane landed on a strip out back of Seth's property. I should have gone and seen Eddy, despite the court order, but I didn't.

I did a three-point turn, hand over hand, forward and reverse, each time looking back, at the house, the plane in the background, then I got facing the other way.

"Why are you crying, Lawrence?"

It didn't do any good explaining.

We meandered through the country roads after that, until I arrived at the bridge where Cheryl Carpenter had been found. There were small toy bears and flowers placed along the edge of the bridge, though soiled and wet. A simple sign said, "Why Jesus, Why?"

I got out and stood in the cold. It seemed like a million years ago, all of it, Kyle and Cheryl, the run at the championship.

The sun fell so low the day was nearly dead. Everything was losing its edge, its definition, dissolving into darkness.

28 Bains smelt of mint candy. When I looked up, he was staring down at me. I had come back from my morning rounds and was filling out my time sheet. It took a moment to take in his size again, to understand just how fat he really was. I think I concentrated on his size just to keep myself calm.

"Can I buy you a coffee, Lawrence?" I could tell it wasn't a casual visit.

We didn't go by the break room. Instead, Bains led me to his own makeshift office, which used to be a closet before he came to investigate Cheryl Carpenter's death.

He had a hot plate with coffee brewing. His back was to me. "Sit." He went about getting me a cup.

On his desk, Bains had a copy of my insurance claim. It was there for me to see, the evidence out before me. I could make out a cover letter. The heading on the letter said "Mutual of Omaha—Fraud Investigation Unit." Their logo, that picture of an Indian in a headdress, was in the upper right-hand corner. I also saw my credit report. My name was printed in bold. Bains had used a highlighter over some of the delinquent payments.

"How do you take your coffee?"

"Black."

He turned and handed me the cup.

Somehow I managed to take a drink of the coffee. It was hot and tasted bitter. I said, "This is good coffee."

The room had no windows, nothing but boxes piled up behind him. I said, "It smells like polish . . . like floor wax in here. This was the janitor's storage room at one point."

"Is that what that is, floor polish?" Bains seemed to take a sniff. "So the mayor put me up in the janitor's room. I'll have to tell him you told me his dirty little secret." The way he said dirty little secret gave me goose bumps. "Sometimes you just don't know what you're dealing with. Am I right or am I wrong?"

Bains looked at me and came forward in his chair. "I'm just clearing things up, getting ready to leave. I was looking through some files. I see you went out to the high school the day Cheryl hemorrhaged."

I nodded.

"Did you get a sense Kyle was homicidal?"

I had my hands cradled around the coffee cup. "No."

"I was hoping you'd say yes . . . I guess you can appreciate the predicament I'm in here?"

"You want me to lie?"

Bains shook his head. "No . . . I'm putting down here in my report that you had no indication that Kyle was homicidal. You mind if I quote you on that?"

"Quote me."

Bains wrote something down. "You know, I took it on the chin here with this investigation. Maybe I made a bad call. I'm willing to concede when a man like Tanner dies, there is some culpability."

I said, "I'd have handled it just like you did."

"Thanks, but I won't quote you on that. That's not a tenable position to hold right now." Bains took a breath. "This is between you and me, but I might be forced into retirement, or at least become a desk jockey for the rest of my career over what happened."

I said in a clichéd way, "Hindsight is twenty-twenty. I think people have become too quick to get lawyers involved. You made a judgment call, and nine times out of ten, it would have been just fine."

"That's it right there. We have become a litigious nation. It's gotten to the point now where you can't say sorry to somebody anymore. I wanted to go to the funeral. I wanted to tell Tanner's wife I was truly sorry. What the hell does she think of me?"

"If it's any consolation, Tanner hated his job. The irony is, he hated football more than anything else in life."

Bains half-smiled. "It helps to know that. I appreciate you telling me that." He pointed at the percolating coffee. "You need a refill there?"

The pot was gurgling like someone on a life-support machine.

When Bains leaned forward to take my cup, he knocked the files related to me off the desk. They fell right at my feet.

That was basically how we got talking about my financial ruin.

The room got so small it was like a box. I picked up the files.

We talked about credit card debt, about sky-high interest rates, or at least Bains did. He did the talking.

"There needs to be credit reform in this country. People are carrying so much debt that someday this country is going to implode. That's my honest feeling on where we are as a nation. We are fed a line of crap from politicians about how prosperous we are, but it's bullshit, that's what it is. Someday people are just going to say, 'I can't pay anymore. I'm maxed out.'"

Bains looked at my credit report. "I'm not judging you here. I'm saying this is the American condition. This is what drives people over the edge." He shook his head. "You ever feel like you are getting close to that edge?"

I said, "I think people have to take responsibility for their own actions."

"That's a good attitude to have, but I'll let you in on a little secret. I'm up to my ass in debt, too. If I get fired, or if I get stuck as a desk jockey, I'm not going to get expenses, and it's expenses, mileage, food . . . that's what keeps me afloat, not the base salary."

I said, "I hear you loud and clear. You want to know something funny and sad?"

"What's that, Lawrence?"

"You know how my dog Max got his name?"

"How?"

"I bought him with a credit card. It maxed out, and I couldn't afford him at the asking price, but the guy at the pet store sold him to me for what he could max the card out at."

Bains hit the desk with his fat hand. "That isn't a true story, is it?"

I said, "Honest to God."

Bains made a whistling noise. "I'm going to use that story, so help me, I am." Then he settled and looked at me. "You know, maybe you're smarter than people give you credit for." He said that like he had just reassessed me, like he felt he was dealing with somebody different.

I sort of dried up after that, and the humor left me. I went to stand up, but Bains said, "Stay a bit. I got just a few more questions."

"About what?"

Bains had a nervous habit of pressing the top of his ballpoint pen. "I see here you met with the mayor's wife about selling your home, is that right?"

It was a question that came out of left field, but I said, "Yes."

"I see here you bought Wealth Tapes on a credit card." He fumbled through some papers. "Right, here it is." He read off the date I bought them and the amount. "Jeez, you paid this much for tapes? And the nature of these Wealth Tapes?"

"Real estate schemes. Things like how to buy real estate with no money down, how to bid on foreclosures, stuff like that."

"So, these Wealth Tapes worth it, in your opinion?"

I said coldly, "I never really got around to applying the strategies."

"So there weren't really any *no-money-down* deals?"

"No."

"There never are, Lawrence. Money makes money, that's a simple economic reality. You needed start-up cash, investment capital, right?"

I shook my head. "I didn't need start-up cash because I wasn't buying anything. All I did was get advice from the mayor's wife. I wasn't seriously considering anything at the time. She manages properties. She's an expert in real estate. I was just considering my options." I felt like I was talking in circles.

Bains stopped writing and closed his notebook. It was hot in the office. A moustache of perspiration showed above Bains's upper lip. He wiped his lip with the back of his hand. "You were lucky to survive that fire up at your cabin." He said it more like it was a question than a comment. "I see here your claim is under review. The fire's been ruled arson."

I stood up, and Bains did also. He said, "I heard your dog wasn't so lucky. He got hung up in a tree with his throat slashed, isn't that what happened to him?"

As I turned to leave, Bains produced a business card like a magician doing a cheap trick. "If you want to talk, call me."

29 I went into a free fall in the hours after meeting with Bains. I went out on patrol. On the way back I passed the mayor's lot. He was inside his trailer.

The mayor didn't exactly light up the trailer with conversation. "I'm real busy here, Lawrence, real busy."

I said, "Bains is following up on an insurance claim I filed against that fire at my cabin. Investigators have ruled it arson."

The mayor's voice was calm and even. "If you felt Earl set the fire, like you told me back then, why did you file the claim?"

The mayor settled himself in his chair. "Maybe there was no Earl. Maybe you needed a down payment on that house you were talking to Jean about? Is that how you came up with the idea for the fire?"

"You got all bases covered, don't you?"

The mayor leaned back in his chair. "I didn't file that claim. You came up with that one. Sometimes I wonder what I'm really dealing with when I look at you. Who are you really in there?" The mayor pointed to his head.

I felt lost for words. "I'm not getting that promotion, am I?"

"Don't put words in my mouth. It's just the chief's not retiring just yet. He's going to hang on a while longer . . . But maybe you should follow your instinct and think about moving on. You're in a rut here."

He looked up at me from his desk. He was holding a pen in his hand. "Those tapes you got, you might be onto something big. There's a big world out there, and it's got a For Sale sign on it. Who is it that said, 'Buy land, God quit making it,' was that Twain? I think it was."

A fax machine made a noise in the background, and a tongue of paper began curling out. Globs of darkness floated before me.

"You're on your own now, Lawrence."

"You'd love to see me go."

"I want what's best for you."

He smiled, and his smile was an infuriating sneer. I drew my gun. I hadn't even contemplated doing something like that, but suddenly I had the gun pointed at the mayor.

I said, "What makes you think I won't blow you away right now? Where the hell do you get off talking to me like garbage?"

The mayor's expression didn't change. He turned and pulled the fax from the machine and said, matter-of-factly, "You are fighting with demons inside you. I'm not the enemy here. I didn't do anything to you." He managed a concerned, condescending smile. "I'm willing to forget what you just did, if you turn around and leave right now. I'm putting it down to stress."

I took a step back and extended my arms so they were shaking. I was looking down the barrel of the gun, and when the mayor had the audacity to start writing on the paper, I shot just to the left of him, shot a hole in his trailer.

The mayor screamed like he'd been shot, instinctively putting his hands up to stop his brains spilling out on to his desk.

I said, "That's the first true emotion you ever showed, you son of a bitch!" I turned and walked out of his office.

By three o'clock, I ended up out at the mall. I felt my heart pounding as I waited for the mayor's wife, Jean, to get done with some women she was dealing with at her office. I wanted her financial advice. Or the truth was, I thought maybe if the mayor had told her how desperate I was, they, or maybe she, would do something to help me out, some program or scheme to get that house in Chicago. I wanted out.

But when I'd got to Jean's office, her office blinds had been drawn, though I'd put my face to the glass and through a broken slat in the blinds caught a glimpse of women with arms raised like they were in a holdup. It had taken a moment to understand what was going on. Jean was conducting a breast self-examination seminar.

I waited by Orange Julius, thought about leaving, got up to go, but sat down again until the women left. Somehow, Jean saw me before I saw her. She was dressed impeccably again in her nautical attire, her face overdone with makeup in a way that only the rich can pull off. A young woman was still with Jean. I could tell the woman had been crying.

Jean looked at me, then toward her office, "Why don't you wait in my office?"

I could see the young woman was shaking slightly.

When I entered Jean's office there was a tripod setup with a stylized text that read, "Pain is inevitable—Suffering is optional."

Under it was a diagram of a breast with a wedge-shaped relief of layered tissue. It looked like a pie chart. I read one of the captions—"The lobules are glands that make milk; the ducts are tubes that link the lobules to the nipple," and another that read "Stage 4—known as metastatic; cancer has spread from the breast and lymph nodes under the arm to other parts of the body, such as bone, liver, lung, or brain."

Before Jean had time to come back into the office, I left through the back exit into the concrete grayness of the service corridor where I had to go down on my haunches just to stop myself from being sick.

I didn't want to go home. I felt sure the mayor had called Bains. As evening settled, I stopped across from Lois's house. Petey was out of his cage, perched on her shoulder. I could see that through her kitchen window. Lois had her small portable TV on the table. They were watching something together. Lois had made popcorn. She was putting her hand above her shoulder, and Petey was craning his head and taking the popcorn. I felt like I couldn't break in on them, on that serenity.

When I eventually went home, I got out my hunting rifles and my boxes of ammunition. I set them on the living room table. I kept waiting for lights to appear in my driveway. There were moments when I picked up my service gun and breathed in its recently discharged, bittersweet metallic smell. I was vacillating between sanity and desperation. I knew Bains was coming. I could feel it.

By six-thirty in the morning, after a night without sleep, I had lived and died a thousand deaths, and drunk two pots of coffee. I ordered the Wealth Tapes again to replace what had been burned in the fire, and listened to the remaining ones. I contemplated blowing my own brains out at one point. And in the end, I kept telling myself there was nothing to worry about. Kyle was dead. I was being implicated in fraud at worst. I said that to myself so many times during the course of the night.

I saw somebody outside in the backyard, and I knew that I was getting picked up. Bains wasn't making the same mistake again.

I got dressed in my uniform. As I was opening the door of my car, someone shouted, "Don't move! Put your hands up slowly."

Before I could even get my hands up, I was pushed hard against the door.

The story had leaked to the TV. A camera crew filmed my arrest.

Bains was still in the same clothes he'd worn the day before, a Hawaiian polyester shirt of muted brown-toned leaves. I sat stuck between him and this other cop, handcuffed in the backseat. We said nothing for the entire ride to the jail at the other side of the county.

Bains's body jiggled, the fat loose on his frame.

30 In an interrogation room in the bowels of the county jail, Bains began his questioning. He slapped down my report from my interview with Kyle the night after the child was run over. He got to the heart of the matter.

The connection had been made. I felt my heart beating fast.

"You remember filing this?"

The room closed in around me. "Yes."

"You want to elaborate on its content?"

I met his stare.

"Well?"

My throat felt dry when I started to speak. "It's the report . . ." I cleared my throat. "A report from my interview with Kyle Johnson pertaining to his possible connection with the death of a child in a road accident."

"An accident or hit-and-run?"

"All indications led us to believe it was an accident. They still do."

"Who's the 'us' you are talking about?"

"Me and the mayor and chief." I felt myself tense. "I was called into the mayor's office the morning after the child was discovered . . ." I hesitated. "I was the one who discovered the child." I reached for a glass of water on the table, drank, and wiped my mouth with the back of my arm.

"How would you describe the nature of your conversation with them?"

"Information gathering . . . They wanted a status report, wanted to know what I'd seen when I found the child."

"What did you discover?"

"It's in the accident report."

"Indulge me."

"After a night of searching, I found the child off to the side of the road, lying in a pile of leaves." I looked at Bains. "She was dead . . . dead a long time. Her body was cold to the touch."

"When were you informed about the possible connection to Kyle Johnson?"

"At the meeting with the mayor and the chief."

"What did they ask you to do?"

"Check Kyle's truck."

"And did you?"

I blinked.

"If you wouldn't mind answering verbally."

"What was the question?"

"Did you check the truck?" Bains's armpits were stained with sweat.

"Yes."

"I'm curious, how did you check the truck?"

"I looked for marks, signs of something being dragged . . . blood stains along the bumper and undercarriage, bits of clothing."

"So the child was dragged, in your opinion?"

"No."

Bains interrupted. "You just said . . ."

I cut him off. "She *wasn't* dragged. Let me restate what I said. She was lying . . . lying in the leaves."

Bains raised one of his fat arms. "I want you to go slow, concentrate on the details. I want you to think before you answer, okay?"

A sudden coldness ran down my spine, despite the hotness of the room.

Bains lit a cigarette and inhaled, then let a trail of smoke out of the corner of his mouth. "So, again, how did you eliminate Kyle's truck as a potential vehicle?"

"I checked the undercarriage, checked the bumper . . ."

"Did you take a cast of the tires?"

"No . . . I didn't have whatever it is you use to do something like that."

"You didn't think something like that might be essential to making a clear determination regarding whether the truck had been involved or not?"

I looked down at the table, then at Bains, who was shaking his head.

"Let's just go on for now. So how did you make your determination if you didn't use anything scientific?"

"I gauged Kyle's reaction to me being there. I think what I lacked in technical expertise, I made up for with gut instinct."

Bains's tongue came out and licked perspiration from his upper lip, and he seemed to accept that answer. "So how would you characterize your interview with Kyle?"

I took another drink of water.

"The kid was a straight arrow. He acknowledged he'd been on the street, but he told me he hadn't seen anything."

Bains touched his temple with the hand that was holding his cigarette so it looked like his head was smoking. "So Kyle was forthcoming?"

"Yes."

"How would you describe his emotional state, given what you told him you were there to investigate?"

"Scared . . . no, more nervous, but cooperative." I resettled myself on the chair.

"It must have been a hell of a thing to confront somebody with the possibility they might have run a child down."

"I guess . . . Like I said, Kyle was an honest kid. I asked him if he'd seen anything that night. He hadn't. The meeting didn't last long. He cooperated. I got his story. It all checked out. There was nothing on the truck that indicated any damage, anything in keeping with his having hit a child." When I finished, I had to stop and catch my breath.

Bains pulled at his fat chin, like he was thinking. "That's something I wanted to ask you. Would there be a mark left if a truck hit a child?"

"I checked as best I could."

Bains stared at me. "That's not answering my question."

"What was the question?"

Bains asked again.

I said calmly, "I don't know the answer." I met his stare. "I don't. I did my best. This job is gut instinct. Like I said, I didn't have access to whatever you'd use to make that clear determination."

"I would have thought a clear determination would have been utmost on your mind in a case like this. We're talking about the death of a child here." Bains's stare was fixed on me. "I find it hard to believe you glossed over the only potential suspect in the case by *gut instinct*."

I lowered my head and felt a whoosh of blood in my ears.

Bains stubbed his cigarette out in his glass of water. It hissed for a moment.

I felt disorientated. The string of questions had blurred, so I couldn't tell exactly what we'd already discussed, or how long I'd been there.

Bains clicked his fingers, and I was suddenly aware that he was speaking. "Let me ask you. Did Kyle mention anything about his girlfriend being pregnant when you met him?"

I felt a thrill of adrenaline shoot down my legs. I said, "No . . . No, he didn't."

"Did he say *anything* about his girlfriend?"

My voice tightened. "No."

Bains leaned forward so his chair scraped the floor. "Were you aware Cheryl Carpenter was a passenger in the truck the night the incident happened?"

I shook my head.

Bains raised his voice. "Could you give a verbal answer to the question posed?"

My chest felt compressed when I tried to talk. "No, I wasn't."

"Wasn't what?" I could smell Bains breathing in my face.

I moved back from him and said, "I wasn't aware Cheryl Carpenter was a passenger in the truck."

Bains's voice took on a measure of incredulity. "You're telling me you didn't ask Kyle if there was anybody in the truck with him?"

I reset my feet on the hard bare floor. "No, I didn't ask him."

I could feel Bains's mounting frustration, but he kept his calm. "You didn't think it strange that Kyle would have been out driving around alone Halloween night?"

I felt my breath go shallow. "At the time I wasn't thinking straight. I hadn't slept in over twenty-four hours."

"You didn't go home before going out to interview Kyle?"

"I did." I felt myself losing the train of his questions.

"So, what did you do at home?"

"I slept."

"So you did sleep. You just said you hadn't slept in over twenty-four hours by the time you interviewed Kyle Johnson."

I closed my eyes. I said with a sudden sense of bewilderment, "What the hell are you after here? I slept maybe for an hour, so what?" I raised my voice. "What do you want from me?"

Bains tilted his head slightly and raised both his hands, like he was backing down. "I'm just trying to establish your frame of mind when you interviewed Kyle, that's all."

I had that gritty feeling in my eyes that you get when you haven't slept in a long time. My eyes watered. When I looked at Bains again, he seemed to swim in a membrane of fluid.

Bains shifted and extracted his huge frame from the steel chair and said, "Maybe we'll take five?" When he turned to leave, I could see the sweat had spread to the small of his back.

When Bains returned, he brought with him a waft of fecal matter. His face was soft and relaxed. He even smiled at me. He'd combed his hair with water so it was slick and plastered across his pinkish forehead.

I said, "Are you charging me with something or not?"

Bains reset himself in the chair and lit another cigarette. "All I'm doing is fact-checking here, corroborating details."

I sat down again. My eyes flickered between the mirrored glass and Bains.

Bains leaned forward in a conspiratorial way. "I'll let you in on a little secret. There's nobody there. Okay, let's get back to what we were talking about. I assume you're going to tell me you didn't know there were three other people in the truck with Kyle the night of the incident?"

I averted my eyes. "No, I wasn't aware of that fact."

"Well, some of the individuals in the truck have subsequently come forward. They've made statements that Kyle hit *something*." Bains hit the steel table with such force that I jerked back. "I suppose you also didn't know Kyle went back later that evening with Cheryl Carpenter?"

I hadn't quite recovered from Bains having hit the table. All I did was shake my head. "No, I didn't."

Bains tapped the back of my hand with his fat index finger. "Well, he did. Cheryl confided in a friend afterward that she'd returned to the scene. You know what Kyle and Cheryl discovered when they went back?"

I said nothing.

Bains's breath was heavy, like a bellows. "They found the body of a child in the leaves. Can you imagine something like that, finding out you'd done that, and knowing you'd left the scene of an accident?" His face reddened. Spittle had formed at the corner of his lips. "And you're telling me Kyle showed no emotion when you went out to his house? Is that what you want me to believe? After witnessing what he did, after finding a child dead in a pile of leaves, he was stone-faced when you questioned him?"

I answered him coldly. "What I said was he was cooperative. I didn't say he wasn't scared or emotional."

Bains shot back. "The guy deserved an Oscar for a performance like that, that's what I think. Was he in drama? I'm going to have to check the school records. This was some performance . . . either that, or you're lying."

Bains sat back, his head bobbing. "You want to tell me what really happened?" Sweat had spread out from Bains's armpits across his chest, the fat around his neck wobbling. "Well?"

And right then I realized Bains had nothing on me. I had survived. I was guilty of nothing. All I'd done was mishandle an interview with Kyle, no more than that. I remained calm. I said, "I told you how I found Kyle. He was cooperative. I just took his statement and left."

Bains poured a glass of water. We were on the downside of whatever he'd wanted to say. He made a smacking sound with his lips. His body was still visibly trembling. He said in a low voice, tipping his head forward, "Let's move on. There was something else going on with Kyle the weekend after all this happened, right, the state quarterfinals, wasn't that right?" Bains reset himself on the seat.

"The way I hear it, Kyle was destined for big things. A potential contract could have yielded millions, couldn't it? It's what I've heard from those who saw the kid play."

"Maybe."

"Maybe?" Bains said incredulously. He mock-smiled, then the smile faded. "You know, you are the only person I've talked to who was pessimistic about what Kyle's prospects might have been. I find that strange, that you didn't believe in his future."

I kept my voice level. "I'm just saying the kid wasn't even out of high school. There were no guarantees. The kid had all of college to get through first. Kids get injured in college. That's what I meant when I said there were no guarantees. I'm being a realist. I'm not denying he was something special."

Bains's face brightened again in a fake smile of understanding. "Let's hear it for the realists." He just kept smiling at me with a mock sense of admiration. "There aren't enough realists in this world, people who can take stock of their place in time and space, people who have it within themselves to evaluate who and what they are."

Bains had ratcheted the tension again. "I'm glad you cleared up your feeling concerning Kyle, because I was having a hard time trying to reconcile a statement I have here . . ." Bains held up a piece of paper. "A statement from Earl Johnson stating you proposed filing a false report regarding the death of the child Halloween night in exchange for hush money."

My throat tightened. "He's lying."

"Earl Johnson says he didn't find out for weeks that you'd blackmailed his son. He said one Sunday morning he found you stalking his son, waiting at the crack of dawn near their property for Kyle to emerge." Bains picked up another piece of paper. "I've also a statement here from Helen Johnson to that effect. Do you deny being out near their property?"

"They're lying. I wasn't . . ."

Bains shouted over me. "I've a witness who saw you, a Mrs. Vanderhagen. She thought you'd broken down. She stopped and asked if you were okay. You remember seeing her?"

I felt everything caving in around me.

Bains raised his voice again. "How would you characterize your financial situation?" He leaned forward so the fat of his chest fell like two breasts. "How much do you owe in credit card debt? How much back child support do you owe?"

I didn't answer him. I made like I was getting up from the table, but Bains put his slab of a hand on mine and held it. His face was inches from mine. "Answer me!" Bains glared at me. "Isn't it true that you recently purchased Wealth Tapes, a series of tapes pertaining to real estate investment strategies? And isn't it true you sought financial advice as to how best to invest in properties?"

Bains let go of my hand. He picked up another piece of paper.

"I have a claim here that you filed against a fire that took place at your cabin. Did you know the claim is under investigation, that the fire has been ruled an act of arson? Do you have any explanation concerning the fire? You needed capital if you were going to enter the realty market, isn't that right? You want to reconcile the coincidence of the fire and your sudden entry into the realty market? I'm waiting for you to answer me! Isn't it true a realty agent told you you'd need over ten thousand in start-up cash just to enter the market?"

Bains's face was beet red. "You're going to answer every one of my questions, so help me, you son of a bitch!"

I had somehow shut down. I didn't shout or say anything, didn't talk again, until two cops came in and took me to a holding cell.

31 I made one phone call to Lois at work, hours later. She answered. I could tell from her voice she knew where I was. The chief must have told her.

Lois broke down. She sniffled and took a deep breath. "I told myself I wasn't going to cry. God almighty. Give me a moment." She blew her nose and sniffled again.

I felt raw inside my gut. I was shivering. Even as I was on the phone, all that was running through my mind was, how the hell had I waited for Kyle like that out on the road, how had I let myself be seen out there?

Lois said, "I want to ask you a question, Lawrence. That story you told me about your wife . . . Why didn't you tell me you brought a gun with you? How could you pull a gun on your wife with your kid hiding behind her?"

"Please, Lois."

Lois raised her voice. "Just answer me. How could you do that?"

It was the continuation of the same interrogation. I guess, if you strung up enough coincidences, enough of any person's life's actions, patterns were going to emerge.

"Why did you call me up to the cabin? How come you didn't see Max until I got there, how come?"

I said her name again.

"Just answer me, damn you." I heard her crying hard.

I leaned into the phone.

I said softly, "Are you accusing me of killing Max?"

Lois struggled, sniffling on the end of the line. "I'm just asking you to be honest with me. Did you burn down your cabin?"

"No."

"You filed an insurance claim against the cabin, though, didn't you?"

"Yes."

"Why?"

"I don't know . . ."

A cop pointed at his watch.

"Lois, listen to me, I'm asking you, please. I don't know how long I got on this call. I need you to find me a criminal defense lawyer."

Lois hesitated. "Why should I?"

I said, "I can't think of a reason."

In the silence, I heard Lois gathering herself together. She said, "I hope to God you are not lying to me about everything." Her voice had regained some of its composure, though it was still shaky.

"If I were guilty, I wouldn't take your money. I swear to you on a stack of Bibles, I wouldn't do that to you."

I met in the late afternoon with my lawyer, a guy named Hayden Mills, who wore an ill-fitting brown suit and stunk of Brut aftershave. He had the makings of a guy who worked cheap. We spoke in my cell, which consisted of a room with a basin, a metal frame bed, and a bare ceramic bowl that passed for a toilet.

Hayden gave me the gist of how things would run, that I was being held for forty-eight hours, and that within that time, I would appear before a court, and charges would be filed and bail set, or I'd be released. Then he said, "For starters, let's go over your interview with the police. What are they accusing you of exactly?"

I said, "Insurance fraud . . . and arson . . . It's about a claim I made on a fire that destroyed a cabin I owned up north."

Hayden gave me a skeptical look. "That's what this is about, an insurance fraud allegation? You got pulled in here for something like that?"

I couldn't bring myself to say anything else right then.

Hayden looked toward the cell door. "Look, if you're not ready to talk . . ." He made like he was getting ready to leave.

I said, "Wait!" I felt my hands become fists. I looked at him. "Okay! There's more. I'm being accused of blackmail."

Hayden's eyebrows arched. "Blackmailing who?"

When I said the name Kyle Johnson, Hayden flinched. "The same Kyle Johnson who murdered his girlfriend, the football star?"

"The same one."

Hayden leaned forward. "Kyle's dead."

"It's his father, Earl. He's the one accusing me of blackmail."

"Over what?"

I half-sighed, shaking my head. "How much time you got?"

Hayden took out a yellow notepad. "However long it takes."

A guard passed outside the door, pulled back the slat, and looked at us. Hayden turned, but the guard said nothing, just scanned the room, drawing the slat closed again. Hayden waited a moment.

We both listened to the hollow sound of the guard's shoes on the cold concrete floor, heard the rattle of his keys. Somehow that sound brought the full gravity of where I was into focus. I was divorced, broke, and sitting in a prison cell facing charges of fraud and blackmail.

"You ready?" Hayden had to say my name before I looked at him.

I said, "I don't know where to begin . . ."

"At the beginning works just fine, usually."

"The beginning . . ." I took a deep breath, nodding. "This all goes back to Halloween. A child was killed . . . run over by a car. She had been lying in a pile of leaves. You hear about that case?"

Hayden shook his head.

"A call had come in that night . . . a reckless driving complaint, near where the child was found. They ran the plate. It came back registered to the Johnsons."

"So what happened?"

"Kyle . . . He became a potential suspect, or at least a lead we had to follow up on. I met with the mayor and chief." I hesitated, realizing I didn't have to tell Hayden everything. "We decided against releasing Kyle's name as a suspect. There was already enough interest in Kyle.

The state football quarterfinals were that weekend. The mayor and the chief thought it would be better to go about the investigation without drawing attention to Kyle."

Hayden had been writing on his pad, but he stopped and looked at me. He didn't challenge me, though I knew he didn't believe what I was telling him about the meeting.

I started talking again. "Like I said, we weren't hiding anything. I ended up making a routine call to the Johnsons' property to inspect the vehicle and then interview the suspect. It's all in a report I filed. I felt satisfied Kyle hadn't been involved in the child's death. There were no marks on his truck, nothing suggesting he'd hit anything."

Hayden wrote something down, then looked at me again with that lawyer's skepticism. He was using his briefcase, balanced on his knees, as a desk. "So, just let me get this straight, you and the mayor and chief agreed to this behind-the-scenes investigation, is that right?"

"I wouldn't put it exactly like you said it there. We were protecting the rights of an individual while pursuing a detailed investigation. That's how I'd put it."

Hayden repeated what I said and wrote it down on his yellow notepad. "You think this chief and mayor can be relied upon to corroborate what you're saying here?"

I met his stare, and nodded.

"You don't seem so sure."

"It's a long story, but they will."

"Okay . . . I'll have to get statements from them."

Hayden let a silence hang between us for a few moments before speaking. "If everything checked out, and you ruled Kyle out of any involvement in the death of the child, how do we get to this claim you blackmailed Kyle Johnson?"

"That cop, Bains, the guy who took me in here, says there were passengers in Kyle's truck. They saw Kyle run down the child."

"That doesn't exactly answer my question about how you ended up being accused of blackmail, but for right now, tell me anyway, how come you didn't know there'd been other kids in the truck? You never asked Kyle when you interviewed him?"

I said, "You know, you're asking the same questions as that cop."

"We're working from the same set of facts . . ." Hayden went on staring at me. "So you never asked Kyle if there'd been anyone else in the truck with him?"

I said quietly, "No," shaking my head. "I know it was an oversight, but, like I told Bains, I'd been up most of the previous night. I was pretty much exhausted. I don't know if I said this already, but I was the one who found the child."

"No, you didn't tell me that." Hayden wrote something down again, and I leaned forward, touching the sides of my head. I looked across the starkness of the cell at Hayden and said, "I was pretty much the way I am now when I interviewed Kyle, exhausted."

Hayden nodded. "Sleep deprivation. That's good. That's something we can work with here."

Our eyes met.

"Let's fast-forward to Kyle Johnson's father. What exactly is his allegation?"

"I just know what Bains said."

"Which was?"

"Earl's accusing me of having blackmailed Kyle. He said I made a deal with Kyle the night I went and interviewed him about the child's death."

Hayden's lower lip showed, like he was thinking. "Why do you think Earl's making that sort of allegation now? Kyle's been dead how long?"

"Three weeks."

"Okay, so why now?"

"Bains."

"What about Bains?"

"Bains has a grudge against us. I guess you know what happened out at the high school, Kyle's killing the principal before he shot himself?"

Hayden nodded. "Sure. It was a fiasco."

"It was Bains's fiasco. Everybody blamed Bains for the principal's death, for not picking Kyle up sooner, for waiting until Kyle was at school. Kyle was paged over the PA system. He was given time to get scared." I looked over at Hayden. "People think we got off lightly that morning, lucky that *only* the principal was killed."

"So Bains became a scapegoat."

"Yes . . . He sort of lost it after what happened at the high school.

Ever since, he's fixated on uncovering something, trying to vindicate himself. Bains feels he's been led astray by us."

"This isn't the same *us*—you, the mayor and chief—that decided to quietly investigate Kyle's potential involvement in the hit-and-run, is it?"

"Yes."

"So how does Bains feel he was led astray?"

"He came to the town hall after Cheryl's death was ruled a homicide. I showed up after the meeting had started. It was informal, just Bains trawling for information, for background on Cheryl. But by the time I got there, they'd already developed a theory that Owensboro, the team we'd been set to meet in the final, might have been involved in murdering Cheryl."

"What?"

"Given how Cheryl had been stabbed repeatedly, there was a suggestion that maybe there'd been multiple perpetrators involved. At the time, we were just searching for anything that might make sense. Cheryl was murdered the week of the state football final. Back then, who would have believed Kyle would destroy his life like that? We just felt . . . the mayor, that is, he just wanted Bains to not go for the obvious suspect. The mayor was looking out for Kyle, not trying to do anything but give him a fair shot in life."

"But Kyle did kill Cheryl."

I said softly, "We know that now."

Hayden stopped writing. His pen was flat against his notepad.

I said, "It was the school principal's death that got to Bains. He told me he'd wanted to go to Tanner's funeral, to say sorry to Tanner's widow, but he was told to keep away. I think that's when Bains started his vendetta. He thinks we covered up for Kyle that night."

Hayden took up his pen again, "Bains became too personally involved."

I nodded. "That's why I'm in here. Bains wants revenge. I met him a day or so before he was supposed to leave. He basically accosted me in the hallway, steering me to the office he had at the town hall. That's when I realized just how bad he had it in for me. He'd been digging around in my personal life, rutting around for something to ruin me. He found out I was divorced, that I was broke, that I was behind in my child support payments. By the end of the meeting he asked me about the fire at my cabin. He'd found out the claim I'd made against the fire was being contested. I thought what he was driving at was that he was going to pass all that financial information on to the insurance investigators. I figured that was going to be his revenge against me."

I stopped and shook my head. "Of course, that wasn't the half of it. The next morning, when I was leaving for work, Bains had me hauled in here. That's when I found out where he was really going with everything. It's when he said Earl Johnson had come forward accusing me of blackmailing Kyle."

Hayden turned over a sheet of paper and kept writing. "So now we're getting somewhere. Did Bains tell you what proof Earl has that you blackmailed Kyle?"

"There is no proof. I didn't blackmail Kyle."

"So what did Bains exactly say to you?"

"He just told me Earl said that he'd found me waiting for Kyle one Sunday morning near their property, that afterwards Kyle told him I was looking for money."

Hayden tapped his pen against his notepad. "You make any unusual deposits into your bank account over the last few months?"

"No!"

"You sure?"

"Yes."

"And regarding this fire at your cabin. You fill up any containers of gas at a local gas station, buy anything flammable recently, anything on a credit card that can be traced?"

"No."

"They're going to check into all that stuff. I just need to know right now if there's something they're going to find."

I felt cold again. I said flatly, "There isn't."

A guard passed again outside. He didn't stop.

The echo of his shoes faded.

Hayden looked at me frankly. "I think I got the picture here. Like you said, we got a cop, deep into a tragedy, who is looking for any out, anything to shift emphasis away from him. Maybe he's uncovered something you missed, maybe Kyle did run over this child Halloween night. Maybe there are even witnesses. So what? I don't see the connection to you. You filed a report, given what you put together after going out to inspect Kyle's truck and interview him, end of story. It was a dead lead, right?" It was a leading question.

I said, "Yes."

"As for Bains . . . I think it's a typical police maneuver, trying to shore up a half-assed theory by pulling you in here. He was working on a hunch. He discovered that report you filed after going out to investigate Kyle, then he put that together with your financial situation, along with that meeting all of you had with him at the town hall, cooking up that absurd theory about Owensboro. So, I can see where he was going, how he was working on a hunch." Hayden was facing me. "But it doesn't matter how close Bains got to the truth, or part of the truth, because, as long as there's absolute silence and resolve amongst those involved, all Bains has is conjecture."

I said quietly, "I didn't blackmail Kyle."

"I didn't say you did, okay?"

"I just want you to know I didn't. I'm giving you my word."

Hayden nodded. "Okay, I appreciate you telling me that."

But I could tell he didn't really care.

He kept talking. "The way I see it, the person who could tell us what happened is dead, that's the central fact we are dealing with here, and dead men don't make good witnesses. There's no money trail, and, the more I think about it, where the hell would a kid like Kyle have gotten the sort of money you need? It doesn't make sense. You owe something like . . . how much on credit card debt?"

"Twenty-two thousand dollars."

Hayden made a whistling noise. "What's Bains going to do, tie your financial distress to you coming up with a scheme to shake down a high school kid? Give me a break."

Hayden was talking with perfect incredulity, like he was in court. He closed his legal pad and put it into his briefcase, then stood up.

"Look, you're being arraigned tomorrow at ten-thirty, so how about we see what the DA comes up with? They have to have actual evidence, probable cause and the like, before you can be charged with anything. This is all circumstantial bullshit. In the meantime, I'm going to petition the court that Bains be removed from the case."

Hayden's head was moving fitfully. "Look, I didn't want to influence you in any way, so I didn't let you in on the fact that I know Bains. He's an intimidator, a heavy, walks a legal tightrope when it comes to dealing with people. He plays dirty pool."

Hayden put a hand on my shoulder. "I think you survived the worst. The way I see it, I wouldn't put it past Bains to have put this suggestion of blackmail Earl Johnson's way. From a public relations perspective, you see how that might work in Earl's favor? Earl's got to live out the rest of his life here, right? Pinning a blackmail charge against you would go a long way to making Kyle the victim. Even if it's never proved that you blackmailed Kyle, the suggestion could raise just enough sympathy for Kyle. And, in the process, Bains could vindicate himself too, positioning himself as a cop who walked into some small-town conspiracy."

I said, "Earl Johnson is not in the public relations business."

"Look, when it comes to money, people get smart quick. Let's say Earl might be angling to file a civil suit against you or the department. I can see Bains leading Earl on with something like that, the possibility of recouping something here, some money. I assume Earl must be dev-astated, right? All his life he's been counting on his son to deliver him from an endless existence on a dead-end farm. I saw on the TV where they're living. I know the kind I'm dealing with here. This would be Earl's last chance at getting anything. If I were Bains, I'd try that tactic to get Earl on my side. I'd tell him how the cop who went out there on official business to interview his son was dead broke, and might have suggested to Kyle that some kind of deal could be worked out." Hayden's voice was hot. "I see Bains's angle here. What Bains is doing is using Earl Johnson for his own end, seeding Earl with the possibility of establishing a case for civil damages in the death of his son, but you know what?"

I was in a sort of hypnotic state, exhausted. I'd stopped really follow-ing what Hayden was saying.

Hayden raised his hands like he was conceding something. He came down a notch and half-smiled. "Okay, I'm racing ahead here, I know. Look, what I'm going to do is pay Earl a visit, share with him a few home truths about how the law works. Admitting to knowing about a bribe opens Earl up to some civil liability, especially in the death of the principal, if the principal's wife wanted to go that route. I'm going to show this Earl how Bains has been angling here to make something out of nothing. I don't think it's too late to get Earl to retract his statement. I'll show him how Bains is using him."

I said, "You can try."

Hayden put his hand on my shoulder again. "People get smart quick when they need to. We all have that instinct for self-preservation."

I said, "So you don't necessarily want to hear that I've been thinking about suicide . . ."

Hayden winked. "We'll work on an insanity plea if the time comes."

With that, he knocked on the steel cell door, and a small sliding panel opened.

The guard outside asked me to stand against the far wall. Hayden left and the door shut, the locking mechanism clicking into place.

It sounded just like it did in the movies.

Despite the sudden sense of deflation, or maybe because of it, I slept for I don't know how long.

I was woken up when a tray of food was sent through the slot in my cell door. I was curled on the small prison bed. I opened my eyes.

Bains was standing outside, his fat head framed in the square of the door slot.

He said, "I think we're on the same side, Lawrence. I really do."

I turned away from Bains, faced the cold wall. "Under the advice of my lawyer, I have nothing to say."

"I'm here to help you. Just hear me out. I want to run this by you, this coincidence. I see that you nearly died the same weekend Cheryl was murdered. That is some coincidence. You believe in coincidence?"

I resisted turning around.

Bains started talking again. "I could maybe be convinced of the coincidence except for how your dog was killed. Your dog's throat was slit with a knife, right? And then there's Cheryl Carpenter, she was not only strangled, but also stabbed—stabbed with a *knife*. Maybe if it was only the fire, then I might concede it was just that, coincidence, but a knife was used in both cases. That makes it suspicious."

I kept my back to Bains, but my eyes were wide open.

"Did someone try to kill you the same weekend Cheryl was murdered?"

And for the first time I turned and faced Bains. The lower part of his face was hidden, so everything he said sounded disembodied. His eyes became slits.

"Help me out here, Lawrence. You met with the mayor and chief at ten A.M., but didn't check Kyle's truck until after five-thirty in the afternoon. That's what it says here in your report. Five forty-five P.M. That seems a hell of a long time to wait to check up on a potential lead."

I spoke for the first time. "I'd been up all night searching for the child." The hair on my arms came up in goose pimples.

Bains said, "Who arranged the time for you to check on Kyle's truck, the mayor or the chief? It had all been prearranged, right, between all of you? You want to work with me, Lawrence? I'm not after you. God knows you and I are alike. What I'm after is the chief and the mayor. That's who I'm after here. Just talk to me."

Our eyes locked in the silence that settled between us. I could hear again the wheeze in his breath. His head moved in the oblong viewing portal of the cell door, like some giant puppet.

He spoke again with a hypnotic softness. "I'm not out to get you. I got you in here because I wanted to talk to you. You think I didn't know something was wrong when we met in the mayor's office? You don't think I felt the tension between you and them—that crock of shit the chief proposed about Owensboro? I'm not a fool. I may be many things, but I'm not that."

I felt myself being pulled toward his words. I didn't want to face the morning before a judge. I was being accused of blackmailing a kid who'd killed two people.

The weight of that, of what sort of charge and time I could serve, pressed heavy on my mind.

Bains's head occupied the small frame opening in the door. "What I'm doing is giving you a chance to talk first. I think Earl knew all along. This was all set up from the very start, with the mayor and chief and Earl, wasn't it? Come on, Lawrence. Just tell me what you know. Someone will talk eventually. Whoever makes the deal first can plea-bargain with the DA's office. You want to spend the next ten years in a cell like this? You want to take that gamble?"

I was on the verge of telling him everything.

"I want you to sign a statement I have here that the chief and the mayor initiated the cover-up for Kyle." Bains pushed a scroll of paper through the slot in the door. "Sign it," and, as he spoke, his voice rose. "Come on, Lawrence, sign it! We can work together, you and me. We're from the same side of the tracks."

His face softened into a weak smile, and somehow that broke the spell of his persuasion. He'd had the paper with him all along. "Sign it, Lawrence."

I just turned again toward the white wall of my cell, and said, "Leave me alone."

Bains's voice retained its equanimity, though I could tell he was holding back from raising his voice. "This is your last chance. I'm going to work with whoever works with me here. I'd just as soon work with the innocent, but if you don't want to help me, then I have no choice." He breathed deep again.

"Sign it. Are you going to bankrupt that woman friend of yours, Lois, is it? Is that what you intend to do? Why are you wasting her hard-earned money on that two-bit lawyer? Haven't all of you ruined enough lives? What's your son going to think when this all gets dragged out in a court of law? There's no medication for that."

32 I passed in and out of sleep throughout countless hours, awaking finally into a morning that surfaced without sunrise in my windowless cell. Only a tray of food punctuated night from day.

Bains never showed again. I'd expected him to be there when the food tray was pushed through the slot in the door, but he never materialized. Had my one chance at a plea bargain passed?

By midmorning, I was led through the long catacombs under the county courthouse, through a series of security gates where I was patted down a total of three times. I ended up waiting for over an hour in a holding area as each defendant was called and led to the court.

It smelt of despair, a whole county's worth of sin. When it came to my turn, I saw Hayden in the courtroom. He was in the same suit as yesterday. It was wrinkled, like he'd slept in it. He said simply, "You don't look good."

"Bains came to my cell last night."

"I thought I told you not to talk to him again." Hayden pointed to an empty wooden bench where jurors sat. "Let's sit over there."

Hayden took my arm and steered me off to the side. The courtroom was vast but empty, except for prosecutors milling around a table and defense lawyers around another table, all of them looking at papers.

I said, "I want to amend my statement."

"You haven't made a statement yet."

"Well, I want to make one now. I want to tell what really happened."

Hayden shook his head. "This isn't the time or place." He took me by the arm. "This is a poker game. We're ahead." He was inches from me.

I pulled away from his grip. "This is my freedom we're talking about." I felt myself trembling. "I want it on record that I'm stating here and now that the chief and mayor initiated the cover-up. I want that on the record. There was no blackmail. All we did was try to save Kyle. I want that established now."

I must have raised my voice, because an attorney at the table across from us looked over, then looked down at his own brief.

Hayden took hold of my forearm again. "That's an assistant to the DA assigned to your case. You want to blow everything right now?"

"I don't care! Bains is after the chief and the mayor, not me. He told me that last night."

Hayden's voice was hushed. "Am I wasting my breath here? Did you sign anything with Bains last night?"

"No."

"Think about it, do you really want to take on the chief and the mayor, or do you have a better shot at attacking Earl's credibility? That's what this comes down to, you hear that? And anyway, implicating the mayor and chief doesn't preclude that you also blackmailed Kyle. In fact, you admit to the first charge and you shoot your credibility to hell with any jury."

And again, in that moment of indeterminacy, I stopped dead. Things swirled in my head. I had this vertigo feeling. The proceedings around me grew louder.

I said nothing else to Hayden.

The old-fashioned radiators hissed hotly.

There was a hearing before mine. The prosecuting and defending lawyers approached the bench. The defendant was accused of raping a woman. We'd been in the same holding area before coming into court. I turned, and, in the background, saw the family of the victim. They were gathered together holding hands, trembling.

Hayden checked his watch and touched the noose of his tie. He kept stacking and restacking papers on the desk in front of him.

We avoided eye contact. Then the lawyers in the preceding case left the bench, and the judge said, "Bail set at thirty thousand dollars."

It was like somebody had let the air out of the room.

The family broke down, crying, and one of them screamed, "You can't do this! He'll come after my sister! He said he'd kill her if she ever told on him!"

The guy looked right at the family as he was led away by two armed guards.

Hayden tapped me on the shoulder. "You're up."

In a series of statements that I didn't follow, and during which Hayden sometimes objected, I was eventually formally charged on two counts: extortion and insurance fraud. My bail was set at ten thousand dollars.

An hour later Hayden came by my cell. "We'll worry about the insurance fraud charge later. First things first, though. Earl Johnson is a straw man and we are going to tear him apart on the extortion charge. He's going to have to prove Kyle made payments to you, or come up with some evidence you blackmailed Kyle. Like I told you, dead men don't make good witnesses. It's Earl's word against yours."

Then Hayden stopped for a moment. "Or do you still want to make a statement admitting to an initial cover-up?"

I said, "No."

"Good. Earl Johnson's word isn't going to stand against yours, not if we have that chief and mayor on your side. We're going to need their full cooperation and support. Now what was this problem you mentioned yesterday between you and them?"

I said, "The last time I saw the mayor, I pulled a gun on him."

"Well, you got your work cut out for you then, don't you?"

Lois worked out the payment with a bail bondsman. I was standing on the steps of the county jail by early afternoon. I looked up into a sky that seemed held up by telephone and power lines.

Lois was parked in a lot and drove up to the steps of the courthouse. She didn't look at me.

I said nothing for a time, and neither did she.

County Road stretched for eighteen miles. I could see the world ahead of me for mile after mile. This is what freedom felt like, this openness.

Lois smoked in a soft, sucking way.

Old snow was piled along the roadside. I saw where people had flung out beer cans and Coke cans and cigarette butts. Somebody had thrown away a shoe and a one-armed teddy bear. Every speed limit sign we passed along the way had been shot up.

Hogs in winter-hardened fields gathered around metal troughs on either side of the road.

We passed a truck collecting metal cans of milk. The guy was wearing hunting plaid. He tipped his baseball cap as we passed, and Lois smiled a forced smile. She finished her cigarette and rolled the window down just far enough to push the cigarette out.

I could smell the hogs.

At the Five Corners bar, we stopped. They were advertising an afternoon special of fried chicken and mashed potatoes.

We were the only customers. We sat in a high-backed vinyl-covered booth. There was a candle in the middle of the table that was really a mosquito repellent candle in one of those glass holders wrapped in plastic mesh netting.

I don't think the owner expected anybody to order food. He foisted two beers on us, which we didn't really want, but felt obliged to order.

Lois got up and went to the toilet, but she left her purse on that table. Sticking partway out of it was the bail bondsman's letter. I took it out and read the terms of payment. Lois had cashed in a life insurance policy to bail me out.

I got this feeling in my chest that made it hard to breathe. I just set the letter back in her purse.

Lois spoke first when she came back to the table. She was looking at the purse, like she knew I'd looked at the letter. She said, "I got a brother in Canada who went there to avoid the draft. He fell in love and got married and has three kids."

"Canada . . . I'm not being sent to the chair, Lois. Jesus Christ, what do you think is going on here?" I leaned forward on the vinyl seat. "What do you think I did?"

"I'm just giving you alternatives."

I tried to reach for her hands, but she moved them.

I said, "I appreciate everything you've done for me."

Lois said coldly, "You're welcome." She looked around at the bar's miserable surroundings, at the cheap dark-paneled room. There wasn't a bulb over forty watts except for the glare from the kitchen in the back.

The chicken was not thawed all the way through. I could taste the hot and then the cold when I bit into it.

Lois's chicken was the same as mine. She got up and had words with the guy, who went into the back of what was really a bar, and I heard him yelling.

I said, "I don't think this is really a restaurant."

Lois raised her voice. "It's what it said on the outside."

I said, "You're right."

Our dinners arrived again. They were the same pieces. I got what had been Lois's, and she got mine, but I didn't tell the guy.

I tasted the chicken and said, "This chicken is good." I looked at Lois. "I mean, considering that my last meal was served in a prison cell."

33 Later that evening, I got a call from the chief. He called Lois's house, where I was staying. Lois answered it. I tried to stop from taking it, tried to mouth, "Who is it?" but Lois said real loud, "It's the chief."

The chief said, "You're on administrative leave until further notice."

"What exactly is administrative leave?"

"We pay you to stay away for a while."

"That sounds like a good deal."

"I want you to hand in your badge and gun."

"Chief, please, any chance we could meet, just to talk things over?"

"I don't think I have anything to say to you."

"Why are you doing this to me?"

He said with a sudden finality, "This is all your own doing."

I shouted, "Don't stonewall me. I know you're busy, that you're a real . . . *impotent* man!"

There was a click when the chief hung up.

Lois stared at me, but I just looked away and said, "I'm sorry."

A beam of light showed through the hole I shot in the mayor's trailer as I ascended his metal stairs. He looked up at me and said severely, "I hope you're not carrying a gun this time." Then he beamed his patent smile.

I followed his lead and smiled. "No, I'm not." I said, "I guess you heard I've been charged with extortion and insurance fraud?" I let out a long breath. "I don't know where it all went wrong. I mean my own life, how I keep making mistakes."

"You got a good lawyer?"

I nodded.

"We're behind you, Lawrence. I want you to know that."

I said, "Good. You might be called yet in this case."

"I hope that's not a veiled threat?"

"It's not. I just want you to help me." I felt lost for words. I said, "Bains got a statement from a kid who was in the truck with Kyle . . . Bains knows Kyle ran the child over."

The mayor kept his composure. "Well, then it looks like you didn't do your job when you interviewed Kyle. You never asked him if there'd been anybody else in the truck?"

I swallowed hard.

The mayor scanned his teeth with his tongue, waiting. "You know what I find most distressing, Lawrence, most emblematic of your . . . let's call it your *mental breakdown,* is how you killed your dog." The mayor leaned forward. "Bains found out there were at least six complaints filed against you for having that dog barking in your basement. That's a fact. You abused that dog. You wanted to get rid of it, didn't you? I thought you pulling that gun on your wife was an isolated incident, but I guess I was wrong. I misjudged you."

I felt my throat tighten. "Is this what you've rehearsed to say if you take the stand?"

"I'm just telling it like I see it from where I stand. You're an unreliable man. Look what you did to me already, shooting at me."

"You're a son of a bitch, you know that, Mayor?"

The mayor leaned back and fumbled inside his desk for a moment, then brought a gun level with the desk, the barrel aimed at my chest. His voice was shaky. The left side of his face twitched. "A simple act of self-defense—that's what I'll say. It all adds up—your financial stress, not paying child support, going to my wife for financial advice, wanting to sell your house, finding out you needed start-up cash, the mysterious fire at your cabin. I'm through with being held hostage by you."

I saw his finger curl around the trigger, but somehow I said, with a cool resolve, "I'm wired, Mayor. My lawyer has me wired." I went to lift up my shirt like they did in the movies, but stopped.

The mayor was still holding the gun, but he looked past me as if somebody was going to bust in the door of the trailer, then he looked at me again and lowered the gun.

I said, "My lawyer checked on the title and registration of the car you sold Earl. You sold it to him for a *penny*. Are you in the business of selling cars for a penny, or did Earl have you over a barrel?"

I had to ask the question again.

The mayor was staring at my chest. His eyes blinked, then he looked into my eyes. "Kyle Johnson was an exceptional kid. I wanted to do something for him, for his family, what with how he was helping this town, winning the way he did."

The mayor's voice didn't quite have its usual authority. He'd been a moment away from killing me. He looked up toward his wall of Little League photographs and pointed.

"Your son is up there. What have I been doing for years but supporting kids with dreams? I've been buying the cookies and the candy bars from Girl Scouts. I put back in what I take out of this community. I've been selling cars off this lot with no money down, with minimum payments. I put kids in a dream, in a car that buys them their liberty to go out on that first real date, to go to a drive-in movie, to hold hands, to kiss for that first time." The mayor let the sentiment hang in the air.

"They come in here with jars of coins. Kids saving like that, working jobs after school, working toward a goal, toward independence. That's what it's about, *independence*. I tie holidays and goodwill to the economy. That's what the hell those flags outside are about, a celebration of freedom; that's what the automobile means, it's part of our destiny!"

The mayor's voice had found its full measure now. He was talking to the recorder I didn't have strapped to my chest.

"You going to damn me for caring? It's an abomination, what we do to our high school and college players, kids working their asses off, and what do we give them, praise, a slap on the back? All you got to do is look around you at how others profit, the guy selling hot dogs, the school selling more sweaters, not to mention the intangibles, the goodwill that gets people down to my lot, gets people out to the mall because they feel good about themselves!

"Strength of character was never compromised by giving someone their hard-earned wages! So, I gave Earl Johnson a car. If that's your question, if that's your charge, I stand guilty as charged, but so help me God, I never told you to go out there to the Johnsons and cut a deal for yourself."

The mayor shook his head. "That was all you, Lawrence, all your doing."

That afternoon I called Hayden from Lois's house while she was at work. I told Hayden the mayor pulled a gun on me, told him about the mayor giving a car to Earl for free.

I said, "The mayor's denying any involvement in covering up for Kyle."

"I thought we agreed we weren't going to bring up the notion of a cover-up? So what you're telling me is you've alienated a potential character witness?" Hayden stopped, "Hold the line a moment."

He got back a moment later. "Right now I got other fires to put out. I had a guy check out where you went around the time your cabin burned down. My guy tracked where you used your credit card. I got a real problem here."

"What problem?"

"The owner of a German restaurant you ate at says he remembers you. He remembers you had some heated argument with a woman. You remember eating at a German restaurant?"

"Yes."

"And the woman was?"

"Lois."

"You remember the nature of that argument?"

"I don't know . . ."

"Did you say anything to the effect that you would burn your house down and collect on the insurance?"

It was like getting sucker punched.

"You there?"

I breathed down the line.

"I don't know if the prosecution is going to dig that up. We're going to have to wait and see, but it doesn't look good."

I raised my voice. "He took what I said out of context."

"Don't even pretend there was a context. You admit that to a jury, this case is done."

Petey was in his cage, but he was quiet. I think he'd come to accept my presence. He was listening, like a juror.

Hayden was talking loud in my ear. "The thing is here, that the more digging I do, the more points of contact I'm finding between you and Kyle. I have a statement here from the high school secretary that you interviewed Kyle at the high school right after Cheryl was rushed to the hospital?"

Hayden stopped for a moment. "Well?"

I didn't answer him.

"Okay, let me ask you another question. Have you ever called the Johnsons' house?"

"No."

"Jesus, don't lie to me, Lawrence. I'm looking at your phone records."

I lowered my head. "I called him once."

"Why?"

"I don't know."

"Come on, you're going to have to do better than that."

I felt my face flush. "I called to tell them that I knew they'd tried to kill me at the cabin, but that I had one up on them."

Hayden made a whooshing sound. "Who answered?"

"Earl did."

"You're telling me Earl tried to kill you?"

I waited a moment. "Yes." My heart was pounding. "Cheryl and I were the weak links in the cover-up. They tried to eliminate both of us the same weekend."

I could hear Hayden nervously pressing his pen. "I'm going to have to think about that one . . . Tell me, this call to Earl, was that before or after you filed the insurance claim?"

"I don't know . . ."

"Think!"

"After . . ."

"So you're admitting to filing an insurance claim when you suspected the fire was arson? That's insurance fraud. Case closed on that charge! Now, you got anything for an airtight conviction on your extortion charge?"

I didn't say anything.

Hayden lost the tone of sarcasm and said frankly, "I'm looking at some more phone records. What about calling Lisa Kendall, what was that about?"

I felt like putting the phone down.

"Lawrence?"

I said, "Look, I don't think I can go through with this."

"I got a complaint filed here that says you were spotted outside Kendall's house. What were you doing?"

Petey's head swiveled. He pecked at something in his feathers.

My chest tightened. "I don't have an answer."

"Do you know Kendall's disappeared?"

I instinctively shook my head.

"Lawrence? Answer me!"

"No, I didn't know she was missing." I said coldly, "Can we get back to my case?"

"You ever go up to her apartment?" And just by the way he asked it, I knew he'd talked to Laycock. "I've a witness who says he saw you dropping off casseroles outside her apartment."

I squatted down, cradling the phone against my chin and shoulder. My arms came up in goose bumps. I said, "I felt sorry for her. I'd found her child."

"You're telling me you *fell* for this woman?"

"What I said was, I felt sorry for her!"

"So you started calling her, stalking her, and dropping off casseroles. Did you ever speak with her in person?"

"Look, it's not how you're making it out. I'm not a pervert, if that's what you're insinuating."

"You haven't answered my question."

"No. I never met her. Look, I don't see what this has to do with anything. So I called her on the phone, so what? I told you, I found her child. I felt sorry for her. What's wrong with wanting to help someone? Why am I having to defend myself to you?"

"Tell me, are you aware that a final report on issues related to this woman's child's death has determined two different vehicles ran over the child Halloween night?"

"Yes."

"You think that strange?"

"What are you asking me?"

"What I'm asking is, was it like you said, you feeling sorry for her, or did you *suspect* something was going on?"

I had my eyes closed and pinched the bridge of my nose. I was still down on my haunches, holding the phone. "Are you asking me or telling me what I felt?"

"Let me put it like this: we are going to have to make a reasonable argument for why you called Kendall. I know Bains already interviewed Laycock. Bains has you tied to Kendall. I think we can work from the premise that you suspected there might have been something else going on, given the findings that a second car had also struck the child the night she died. Okay?"

I raised my voice. "Are you accusing me of doing something to her?"

"Calm down, Lawrence. I'm just telling you you're going to have to justify why you were watching Kendall, why you called her house."

I said, "Look, I'm going to tell you something I should have told you before, but I didn't. I know it's not going to make sense. It's about why I was out there at the Johnsons' property, waiting on Kyle when that Mrs. Vanderhagen saw me."

"I'm listening."

"Kyle knew Kendall."

I heard the surprise in Hayden's voice. "What?"

"Kyle knew Kendall, or had gotten to know her after the accident. The night the complaint was filed against me for being parked outside her apartment, I saw Kyle dropping Kendall off at her apartment."

I could sense Hayden's disbelief. "I think Kyle told Kendall what he did was an accident."

"Why?"

"You didn't know Kyle. He was simple. That time I met with him after Cheryl collapsed at the high school, he'd just about lost it. He didn't know Cheryl had an abortion, not then anyway. He thought God had taken his child, like eye-for-an-eye vengeance. That was the kind of God he believed in. He wanted to turn himself in. I told Kyle that what he had to do was go on to greatness, to save women like Kendall who had no husbands, women abandoned like her, that he should give money away when he got rich. I told him that was how he could redeem himself."

I heard Hayden's office chair creak. "How come this Laycock mentioned seeing you, but never mentioned Kyle going to see her?"

"You know the guy's a small-time pusher? What he says isn't worth a hill of beans."

"That's not answering my question."

"Kyle did go there. Ask him again."

I heard Hayden shuffling through papers. "What Laycock said was that numerous kids from the football team came by the apartment. He said, somehow they got the impression that Kendall had died and come back as a ghost."

I raised my voice. "They got that impression from Laycock. That was his urban myth, spread just to lure kids to his apartment."

Hayden cut me off. "Well, if we can just locate her, we'll know, right?" But I got a sense he felt she wasn't going to be found.

I said, "Find her."

Hayden cleared his throat. "I don't know if that's entirely my job . . . which brings me to my next point. We're going to have to renegotiate terms before I can proceed. This is far more complicated than you led me to believe.

"Let me just recap what you've told me so far, for both our benefit, because right now I can't see the forest for the trees, and maybe neither can you. To begin with, you denied everything, then you positioned yourself simply as a victim, party to a cover-up, wanting to come forward and expose those who were behind it—the chief and the mayor. That was your initial feeling, the morning you were arraigned, to just come forward, but we decided against that strategy. Then it turns out you were entangled with Kyle and his family, not only meeting with Kyle, but also calling the Johnsons' house at two o'clock in the morning, denying that fact, then admitting it only when presented with proof, and now it appears you had some interest in the woman Kendall that you've yet to adequately explain—a woman who, it turns out, has disappeared, a woman whose child was run down, by not one but two cars—and now you're telling me Kyle had befriended Kendall, that he might have told her he'd run her child over. You following all this?"

I said curtly, "How much do you want?"

I heard Hayden's chair squeak again. "You want to get high and mighty, then we've nothing more to discuss."

"I just want to know how much I've got to come up with."

"I'm going to have to think it over."

"Give me a price when you're ready." I waited for him to say something, then said, "Anything else I should know?"

Hayden said flatly, "I interviewed your wife yesterday."

"And?"

"Put it this way, I don't see you two getting back together anytime soon. She told me you pulled a gun on her when she tried to leave you. You remember kicking in a motel door and screaming you were going to kill her?"

"The gun wasn't loaded."

"I'm glad you cleared that up." Hayden's voice held a measure of disdain. "That'll work with a jury. 'Ladies and gentlemen, the gun wasn't loaded . . . ' Let me tell you, a pattern is emerging here, a damning pattern of erratic and potentially homicidal behavior. I cannot, for the life of me, figure out what's going on, and maybe that will work to your advantage in the end. I don't know. But what I want you to do is, reconsider why the hell you hired me."

There was a muffled sound on the phone. "Look, I got another call waiting. We'll have to meet in person to discuss where we want to go from here."

I was about to hang up when he said, "By the way, did you ever speak with that chief of yours, seeing you blew it with the mayor, and your wife's a washout?"

I said, "That's a complicated situation. We're not on speaking terms."

"Why?"

"The chief is in love with the woman who bailed me out."

"With that dispatcher, your friend, Lois?"

"Yes."

"Okay, I'm waiting for the punch line."

34

The Canadian border is just a line on the map. There is no appreciable divide, no physical barrier.

I said, "Does Canada have any extradition treaties with America?"

Lois was sitting at the kitchen table. The map was set out before us. "I don't know. They never went to get Sam. They could never touch any draft dodger that went up there during Vietnam."

"Maybe it's different for felonies?"

Lois said, "I don't know."

Lois's brother, Sam, lived along the St. Lawrence. We got out Lois's set of encyclopedias and checked out Canada, then cross-referenced with Quebec, and then found the town where Sam lived. Lois told me he traveled the world as a merchant marine when he was younger and made out real good.

Lois said, "I already called him. He told me you could get work easy. You don't got to have any experience." She was inches from me, both of us staring at the encyclopedia.

"Come on, you could end up seeing the world out of this. Think of it that way."

I looked at her. "What about that bail money you posted to get me released?"

"Ten thousand is worth it to buy your freedom."

"If I run, I'm basically saying I'm *guilty* of something."

I'd found out the previous day from Hayden that Kendall might have been using an alias. It was going to be hard tracking her down. I hadn't told Lois about Kendall's disappearance. I'd been holding out all along that Kendall would show up, that my association with her would prove nothing other than my sense of loneliness.

For the remainder of that day, I'd tried to hide from the possibility that she was dead. But I'd been in her apartment, and maybe even back then I knew, not that she was dead, but that she'd gone, that she'd faded from our lives. Who would leave behind the last remaining relics of their child's existence?

Amidst everything with Kyle, some deeper mystery had emerged. I was sure of that. At times I saw, in my mind's eye, Kyle killing Kendall. He'd confessed to her, then backtracked and killed her. Hadn't he killed Cheryl, hadn't he tried to kill me? At other times, I thought of that pleading voice of hers that night on the phone, begging forgiveness—from whom and for what?

When I closed my eyes I saw one car, then another, hitting that pile of leaves in the road.

Then later that evening, Hayden had called again. I didn't pick up, but listened to the message. Janine had told Hayden about the eight hundred cash I'd paid toward child support. He wanted to know where I got the money. He called back, talking to the machine again. He said, "The report outlining the chemicals used to start the fire at the cabin has come back. It's definitely arson."

Hayden never mentioned Kendall, which meant he hadn't found her. She was still missing.

I think it was her disappearance that affected his commitment to the case most of all, a thread of coincidence that made a strong circumstantial case against me in his mind, that and how I got the eight hundred dollars. In a way, I couldn't blame him.

In the end, there was only one escape—Canada.

Lois made a light lunch, grilled cheese sandwiches with a pickle on the side. We didn't talk. I didn't tell her about Hayden asking about the eight hundred. I'd already made up my mind to run for it.

When we finished, Lois got up and cleaned the plates. I began to stack the dishwasher. Lois touched my hand. "That's not how you do it. You have to pack a dishwasher like you fill a church, from the back forward."

It was one of those perfect moments when I wished we were married, when I wished things could have been different, that I could have turned back time. I think she knew what I was thinking.

Lois got the paper out of the driveway. She came back into the living room and gave Petey the *Parade* section of Sunday's newspaper, and the Jane Fonda cassette box. Jane's picture was on the box. Petey dragged her into his cage, pecked her for a while. Then he went about building a nest. He did that through the afternoon, tearing and chewing and making an elaborate home.

Lois put a roast in the oven, and the smell of meat filled the house. I sat with her at the kitchen table for a bit. She was going through the papers, cutting out coupons.

I got up and saw Petey was still making his house, rustling around inside his cage.

I said, "How the hell did Fonda go from fatigues to leotards, from antiwar and feminism to this?"

Lois didn't look up. I guess she knew I was talking to myself.

I said, "All I think of when Fonda says, 'Go for the burn!' is napalm." I went into the living room and peered in at Petey. I was talking for the sake of talking.

In the back of the cage, Petey's eyes shone out at me. He had Jane Fonda set on top of the nest.

I stood in the doorway between the kitchen and the living room. The roast hissed in the oven.

Lois looked up. She had a pile of coupons cut for me. She said, "I could save you bundles. This is like cutting out money . . ."

Her face was puffy from lack of sleep. She was still talking, but I put a finger to her mouth, and right there, under the glare of the kitchen light, on the kitchen table, amidst the coupons, we made love.

Through the dark hours of early morning Lois drove me to my neighborhood. I crept through the obscurity of night, went in through the back door of my house and didn't turn on the lights, working against moonlight. I packed a few items of clothing, but what I'd really gone for was a photograph of Eddy and Max, taken when Eddy was less than two years old. It was in the room I kept for him when he came over to spend the night. He had a picture of Luke Skywalker on his wall, along with another of Obi-Wan Kenobi, Luke's surrogate father. I closed the door, went downstairs and took the answering machine as well, just to have Eddy's voice with me. Then I shut the back door and walked away from the only life I'd ever really known.

It ended that quickly and unceremoniously.

Lois was startled when I put my face to the driver's-side window. I got in. She pulled away without turning on her lights, waiting almost two blocks before she did so.

I looked around to see if there was anybody following us.

At a twenty-four-hour gas station, I filled a canister of gas. Its sweet odor filled the car.

At the same storage facility where I rented my unit, Lois had a carport rented where she stored Lionel's car. She'd never sold it. Originally, a brother of Lionel was going to buy it. That's what he told Lois at the funeral, but then he never did. She'd had it towed back from the town where Lionel had hung himself. She'd told me all this back at her house. I'd just listened. I figured she was coping with me leaving in her own way.

But I admit, there were moments when I thought, despite everything she was doing for me, that maybe she wanted me gone.

Track lighting ran the perimeter fencing, making everything faintly glow as we arrived. We used a key to get into the compound.

Lionel's car had a musty, cold smell. I poured the gas into the car and rolled it out into the lot. The battery was dead. I stood, shivering, uncoiling the jumper cables we'd brought, then, leaning into the yawn of the opened hood, felt the cold metal teeth on each jumper lead bite the charged battery mounts.

I turned, and Lois was watching me. I stopped for a moment, struck by the desperation of what I was doing.

I think we were sharing the same thought.

The ignition clicked, but the engine didn't turn over, though the interior light came on. Pasted to the glove box was a sticker that said, "Into every life, a little rain must fall."

I said Lionel's name to myself. I couldn't see Lois, because the hood was raised. Leaning out the door, I shouted, "Rev it more, Lois," and she did, and I pumped the gas pedal until it built up pressure, turned the key, and the car roared to life for the first time since Lionel had killed himself.

By four-thirty, I had a suitcase full of Lionel's clothes on the back-seat, and Petey. Lois had put him into the car just as I was leaving, along with the Jane Fonda cassette box with its tape.

She had tears in her eyes. "I told you, Petey, I won't stand being cheated on." She said that as she'd put Petey into the backseat.

"You know, Lawrence, parrots are supposed to mate for life. Petey has committed the highest infidelity you can imagine."

She came and put her head into the driver's-side window. I could see the strain in her face.

"My brother's kids always wanted a parrot. I cleared it with him. They'll take him off your hands when you get there."

Petey was perched on the passenger side headrest, rocking back and forth. He said, "Go for the burn."

It was the diversion we both needed.

35 I drove Lionel's car through a blur of hours, away from everything I'd known, letting the semistatic of AM radio fill my head.

I was three hours on the road when I realized there was a cassette deck in the car. I pushed in a tape Lionel had been playing the day he died.

It was a Burt Bacharach song, "Wives and Lovers," and maybe I learned more about Lionel than I could ever have otherwise, listening to that crooning voice:

> "Don't send him off with your hair still in curlers.
> You may not see him again."

I kept driving through a smear of mile markers, replaying that song again and again, and each time I saw Lois with curlers in her hair.

I arrived in Niagara Falls in the late evening. Petey was in his cage, his black eyes shining. It was freezing and deserted, not like I'd seen it in those fifties summer movies of romance and intrigue.

The American side was just a desolate park leading to lookout points where it seemed like people might contemplate jumping.

I know I did.

I pulled into a motel near the park, and that's when Petey lost it. Maybe it was some residual memory of what he'd seen happen to Lionel, maybe he picked up on some sense of desperation. I had to pull the sheet over his cage just to get him quiet, but even that didn't fully quiet him.

I ended up leaving the motel and driving around the grim nether regions of the park before pulling into a dilapidated motel called The Honeymooners' Getaway that had seen better days. The Getaway part was somehow ironic.

I took a suite at the off-season rate. It came complete with a heart-shaped bed and a Jacuzzi that didn't work. But it also came with a VCR you could rent with a deposit. I put the Jane Fonda video into the VCR, and Petey settled.

I was supposed to call Lois's brother, Sam, at 11:00 P.M., so I set the clock radio, lay out on the bed, and slept. The alarm sounded, and I woke like I'd not slept at all, no dreams, nothing, just the cold sterility of the room.

Time had stopped meaning anything. I felt maybe how Janine had felt when she left me, and for a moment I was truly sorry for what I'd done to her.

The TV was on in the background. It was a movie about a wife who killed her husband by hitting him over the head with a frozen leg of lamb. The police arrived but couldn't find the murder weapon. The wife was cooking the leg of lamb, even as the police were searching the house.

I went out into the night. I still had some time left to kill before I was supposed to call Sam. There was an amusement arcade across from the motel parking lot. Everything looked rundown.

In the distance, I could hear the sound of the falls. Mist was falling, making everything gleam. A billboard advertised a *Maid of the Mist* tour of the falls.

I don't know why I ended up calling Janine, but I did, maybe to say goodbye. I was a fugitive, and all my calls would be traced from here on out. Even calling from here, I figured the police would know I'd gone to Canada, but still I called.

I was shivering. The phone booth was near the falls. Seth answered, not Janine. He caught me off guard.

I said, "Where'd you learn to fly a plane, Seth?" I said it in a civil way.

It took Seth a moment to wake up, then he said, "Oh, you mean about Thanksgiving?"

"Yeah, Thanksgiving. Where'd you learn to fly?"

I heard Seth yawn, a faint snapping sound of his jaw. "The Air Force."

"I didn't know you were ex-military. I didn't know that, Seth."

Seth said, "How would you?"

"I guess I wouldn't, Seth." I said, "This is probably the longest conversation we have ever had right here."

"I think you're right. I think it is."

I said, "That's not a good situation, when you're raising my kid. I think we should have become friends, or been on speaking terms at least."

"It's never too late to start."

I said, "I like your attitude, Seth."

"Thank you."

I felt I was coming off a hangover. "You mind if I ask you something, Seth?"

"Shoot."

"I hope you don't mind me asking you this, but do you think of Eddy as your son, or do you think of him as Janine's kid?"

"What are you doing right now, Lawrence? You okay? I hear something in the background."

"Seth, if you don't mind, I'm asking the questions. We've got a nice conversation going here."

"Sure thing."

I turned and stared out across the park, and through the scarves of mist from the falls, I could see pulses of light coming from the other side.

Seth was talking. "I never told anybody this, but I was adopted. I was left in a department store in downtown St. Louis. It was during the Great Depression."

I said, "I didn't know that."

"How would you?"

"I appreciate you taking me into your confidence. I just want to say, I hope you don't think badly of me not paying for Eddy, but I'm strung out right now. That's just the plain economics of it. It's got nothing to do with not loving my kid. I just thought I should put the record straight."

"I never thought badly of my mother for leaving me in that department store. There are bigger forces at work sometimes than mere willpower or faith can overcome."

"I'm not asking to be let off the hook here, Seth."

"I'm talking in the abstract, not about you specifically. It's just an opinion I hold."

I said, "Oh . . ." My breath was shallow, my feet numb. It was like I was whispering, which I guess I was. "Maybe you could explain things to Eddy, if I don't get the chance, Seth." I was getting soaked from the mist.

"Sure, I will."

"One other thing."

"What's that?"

"Wasn't there any way you could have found somebody who didn't have a kid? I'm just asking here, Seth. It's not an accusation. I'm just trying to understand your motivations."

"I don't think people plan on falling in love. It just happens."

I said, "I guess I can buy that." It pained me to hear him use the word love in connection with Janine. I wasn't as big a man as I thought I was right then.

"I've got to level with you, Lawrence, I'm breaking a court order by speaking to you."

I said, "Seth, I'm glad we had this chance to talk like human beings."

"So am I."

"Good night, Seth."

"Good night, Lawrence."

I called Lois's brother, Sam the draft dodger, from the same phone booth. He was to pick me up the following day. He was talking about being a draft dodger though I wasn't really listening. I was staring out at the falls.

It seemed like the end of the earth with that noise beyond, like everything was getting sucked into its center.

Sam said my name, and I said, "Yeah."

"You brought the title to the car with you, right?" That was the deal. He was getting Lionel's car for helping me out.

I said, "I have Petey too."

Sam said, "I don't think we can take him right now."

I passed a solitary couple huddled together on a lookout point, and then went down to another lookout. As I got close, I saw a cauldron of illuminated ruby mist. The ground was iced over. I had to walk crablike just to get to the railing edge.

I looked over and saw the falls half-frozen in tongues of ice, chandelier icicles hanging from the cragged walls.

I called Lois from the same telephone I'd used to call Sam. She was waiting at a bar we'd decided on before I left so the call couldn't be traced.

When she picked up, I could tell something was wrong. She didn't say anything for a few moments. I had to say her name, then she said coldly, "Where are you?"

"Niagara Falls. What's wrong?"

There was the sound of a pinball machine in the background.

"Lois, what is it?"

I heard Lois swallow and let out a long breath. "Your lawyer called me looking for you. He wanted to speak with you. You know why?" Lois's voice cracked. "He told me Lisa Kendall is missing. He told me you *knew* she was missing. How come you didn't tell me?"

I leaned against the cold metal of the phone box.

"What's going on, Lawrence—please, I gave you everything I had."

I was shivering. "I don't know what's going on." I hesitated. "What's her disappearance got to do with me, Lois? Maybe she just left."

"She's disappeared. She left everything behind, even those mementos of her child. A mother wouldn't leave those behind, she wouldn't." Lois had begun crying. "You were in her apartment, weren't you?"

I felt sick in the pit of my stomach. I wanted to say something, but she sobbed down the line, "Don't deny it, don't! They recovered your prints."

I heard her shudder. Her voice went low. It was brittle. "Oh my God . . ." She was talking under her breath. "I don't know who you are anymore! I don't."

Her voice trailed off.

All I could do was shout, "What the hell are you saying, Lois, that I did something to her? Listen to me, I'm not your goddamn pervert husband, Lionel, you hear me?"

36 That evening I sat at a diner, drinking black coffee, afraid to go back to my motel, and for the first time in my life I wondered what was on the other side of life. Did we look down from above? Were we granted that solace?

I watched people come and go from the diner and understood what freedom was, those throwaway days when we thought of neither illness nor death, where we lived outside the reality that we would one day cease to exist.

I was jittery from the caffeine. My cup trembled. A waitress looked at me like she knew I was in trouble.

I left when her back was turned.

Outside, the evening air knifed my throat. I huddled and got to Lionel's car. The leather seats were stiff. I let the car warm up, sat watching the waitress inside the glass bowl of the diner clear my table.

She looked up for a moment, put the tip into the pocket of her apron, and wiped the table in a slow wave.

A cosmos of lights winked along the strip of eateries and motels. On the radio, they forecasted clear skies and dropping temperatures. I filled up on cheap gas, then circled the motel a few times before deciding I wasn't being watched.

I went into the room and loaded my gun. Petey watched me. It looked like he might yet again be the star witness to another suicide. He swayed to and fro on the bar of his cage, rolling his head in an S pattern, his neck craned forward.

I plugged in the answering machine I'd brought and listened to Eddy's messages, hitting replay over and over again. It's what took me through the dark hours of doubt and fear, took me literally toward the light that streamed around the edges of my motel window.

I woke to someone knocking at the door. I had fallen asleep. I heard a key in the lock, and the door opened. I scrambled across the bed, going for my gun.

Petey squawked and fanned his wings. But when the door opened, it was the maid. It was eleven o'clock in the morning.

I emerged minutes later from the shower into a bank of mist. The bathroom fan didn't work.

I wiped a hole in the mist and shaved. Steam ran down the mirror in silver lines. It was like seeing myself behind steel bars.

I hoarded the miniature shampoos, soaps, and shower cap.

When I opened the door, the daylight made me squint for a moment and shield my eyes. My hands smelt of soapy lavender, my skin dry.

Petey hunkered down in his cage on the heart-shaped bed. It rattled in the cold air. The curtains billowed and settled.

I was on the second floor, above everything. I went outside, stopped and stared across the industrial landscape, antennas on flat black tarp roofs. At the motel across the road, a guy in overalls was working on a heating system unit. Behind him was a huge garish billboard facing the highway that ran on gray pylons. It was advertising an "All-U-Can-Eat Buffet."

I could see cars streaming along the raised highway. The guy looked small against the billboard when he stood up. He looked like he was in the line of oncoming cars from where I was standing. I could hear his radio playing. Somewhere beyond that, a car honked. A phone rang in a bedroom, and Petey squawked.

Down below in the motel lot, the piano-key parking spaces were empty, except for where I'd parked Lionel's car—a solitary flat note.

A squat woman in a maid's uniform was standing by her cleaning cart, smoking.

The teardrop-shaped motel pool was fenced off and closed for the winter.

I left at exactly noon.

I drove aimlessly along the American side of the falls. Across the gorge of Niagara I saw the Skylon tower with its revolving restaurant on top. It was like staring into the future.

I crossed at the border without incident. Petey was in the trunk, covered with a cloth to keep him quiet.

I stopped at a manicured park, got out and shivered, tipped my head back, feeling that disorientation you get when the sky moves fast overhead, when you catch on for a brief moment to what you know to be true but rarely experience, that we are hurtling through the universe on a spinning rock.

I had escaped America. What now?

I began walking by storefronts filled with lace doilies and trinkets, souvenir pens with a miniature of the *Maid of the Mist* that floated from one end of the pen to the other.

I bought one for Eddy. That was the kind of thing a kid would die to have.

There were china plates with the image of Charles and Diana's wedding, dishcloths and calendars bearing the image of the queen and her mother, souvenir silver spoons with family crests—colonial nostalgia for a more subdued time. I saw how that all meant something now. History meant something here.

I walked down along the gorge, and when the wind blew just so, everything was enveloped in a damp, iridescent, onionskin mist.

I read on a placard about a Frenchman who'd walked the falls on a tightrope, about the long history of people going over the falls in barrels.

I went up the beetlelike elevator of the Skylon tower and watched the world turn beneath me. Across the way, I saw America.

I went down into the world again, thinking about nothing, letting time run out before me. Further back from the pristine facade of Niagara, I fell upon the vaudevillian spectacle of sideshows, a world of carnivals and slot machines. Everything was in disrepair, the cogwheels of novelty laid bare, disemboweled machinery reeking of oil.

I entered The Wall of Death, a room that spun with such centrifugal force that I stuck to it even as the floor fell out beneath me. I was the only one on the ride. I went on a Ferris wheel, rose again into the blue sky and stared deep into Ontario and beyond to Quebec.

At a wax museum, I paid to see the world's fattest man, the world's tallest man, and the world's strongest man. I walked through history, came face to face with Napoleon and Genghis Khan, Harry Houdini and Evel Knievel, Elvis Presley and Frank Sinatra, the Beatles, Gandhi and Hitler, Winston Churchill and Dolly Parton—not all in that order.

They were just the ones I remembered.

It was my last chance to hoard a lifetime of memories. I ate cotton candy and, allegedly, the world's greatest fudge. I got my palm read. I was told I was taking a long journey.

I said, without a trace of irony, "You don't know how right you are."

I kept experiencing everything like it was my last day on earth. I got a picture of me going over the falls in a barrel. It was done like the front page of a newspaper.

Back up by the rundown motels, they were renting out spaces for RVs, creating a sort of refugee camp of retirees.

As evening fell, I stood against garish flashing lights, watched the elderly sitting with plastic buckets of nickels and dimes feeding slot machines at a rundown amusement park.

I went over to the bumper cars, to the only attraction drawing people, and when my turn came I stepped into the mesh wire–netted cage and found a car that just swiveled in a circle when the power came on.

It was while I was trying to control it that I felt the jolting impact of one, then a succession of hits, felt the car recoil, and suddenly I was right there again, where it had all started with that child, at the moment of impact and death.

I went down by the falls again, left behind the phantasm of the amusement rides for the quaintness of the colonial facades.

I called Lois one last time from a pay phone. I'd not met with her brother as planned. He'd expected to get the car. I wanted to tell her I was keeping it for a while.

When she answered, her voice was frantic. "Lawrence, thank God . . . thank God you called." I felt taken aback for a moment, as if this was a trick, like they were trying to trace the call.

I said, "I never did meet your brother."

"That's not important now. Listen to me. I got in touch with that friend of mine at the telephone company. She checked up on who Kendall had been talking to the night you called her? You know what she found out?"

"What?"

"She'd been talking to the *mayor* the night you called her! She'd called him on his office phone, down on his lot. She'd been speaking with him for over a half hour before you called her!"

Lois was talking a hundred miles an hour. "There's more. I got my friend to pull Kendall's records going back to when she moved into the apartment. Kendall's been phoning the mayor for at least two years. Two years—you hear that? I have a copy of Kendall's records right in front of me here. Listen to this. This is the kicker. Kendall spoke with the mayor the night her child was killed for going on an hour, you hear that, Lawrence?"

The steel casing of the phone booth was freezing against the side of my face.

"You're not making this up, are you? You trying to draw me back?"

"No." Lois's voice settled. "I'm sorry, please. You want to know the truth? I didn't trust you. That's why I called my friend. I wanted to see how many times you'd called her."

My body was shaking. "So what now?"

"I'm calling your lawyer and telling him what I found out. Now we know why the mayor has always denied there was a cover-up. He was involved with Kendall!"

I don't think what she was saying had really sunk in. I kept shivering.

Lois said my name. "Just get back here as quick as you can, before anybody knows you're gone."

When I turned from the phone booth, I could see the ruby glow from the mouth of the falls, like hell had just frozen over.

37 The meeting at the county courthouse came at the request of the mayor's lawyer. In the car in the parking lot of the courthouse, Lois fixed a run in her nylons with nail polish. The smell cut the air like smelling salts. I felt sick to my stomach and had to get out and take deep breaths of air.

In the wide halls of the old building, we were standing around in clusters—the mayor, his wife, along with Bains and some guy from the prosecutor's office. Lois and Hayden were talking with one another alone. There were some other people I didn't know also standing around, holding briefcases.

We were all keeping our distances before the meeting started, avoiding looking at one another as much as possible.

The room in which we were meeting was big, with a long mahogany table running down the middle. There were jugs of water set out, along with a silver tray with glasses.

The mayor, in his checkered blazer, and his wife, in her fake admiral's jacket, were holding hands, which was something I had never seen them do before. In fact, I'd never actually seen them together.

They had their own lawyer present. He arrived with a young intern, or that's what she looked like. She was carrying a bulging briefcase.

The mayor's lawyer was from a big law firm in Indianapolis, that's what Hayden told me, and he charged over a hundred and twenty dollars an hour.

Hayden said, "You see the deal I'm cutting you, Lawrence?" but I wasn't in a laughing mood. I could tell Hayden was intimidated.

Only a few days had passed since I'd got back from Niagara Falls, and all hell had broken loose.

I went over and stood with Lois. She was dressed like it was Sunday service.

The chief arrived late. He was in uniform. His pomade-flattened hair shone like a beaver's pelt. He said Arnold Fisher was alone on duty. That's all he said by way of explanation. He had a heavyset guy with a double chin with him. I figured it was a lawyer, but the chief didn't introduce him.

Lois had already talked to the chief. They'd gone to lunch the day I drove back from Niagara Falls. The chief wasn't speaking to the mayor, not since he heard what Lois told him about the mayor having whatever dealings he had been having with Lisa Kendall.

A court stenographer was present, and like a silenced pianist began typing as the mayor's lawyer read aloud a statement that acknowledged the mayor had contact with Lisa Kendall, but explained that the property Lisa Kendall rented was managed by the mayor's wife's realty company, thus explaining the contact.

"We have documents supporting this fact." The mayor's lawyer held up a series of papers, but didn't distribute them.

"Let me state that the mayor, along with his wife, developed a platonic relationship with Lisa Kendall, given her personal circumstances. True to their civic and personal sense of compassion, the mayor and his wife took on Lisa Kendall as a charitable cause. That was the extent of their relationship with her."

I could see the mayor's face twitch as his lawyer talked. He reached for his wife's hand and put his hand on hers. She was like a mannequin behind her mask of makeup, abject and sickly.

I made eye contact with her, but she looked away.

The mayor's lawyer continued reading from the prepared statement.

"Let me further reiterate that insinuations related to the mayor having had an extramarital affair with Lisa Kendall are wholly unfounded, and we intend to pursue criminal charges of libel against any persons printing such fabrications. On a final note, I would ask for your consideration for both the mayor and his wife, Jean. Jean's cancer has recurred. She is currently undergoing chemotherapy."

The mayor's lawyer sat down and looked at the mayor, who nodded and stood up and squeezed his wife's bony hand and said, "I love you." Then he cleared his voice. "I am prepared to make a statement related to events on the night of October 31."

Over the course of ten minutes, the mayor outlined his involvement with the case, how, after receiving the information from the chief, he made the decision to call Earl Johnson, and how Earl first denied Kyle's involvement but then began ranting that he was going to kill Kyle for what he'd done.

The mayor said, "I was dealing with a crisis situation, with a known belligerent drunk. At that point, my whole focus centered on protecting Kyle Johnson, protecting him from Earl Johnson, from the domestic quagmire the kid found himself living in . . . There was no intention of covering up any wrongdoing on Kyle's part." The mayor stopped. "I think the chief can corroborate that my concern was protecting Kyle from his father, Earl."

The chief was about to answer, but his lawyer said, "We have no comment at this time." The chief swallowed and stared down at the table.

The mayor turned again to all of us seated at the long table. "It's never been my style to hide behind a political or legal smokescreen. It's not me, not who I am, what I stand for. If you want to damn me for caring, then damn me, because what I did was not out of political or personal gain, nothing like that, what I did was protect a young man from a belligerent alcoholic, a man who lived in the past, a man with failed ambitions, a failed high school quarterback who amounted to nothing, and instead of nurturing and loving his son, instead of sharing in his son's success, rode his son every day of his life, belittling him. When I called Earl Johnson, when I explained Kyle's potential involvement in the hit-and-run, I very quickly knew I was speaking to a time bomb, that the life of a young man with a future would be ruined."

The mayor's face was red. He stopped and took a drink. His lawyer leaned toward him.

The mayor shook his head vigorously. "What my lawyer here wants are the facts, but I want you to know what was going through my mind, I want you to know what I confronted that night I called Earl Johnson."

Hayden interrupted and said, "With all due respect, to get to the heart of the matter, did you call in my client and coerce him into covering up Kyle Johnson's involvement in the hit-and-run of Sarah Kendall?"

"Coerce is not a word I would use in this context."

"Well, let me put it this way, how did you get my client's cooperation?"

"I had kept your client . . . that is, Lawrence, there, out of jail, for an incident with his wife a few years before. I was calling in a favor. I'd kept him out of jail, isn't that right, Lawrence?"

Hayden put his hand on my shoulder.

The mayor looked at me. "That's what I've done all my career, looked out for everybody else. By rights, your client should be in jail for pulling a gun on his wife."

Hayden interrupted. "If we could keep to what happened during the meeting."

The mayor's lawyer stood up and said, "This meeting is over," but the mayor said, "No, I want to finish this. Over the years I've made calculated decisions for the sake of the town, for the *greater good,* and at times I have skirted the law, because the law is an abstract thing. It doesn't deal in the fears and emotions of those involved. There was another law we lived by here not long ago, an older, more compassionate law that took into account the foibles of our humanity, that gave us a second chance." The mayor leaned forward. "I loved my town like a family, a *family.* I never stood above everybody looking down—I was always underneath, holding everybody up."

He raised one of his hands, like he was holding up a great burden, and put the other on his wife's shoulder. "We never did have children, and God knows we tried, so instead, we took this town as a surrogate, as our own." He didn't finish what he was going to say.

The mayor's lawyer said, "This meeting is over," and the mayor sat back in his chair. His wife was just staring across at me.

I could see now her hair was a wig, that she'd already lost it all.

In the lemony afternoon light, I sat with Lois in a coffee shop on the second floor of the courthouse. It was like a great weight had been lifted, almost anticlimactic. The evidence suggested that I had been an unwilling accomplice, that I was guilty in the end of falsifying a report, nothing more. I didn't even think about the arson charge. I felt sure it would be dropped, after what had come to light.

Lois was looking out the window, her cup at lip level, and she was blowing softly. It was like she was in another place.

When I touched her hand, she smiled, but her eyes were glassy.

On a radio, I heard the mayor's lawyer making the same statement he made to all of us inside the court building. Then the mayor's lawyer announced that the mayor was resigning.

Hayden wasn't smiling when he slid into the booth beside us, and that took me by surprise. He said, "The DA told me they are going to begin proceedings against you, for aiding and abetting the mayor in his plan to cover up for Kyle. You're being named in an indictment along with the mayor and the chief."

The euphoria was gone.

Lois raised her voice. "Lawrence was coerced by the mayor!"

Hayden said quietly, "They aren't going to let this go. Lawrence filed a false report. Also, the blackmail charge stands as is. Working with the mayor and chief to initiate a cover-up doesn't preclude you from trying to extort money from Kyle. They have that witness, that woman you told me about, scheduled to testify you were out waiting near the Johnsons' property. It underscores the veracity of Earl's claim that he only found out what had happened after the fact. I think that single fact may well protect Earl from any legal proceedings against his not coming forward sooner. It's a mitigating circumstance. It leads to the conclusion that he wasn't initially in on the cover-up."

Hayden waited a moment. "You heard the mayor in there, talking about civic duty and responsibility to the town. All that will play to Earl's favor. Earl's lawyer can argue the mayor was interested in Kyle's success for his own reasons, he can argue that given Earl's disposition, the mayor might have bypassed asking Earl anything. I can guarantee you the mayor's not going to say he made a deal with Earl."

I just shook my head.

"That's not to mention the eight hundred cash you suddenly came up with for back child support."

Lois cut in, "I gave him that!"

Hayden looked at me and then at Lois. "You gave it to him? Did you withdraw the money from a bank?"

I could see Lois's profile stiffen. "No . . ." Her voice trailed off. "It was money . . . money I was saving for a vacation. I had it . . . It was at the house."

Hayden bit his lower lip, and I could see the vague register in his eyes that maybe he thought I wasn't totally innocent. I was going to have to live with that look for years to come.

Lois flattened her hands on her knees and stared at the tops of her fingers. I saw her lips moving. She looked up at me with a hurt expression, like this was her fault.

For a second I wanted to hit Hayden, wanted to push him against the wall and say, "Whatever you think about me, she's not a goddamn liar!" But instead I said, "Let's round this out. How about the insurance fraud charge?"

Hayden met my stare. "I'm sorry, Lawrence. It stands as is. Bains interviewed the owner of that German restaurant you stopped at. He's going to be subpoenaed to testify that he overheard you and Lois talking about burning down your house." He waited a moment. "You're going to be called as a material witness too, Lois."

She squeezed my hand.

I said, "Anything else?"

"They lifted your prints from Kendall's apartment. You're going to be interviewed with regard to the investigation into her disappearance. She's still missing. It's pretty clear she used an alias."

I felt the world close around me again.

Lois raised her voice. "How about her phone records? She had to phone somebody else, sometime. How far back did they check?"

"It's already been checked. There's nothing." Hayden turned slightly so he was facing me. "They're going to want to know why you went into her apartment."

I couldn't answer that question, not then anyway. It seemed like a lifetime ago since that rush of relief had hit me in Niagara Falls. It had seemed so obvious that the mayor had been involved with Kendall. Had we jumped to the wrong conclusion?

Hayden said my name. I looked at him.

"I think we need to go with the angle that you suspected something when you discovered that two vehicles had run over the child. We need to establish a credible story line. Right now, you've been linked to watching Kendall late at night, dropping off food outside her door, phoning her, and being in her apartment. They're the facts we have to contend with."

The reprieve was well and truly over. The nightmare was only beginning. I said with a sense of bewilderment, "Maybe I should have kept running . . ."

Lois said, "Why would a woman live under an alias? What's going on here?"

Hayden shook his head. "I don't know, but we're going to try and find her."

Lois said almost under her breath, "Can people just disappear without a trace?"

Her eyes looked hollow, a half-crescent of dark under each eye. She'd not slept in days.

I touched my coffee mug. It had gone cold.

There seemed to be no answer to Lois's question. We stayed quiet. But then, amidst the stream of afternoon light, Lois looked up and said, "Could she have been in something like a witness protection program? You hear about people entering them. Do they really exist?" Her voice grew more animated. "That would go a long way to explaining her using an alias. Maybe whoever she'd been hiding from found her out? What if they got to her like they got to her child?"

Lois was talking a million miles an hour. "How do you find out if someone was in a witness protection program?"

38 The mayor's wife collapsed during the mayor's interview on the county courthouse steps and was the lead-in to the floodgate of loose ends that were now being threaded together by journalists.

I saw the images of Jean on the evening news, the way she buckled as she stood beside the mayor. This was how she was going to live out her last months, in the mire and confusion of what her husband had done. I truly felt sorry for her at some gut level.

The mayor's connection to Lisa Kendall broke with the sensationalism that not only was she missing, and had most probably being using an alias, but that her child had been struck by not one, but two, vehicles Halloween night.

Then the story took an even more surreal twist when it was revealed that a witness traveling in one of the vehicles that struck the child had identified Kyle Johnson as the driver. Of course the perfunctory details of who and what Kyle meant added to the cinematic specter of everything as it unfolded. Cameras had again been set up at the Johnsons' property.

Then the report cut to a young woman reporter standing on the street where Sarah Kendall had died. She was explaining the details of the child's death.

It was snowing lightly. A shot widened to take in the white colonial facade of a house that had seen better days, where Lisa Kendall had lived in utter obscurity until that fateful night.

We had come full circle.

But at that moment, caught in the camera lens, the street looked like one of those globed winter scenes that you shake and snow sifts through a miniature world. It belied the reality of what had gone on here.

I saw Raymond Laycock appear off-camera as the reporter was talking. He was huddling against the cold.

The reporter was nodding fitfully. She had one hand to her ear like she was following breaking news. "We are now learning disturbing details surrounding Lisa Kendall's last weeks alive. Seemingly, she had become an object of morbid fascination for high school students as a neighbor can attest to. Right now, we are bringing you an Eyewitness 5 exclusive interview with a young man who lived in the same multi-apartment house."

The reporter closed the distance between herself and Laycock, bringing him into camera. It had such dramatic flair, all of it, that sudden intimacy, her putting her hand on his shoulder.

Laycock looked strung out, dressed in a Pink Floyd T-shirt, his eyes bleary. He inhaled the dregs of a cigarette which he stubbed with the heel of his shoe, then ran his hand through his greasy hair. He looked right into the camera. "Yeah . . . Charlene, it was weird, I mean, real weird. Kids from the high school thought Lisa was a ghost come back looking for her kid. They'd show up drunk some nights, guys pushing girls up the stairwell to Kendall's apartment, shouting to her." His voice trailed off. "I guess it was like a rite of initiation."

The reporter timed it just so. I could tell she'd gone over things with Laycock. She asked knowingly, "Did Kyle Johnson ever come here?"

Laycock looked at his feet and then raised his head slowly. "Yeah . . . I saw him here . . . him and the whole football team."

And just the way he said it brought up again the issue regarding the coroner's initial theory that multiple perpetrators might have been involved in the brutal slaying of Cheryl Carpenter—a point, of course, not lost on the reporter, who right away referred to that theory. It added a macabre, cultish twist to the story, took it a level deeper into the mystery of what had happened. The reporter looked into the camera. "Lisa Kendall remains missing. The question now is, what was her connection to the football team, if any? In light of these recent revelations, and the fact that Sarah Kendall was struck by two vehicles, investigators are set to reexamine Cheryl Carpenter's body as part of this ongoing investigation to try again to determine if multiple perpetrators stabbed her. We'll continue to bring you details of this breaking exclusive as they emerge."

The piece ended with a police sketch of a woman staring out at the world in that unnatural way police composites are always drawn. She looked like anyone and everyone. A toll-free number was listed beneath the sketch.

Lois got up and turned down the sound on the TV, then sat again in silence at a table facing the night. Even Petey was quiet. A clock ticked off time.

Did this go beyond the mayor? Was he covering up a reality far more horrific than any of us could have imagined? It was hard trying to understand what was happening to us.

I looked at Lois and said, "Is this the beginning or the end of something?"

Lois turned her head slowly. She was exhausted. "I don't know anymore." She shuddered like something had passed through her, then yawned and covered her mouth, and I yawned too.

Lois went upstairs. I heard water running.

I didn't want to impinge on her. We had run out of things to say to one another. We had been holding out all night for Hayden to call regarding Kendall being in a witness protection program.

I bided my time, ate cold cereal in the kitchen, and stared at the face of a missing child on a milk carton. The world seemed like it had run out of goodness when children could disappear like that. Seeing the black-and-white shot of the child made me long for Eddy.

I called Janine even though it was late. Janine answered on the second ring, and for the first time since our divorce, I said, "I'm truly sorry for what I did to you, Janine." I was leaning into the phone, talking in a quiet way.

Janine said quietly, "Seth told me he thought you were going to kill yourself when you called from up there in Canada."

I said, "I came close."

Janine hesitated. "That night you called, Seth asked me . . ." Janine took a breath. "He wanted to know what went wrong between us."

I could tell I had called in the middle of something going on between her and Seth. I said, "I didn't mean to cause trouble between you and Seth."

Janine interrupted. "Seth told me something the night you called."

I didn't really want to listen to her. I wanted to hear Eddy's voice.

Janine said my name.

I said, "I'm here."

I could hear the sadness in her voice, a woman I was once married to, and yet I had no feeling for her at that moment.

She said, "You know Seth was a spotter aboard surveillance planes during the Korean War. What he did was identify potential targets, guide bombers to targets. Sometimes those targets were refugees . . . women and children."

Janine let out a long breath. "Seth told me he's someone who can pick out a refugee, a person who's lost. That's who he says he is."

I said, "Where's Seth now?"

"Sitting across from me. He's listening to everything."

And for the first time, I was the one who set the phone down gently.

Johnny Carson had just completed his monologue and was doing that signature putt of his that took him to a commercial break when I came into the living room.

Lois had come down again. She had a tray on her lap with a glass of warm milk and a cookie. Petey was sitting on her shoulder. He didn't even hiss when I came into the room.

Lois smiled like she'd made a decision to endure. She was on the other side of things now. It was something I admired in her. I wanted to say that to her, but I didn't. She said, "You want me to fix you some warm milk, or there's coffee put down already?"

"Coffee."

We watched Elizabeth Taylor talk with Johnny about how much she liked furs and diamonds. She was past her prime. She made you feel your age. Between her and Johnny, they calculated they'd been married thirteen times, and Ed McMahon made three for a total of sixteen times.

Liz's new husband had an earring, which worried Johnny, but Liz was confident about this marriage. She said men who'd pierced their ear were better prepared for marriage. They'd experienced pain and bought jewelry.

Ed McMahon just about toppled over laughing, and Johnny was doing that thing he did with his pencil, tapping it on his desk. Liz was showing the camera her new jewelry.

They were a piece of work. I guess we all needed to end on a note like that.

I got up and poured myself more coffee. A heavy snow fell through the late hours, then abated, leaving the world blanketed. Lois was curled up on the couch. The station went off the air and made that whistling noise. I got up and turned off the set. It faded to a pinpoint of light.

I smoked in Lois's carport. She came out and smoked alongside me. It was long past a reasonable hour for Hayden to call. He'd discovered nothing. There was nothing there to discover. Something else lay at the center of this. We were just too close to understand it. I said to Lois, "In science, they have this maxim—the simplest explanation is usually the right solution." I waited a moment. "There is no witness protection program."

Lois said softly, "Give him time. There might be something there."

I cleared my voice. "I don't know if I can keep on going."

Lois looked at me. "Don't say that. I don't think I could take another man committing suicide."

"I didn't mean that."

Lois shivered against the cold. "You know I have nightmares."

I said, "Let's just go in."

"No! Let me finish." Lois hugged herself and stepped from foot to foot. "I used to have nightmares where I'd see Lionel hanging in that motel room, even though I never did see that. It was an image that just found its way into my head. But now, when I have nightmares, it's different."

Lois took another pull from her cigarette and held the smoke a long time before breathing. "I'm driving along a dark road deep in some forest when something catches my eyes, something gleaming in a tree. I get out, and somehow you are there pointing your light into the tree. You're telling me to go back, but you're still pointing the light into the tree. It's Max, hanging . . . but then suddenly the head lifts, and I see Lionel's face on Max's body."

Lois didn't look at me, just left me and went back inside.

The storm door slammed behind her.

I stayed outside, giving her time, standing against the cold. I thought of Max. When I closed my eyes, I saw Kyle cutting his throat. It was the same knife he'd used to kill Cheryl. No matter what Laycock or the media said about multiple perpetrators, they were wrong. It had been Kyle who'd killed Max and tried to kill me. Showing up in the early morning, waiting for him like that, I'd scared the hell out of him. I was responsible in some way for what he did later that night. Earl had thought I wanted money. He'd asked me how much I wanted. He must have told Kyle that. They'd got scared, that was the plain and simple fact. Maybe Earl really felt I was trying to blackmail them.

I came back into the warmth of the house. My arms came up in goose bumps.

Lois was listening to the Wealth Tapes in the living room. She said, in a serious tone, "I think they're onto something on those tapes. I want to go into business with you. There are people becoming millionaires every day."

I said, "They're crap."

"Maybe you went about it the wrong way."

I told Lois about the guy from the Holocaust who lived just outside Chicago, how he was willing to sell cheap. I said, "That's how you become a millionaire. You've got to be willing to feed on the misfortune of others."

Lois's eyes had the sheen of somebody exhausted or desperate. "Some people call that free enterprise."

"Maybe I don't have it in me to be a millionaire."

Lois said defiantly, "I think I do."

While Lois was getting ready for bed, I poured a measure of whiskey into my coffee. I stared at the photograph I'd taken of Eddy getting a prize for his costume. I imagined his face, those searching eyes in the holes of the mask. And there with Eddy was the mayor, with that capped-tooth smile, his arm crossing his midsection to shake Eddy's hand, done politician-style, so his face was always toward the camera.

I stood up and got Kendall's phone records from Lois's bag in the hallway and sat down again, looked at the times Kendall had called the mayor Halloween night—a long call at 6:35 to the mayor's lot, then a shorter call at 8:40 to his house. That second call lasted three minutes.

It was obvious the mayor had some sort of dealings with Kendall beyond being her landlord. Why had Kendall called the lot? It would've been more natural for her to confide in the mayor's wife, not the mayor. The mayor *was* involved with her. I knew that. He had to be. The thing was, how could you break through to him? And what was he covering up, himself or something far more sinister?

The Wealth Tapes were still playing in the background. I could hear Lois in the bathroom.

I listened to the voice talking for a few moments, then closed my eyes, felt sleep coming on, put my head on the table, using my arms as a pillow.

I jumped when Lois put her lips to the crown of my head. I'd fallen asleep.

When I looked up, she said, "You coming to bed?"

I shivered and looked at the time. It was after two in the morning. Lois rubbed my shoulders. I bent my head and let her work the tension out.

In the long hallway, Lois blew a kiss toward Petey's cage, and as she killed the light, it was as though she had extinguished it with her breath.

The bed creaked when we got in. I turned away from Lois, and at first she leaned into me, but then turned away, so we were back to back.

I said softly, "I'm sorry."

I heard her snore minutes later.

I turned and curled against her warm back, then turned away again, trying to find the sanctuary of sleep. I saw Sarah Kendall again in the leaves, that recurring dream of a car coming at her. I woke with a startle, saw the curtains waver like some spirit had passed through the room.

I left before dawn. I didn't wake Lois.

39 Lois had called and left a message on my answering machine by the time I got home. She was crying. I don't know why I didn't call her back, but I didn't.

I left again while it was still dark and drove around the town. I was going to go back and be with her, but ended up going out by Janine's, then further on toward the Johnsons', and just looked across the flatness of the land. I could see a light on in a window down on their property, and a halo of lights from the camera crews who were again staked out waiting for Earl to show.

Even in death, Kyle was being used as he had while he was alive. I had been with Kyle the night after he'd run over the child. It was as simple as he'd said, his involvement was simply an accident, but for the media it made a more sensational story to follow the notion that he had led multiple perpetrators in the butchering of Cheryl Carpenter. The media fed on the indeterminacy of conjecture, on speculation. Laycock had probably sold his story to some newsstand rag.

It wasn't the truth that mattered anymore.

Just staring across at the Johnsons' house, I knew their lives were ruined forever. At that moment, I wished so badly I could have gone back to that evening when I met Kyle, when all this started. We had all been victims that evening, victims to a far greater mystery. In the dead of night I came to understand that.

I wanted to go down to the Johnsons' and say I was sorry, make them understand I wasn't the enemy. I wanted to speak to them away from lawyers, speak to them like a human being. We had been used. I said that under my breath. That's what I wanted to say to them. I wanted them to give me back my life, to retract their statement that I tried to blackmail them. If I could have got to Helen Johnson, if I could have been assured it was just her awake down there, I would have pleaded with her as a Christian.

But of course, I couldn't be sure that Earl wasn't the one awake. And to go near them now would only have drawn the cameras around all of us anyway.

There was no redemption for any of us. We were long past all that.

I passed by the mayor's lot in the early morning light. A camera crew was on hand there as well, filming footage of the front row of cars with their windows smashed.

The lights of the lot ran against the low moving clouds. It looked like a circus sideshow that had seen better days. There was a banner strung across the entrance that read, "Closeout Sale—Everything Must Go!"

I stayed on the opposite side of the road. I saw the line of new cars the mayor had on his lot, saw there was more than one of those cars he'd given to Earl and Kyle.

And right then, I knew Kyle had not dropped Kendall off. It had been the mayor. I felt sure of it.

It was a revelation that hurt deep inside me. I closed my eyes for a moment, letting that truth sink in. I knew I should have called Hayden right then, told him about the car, but I didn't. There was time enough for that.

I wanted to face the mayor.

I circled the lot one more time, collecting myself, then parked and walked across to the mayor's trailer, avoiding the cameramen.

The mayor was sitting at his desk. He looked at me but didn't say anything. He was wearing a flannel hunter's cap, the flaps down over his ears, his cheeks scarlet from the cold. He looked like a defeated man, the rims of his eyes pink from the cold.

The trailer was freezing. He'd not turned on the heater.

I stood in the doorway for a moment.

I looked back out across the lot, saw the camera crew standing around, cupping their hands and blowing into them. They were waiting for the early morning news to start.

I said, "That two-door '75 Chevy Caprice convertible you got out there, how much is that going for?"

"It has a shot gasket."

I said, "I still might be interested." I looked toward the big window of the trailer facing the lot. The camera crew had turned on their stark lights. I said, "Why don't we get out of here for a while?"

I went and started the Caprice. A camera guy came over to see what was going on, saw me, and thought I just worked at the lot. He went back to the van.

The mayor was standing in the back alley, shivering. He got in when I stopped.

I drove through the icy tracks laid down by other cars. Everything had that morning-after look. Snow was still falling lightly. A solitary snowplow worked Main Street, its yellow lights flashing.

By the town hall, I saw the chief and Arnold Fisher waiting to cross to a coffee shop. I slowed, and they crossed in front of us, not knowing it was the mayor and me. It was like seeing it on a big screen, framed in the window of that huge car.

I took a left on Jackson and headed toward Oak, toward Lisa Kendall's apartment. I stopped right where Sarah Kendall had died. I stared down the long street.

It was almost like a funnel, the way the snow swirled, the canopy of trees laden with an ethereal white.

I let the car idle and said quietly, "Why don't you step out of character, Mayor?"

The mayor didn't look at me. "Sometimes there is nothing behind the character."

I said, "Where is Lisa?"

"I don't know."

I said, "I know it was you, not Kyle, who dropped Lisa back at her apartment. You had an affair with her." My voice rose slightly. "All those calls to your lot, you can't deny it any longer. Everybody knows."

The mayor lowered his head. "Is this how my life is going to end? Why did I hang on to a car lot, to a failed marriage?"

I said again, "Where is Lisa?"

The mayor's lips were moving like he was talking to himself. "I don't know . . . I want people to know it wasn't because of how Jean looked after the mastectomy. It wasn't."

"What?"

"I stuck through everything with her . . . You know, we'd tried for children for years, and they never came. I never put us through the humiliation of finding out which of us had the problem. And then, in one weekend . . ." His voice faltered. "In *one* weekend with Lisa it just happened. It was nature . . . nature telling me something."

The world closed around me. "The child was your daughter?"

The mayor turned to look at me for the first time since we'd gotten into the car. It wasn't a face—just a hole with words coming out of it. "Yes . . ."

I felt sick in the pit of my stomach. I didn't say anything for a few moments, then I said, "What happened that night? Who ran Sarah over?"

The mayor said quietly, "I don't know." He shook his head. "The apartment door was open. Sarah got outside, that's how it happened . . . She just got outside." His voice was shaky. "Just take me back, Lawrence, please."

"You argued with Lisa . . . You spoke to her for over an hour on the phone. Why did she get drunk? Something happened between the two of you."

The mayor moved his head slightly. "She was depressed . . . She wanted me to go see Sarah's costume." His voice was strained. "I couldn't . . . I couldn't meet with her then." He let out a long breath. "It was coming to an end, all of it. I told her that. The survival rate for Jean's type of cancer was less than five years. I told Lisa to hang on, that it was nearly over. She kept pushing against me. She didn't want to wait."

Again he stopped for a moment. "I wanted to give Jean that dignity.

I thought we could wait it out. We were so close to all of it ending . . ." His voice tapered off.

He started talking again, softly. "I'm not a bad person, Lawrence, I'm not. Don't look at me like that." He closed and opened his eyes. "The truth . . . okay." He said it like I'd asked a question.

"The truth is I couldn't leave Jean, okay? My lot hasn't broken even in years. It's been Jean's money that's paid for everything. I had no future without her money. I needed to wait for her to die. I couldn't leave. How could I tell that to Lisa, how could I? I was trapped."

The mayor's hands became fists on his thighs. His Adam's apple disappeared and reappeared in his throat. "I felt I was doing the right thing, you know that? I thought I could handle everything, keep everything going. I stood by Jean all these years. I gave her that dignity."

I said, "Jean must have known about Lisa?"

The mayor turned his head slowly. "No. She didn't. Lisa came up here to live after Sarah was almost a year old. I wanted to be part of her life. I wanted a *family* . . ." The mayor's voice halted. "I sent her into Jean's office looking to rent something. I got Lisa to make up a story about running from a bad relationship, hiding. Jean believed it all. After her cancer, Jean reached out to help people. It was Jean who took Lisa on as a charity case."

"And the alias Lisa used?"

"In case Jean ever did run a check, in case she got suspicious."

I said, "You had it all covered."

"What's wrong with wanting to do the best for everybody? It's what I tried to do. The world changed—not me. I didn't let Lisa abort. I told her we'd work things out. I just needed time . . ."

"Did you do something to her?"

"No!" He raised and then lowered his voice. "No."

I felt him pull me away from getting to the heart of what had happened Halloween night. Even now he was hiding behind his own words. I said, "What happened when Lisa called Jean?"

The mayor shifted. "What do you mean?"

"Lisa called your house when you were already at the mall. I have the phone records. Did Lisa tell Jean Sarah was your daughter then?" But by the time I got it said, the mayor's face turned white. I could see the mayor hadn't known Lisa had called Jean.

Neither woman had told him.

The car idled in the stillness of the cold morning. It had begun to snow again.

I said, "Where is Lisa?" but before he could answer, a TV reporter pounded on the passenger window, and I instinctively hit the gas, the car's wheels spinning, the back end fishtailing before the tires gripped.

I let the mayor out near his lot, but said again, "Where is Lisa?"

He said quietly, "I swear I don't know. I don't. If I did, I'd tell you."

40 I waited out the dying day at my house, confronting the fact that the mayor never knew Lisa had spoken with Jean. What had Lisa said to Jean? Was the child missing at that stage? I tried to go through so many scenarios in my head.

But of course only Lisa, and maybe Jean, knew.

I figured the mayor was confronting that same fact—that the two women in his life had gone behind his back.

I thought back to that time in Jean's office when she'd said Sarah's name. She'd lived with the secret of what happened all this time.

The TV broke live to the mayor's lot, to the stream of flags blowing in the wind, the mayor's trailer empty. The camera lingered on the broken windshields. Then I saw the footage of the mayor and me, parked on the street where the child had died. The camera pulled back to take in the white facade of the house that held the apartment where Kendall had lived, and the road where the child had died. It was framed in that single shot.

It was the shot that defined the story.

Then came the official statement from a police spokesman confirming that investigators were reviewing the circumstances surrounding the child's death. The spokesman asked again for anybody who had been in the vicinity of the street that night to come forward.

The mayor had been questioned throughout the afternoon. He appeared on the steps of the county jail, released on his own recognizance. He looked jaded. He was standing with his attorney shielding him. The mayor was described as "a person of interest" in the ongoing investigation into Kendall's disappearance.

I got a phone call from a member of the town board informing me that, given my involvement in the cover-up, I had been officially terminated from my job.

The phone rang half an hour later. I let the machine pick up. It was Lois. She said she was on her way to getting very drunk. She, too, had been fired, along with the chief.

She said, "I know you're still around. I saw you on the TV . . . I just want to say, I feel like this is a good thing, right, isn't it? I'm listening to a song here called, 'I'll Marry You Tomorrow, But Let's Honeymoon Tonight!' You know that song?" She sniffled and cleared her throat. "Where did you go last night, Lawrence? I hope you haven't up and left me for good. I believe in those Wealth Tapes more and more. What is the name of the Holocaust survivor? I want to call him. I've got a proposition for him."

The phone rang again a half hour later. I didn't answer it.

The machine picked up. It was Janine's voice. She said, "I have somebody here who wants to tell you what he wants for Christmas." I could hear Eddy in the background, then he got on the phone. He talked in a rushed kid way, listing what he wanted—C-3PO, R2-D2, and Chewbacca.

I think I could have listened to him talk for the rest of my life.

In the evening light, I went and stood in Eddy's room, stared at the Star Wars posters on the wall, the trilogy, his favorite movies of all time in his short life. I thought of Darth Vader, a.k.a. Anakin Skywalker, the father who had gone over to the dark side of the force, his face hidden behind a mask, whose son, Luke Skywalker, was to learn who his father was only years later. I'd sat with Eddy for two hours, watched Luke Skywalker searching for a masked father he never knew, watched him redeem his father, bring him back from the dark force. It's how we had come to live and die, behind masks.

———

I fell again to thinking about what Lisa could have told Jean. Lisa was drunk. They'd talked for three minutes. The child was missing at that stage, she must have been. In the heat of panic had Lisa told Jean who Sarah was? Surely she had to have, and just thinking about that I felt a shudder run down my spine.

I waited until after midnight before leaving, drove through the narrowed streets, snow banked up on either side of the road. I passed the town hall. There was no one around.

I parked in one of the abandoned lots in the warehouse district and walked. The lot was half a foot deep in unspoiled snow.

I didn't know if my old key still worked in the annex door, if they'd changed the lock since firing us. They hadn't.

In the dead quiet I followed the emergency track lighting leading from the gangway to the main building, winding my way back to Bains's makeshift office in the janitor's storage room.

I shut the door behind me and turned on the light. I began searching for a copy of the accident report and found it.

There was the description of the child's injuries, associated shots of the body taken at the scene, the grim details of where she'd been hit, each injury circled and referenced by a letter corresponding to the final coroner's report. There were leaves plastered to the child's hair, her face, arms, and legs splotched with dirt. I saw where the twisted wire-hanger frame of the transparent cellophane wings had cut through her back.

I kept skimming through the report until I came across a statement indicating the child had *not* been thrown by the impact. Abrasion patterns along the left torso were consistent with the conclusion that the child was lying amidst the leaves when struck.

I took out the set of records related to the two vehicles, laying out the series of shots that showed the tire pattern of both, the last image in each series a chalk outline of the child's body.

I read through the investigator's summary.

Vehicle B had cut a weaving pattern going back some fifty yards, leaving in its wake exploded bags of leaves, whereas Vehicle A seemed as though it had been pulling over toward the side of the road. The report detailed the tire tread pattern on both vehicles.

There was an unusual slash mark on the right front tire of Vehicle A.

I looked up and stared at the stark light bulb, the truth beginning to surface of what had happened.

I tucked the photographs into my shirt and left, stopping one last time in the milky light of the long hallway, staring at the place in which I would surely have lived out my life, if not for what had happened.

The mayor's home was set back from the old part of town, overlooking the river. The temperature had risen, so the falling snow turned to sleet. A half-moon smoked against the clouds.

I could see lights on up in the mayor's house.

I should have left and called Hayden. In my heart, I knew the mayor was going to be waiting for me, but I couldn't stop myself from going up there. When I looked at my hands, they were shaking.

The windows fogged. I wiped the driver's-side window, stared through the porthole clearing, the house sailing high above me.

I put the photographs inside my jacket, got out into the cold wind, and climbed slowly up the steep embankment of snow. I slid and found it hard to keep my footing, hunched over, using my hands to steady myself. I hesitated before cresting the hill and turned, looking back at the town's faint glow, saw the dark slur of river catch the glint of moon-light. The wind's pull was strong at the top of the hill.

I went around the back to an old carriage house. The lower level served as a garage. Opening one of the doors slightly, I wedged myself into the darkness, closing the door behind me.

Everything reeked of oil. Both cars were there.

I couldn't make out anything else, just the dark shapes. I waited, adjusting to the dark. Wind whistled through the slats of wood, the doors of the carriage house rattling on their hinges.

Slowly, a pale yellow cast of light from the kitchen became more defined. I felt the looming presence of the house. I knew the mayor was waiting there for me. Then I saw him at the window, and still I did not leave.

I turned on my flashlight, a wedge of light cutting a hole in the dark.

I took out the photograph identified as the right front tire track and, crouching, checked the lug nuts on the mayor's wife's car. They had not been removed in a long time. I worked my way around the tire until I found the signature scar on the tire tread that had been circled on the photograph.

It matched.

I had to lean on one knee. The cold wrapped around me. I looked up and let my eyes adjust again. In the cruelest and saddest of ironies, I felt I understood what had happened. In the wake of Lisa revealing to Jean who the child was, and that she was missing, Jean had frantically rushed over to the house. In the confusion of the moment, in pulling over to park, she'd run through the leaves and hit the child.

It's how it must have happened.

Through the slats in the carriage house, I could see the mayor had come out into the yard.

I simply turned off my flashlight.

The carriage house door wavered and swung open, pulled by the wind. I heard it groan and slap against the outer frame.

The mayor raised his voice, though it held a quiver of fear. "I couldn't bring myself to check. But I knew you'd come." He had his gun pointed into the chasm of the carriage house.

I moved and toppled over a gas container.

The mayor turned on his own flashlight. It licked away the dark.

The wind whistled through the carriage house. The door swung again, and the photograph I'd had beside the car lifted and fluttered, drifting to the edge of the door. The mayor followed it with the flashlight, moved tentatively forward, bent and picked it up, keeping his gun trained into the carriage house.

He walked forward. His flashlight found me hunkered down in the far corner of the carriage house. He had the gun pointed at me.

"Put your hands up."

I stood up and faced him. I raised my arms. I was still inside the carriage house.

The mayor was shivering. "I don't think Jean knows Sarah was mine." He shook his head slowly. I could tell he'd not confronted Jean. He was still hiding from the truth.

Of course Jean knew, but the mayor said, "I'd just as soon keep Jean from knowing Sarah was mine. Jean did nothing wrong. It was an accident what happened." He had the gun still pointed at me. I couldn't see his face because the light was bright in my eyes.

He kept talking in a rambling way. "You know Jean is a beautiful person, in here, where it counts." He touched his heart with the flashlight, then lowered his hand so the light was a beam pointed at the ground.

My eyes adjusted to the dark. I still had my hands raised.

"Sometimes we forget why we fall in *love* . . . You know what I mean, Lawrence? You ever have a one-and-only?" There was a searching note in his voice.

I said, "It's over, Mayor." I lowered my hands.

I heard him cock the trigger. "Don't move, Lawrence. Don't move."

The wind swept across the dark, pulled against the carriage house door. It flapped and creaked.

I said, "Where is Lisa?"

Jean had come outside. I heard her raise her voice. She said, "He doesn't know. She's away from him now. She's safe."

The mayor turned his flashlight on her, tried to go toward Jean, but she said, "Keep away from me!"

In the glare of light, in the static of sleet, Jean looked abject and sick. She looked nothing like how I'd seen her before. Her head was bald from the chemotherapy. She was already a ghost, her voice frail. "I know Sarah was your daughter. Lisa called here Halloween night, frantic, drunk . . . She said you'd had a fight. She'd passed out. When she came to, Sarah was on the floor by the coffee table, dead . . . When I got there, Lisa was suicidal."

Jean was facing the mayor. Her housecoat fluttered in the wind. "You know your worst crime? You robbed her of her dignity, made her doubt herself. She couldn't be sure it was just an accident. She was unable to judge what she was capable of doing. I don't think she knew whether she killed her child or not. She couldn't tell . . . You did that to her. Do you think you can use people like that forever?"

Jean was crying, one of her fists clutching her housecoat. "I couldn't let them find Sarah dead in the apartment. Lisa couldn't have faced all the questions about Sarah's death, faced the accusations. She was incoherent, shaking from what you'd made her live through. They'd have put her away, one way or another. She didn't deserve that . . . She didn't."

Jean faltered. "I'm going to die facing what I had to do that night. I put your child out into the street. I ran her over . . . not to save you, or me, but to save *Lisa*."

Jean spoke across the dark. "You've sent me to Hell."

The wind picked up again. The carriage house door swung and flapped closed, and through its slats, I saw the mayor raise his gun, saw my own life flash in the incandescent burn of gunfire, felt things come full circle as the mayor did what I had stopped myself from doing. He pulled the trigger first on his wife, then on himself, finally ending the nightmare of their shared existence.

Epilogue

I arrived at Lois's before morning. She was up sitting in her kitchen. The Wealth Tapes were playing in the background. Petey was watching *Good Morning America*.

Lois had called the Holocaust guy in Chicago. She'd found the listing in a coat I'd left at her house. He was willing to sell.

It was a start.

Lois put down coffee. She wanted me to tell her about the house in Chicago. She was talking in an optimistic way about the future. She made scrambled eggs and toast, her back to me, talking all the time.

I had the TV on in the living room, the sound turned low. I could see it from the kitchen. Maybe this is what it would feel like to know the future, just sitting waiting for it to happen.

The kitchen filled with the smell of the percolating coffee. By stages, outside the kitchen window, everything was becoming visible, like sheaths of membrane were slowly being taken away.

Petey ate wheat toast and egg, watching us from on top of the refrigerator. I said, "Isn't Petey's eating eggs basically cannibalism?"

Just after nine o'clock, the story of the mayor's and Jean's murder-suicide broke. The old house high up on the hill served as a gothic specter against which their deaths were reported, giving the story an Old World feel.

The TV cut to a montage of the mayor's life—him dressed as a pilgrim on his lot with his Thanksgiving turkeys; as the suave Gomez Addams with penciled moustache at the mall, Halloween night; at the pep rally riding in the tricycle race, that beet red of his face, the absurdity of his size on the tricycle; putting his whole fist into his mouth during a campaign speech the year he became mayor.

They had footage, too, of him spreading his arms apart at the pep rally, introducing Kyle Johnson, the other tragic figure in the story. The camera caught Kyle's size and improbable good looks, a combination that only came along once in a while, what a reporter quoted a coach as calling "the total package."

The TV had seemingly abandoned the theory that anybody but Kyle had killed Cheryl. A voice-over gave an account of Kyle's meteoric rise and fall, the sad irony of his involvement in the hit-and-run and the subsequent cover-up, lingering on the quintessential image of Kyle and Cheryl as homecoming king and queen, then cutting starkly to a shot of the abortion clinic Cheryl had visited, then to her car being dredged from the river, flitting to the image of Kyle's body being removed from the high school on a gurney, before settling once more on the dark spires of the mayor's old house sailing against an embankment of clouds.

It played as allegory, high Hicksville tragedy, one of those stories that marked the passing of an era, where all the principal characters died. From the height of the mayor's house, the town looked desolate, emptied of life, the town hall an anachronism amidst the hull of abandoned warehouses down by the dark scar of river.

The town had moved away from its center, moved out fifteen miles to a strip of bleeding neon-sign eateries that looked like some extraterrestrial runway to a huge domed mother-ship mall out amidst snow-covered fields. It served numerous communities.

In a year we would lose control of the mall in a rezoning ruling.

A camera found life there in the early morning, the aged in their track suits and walking shoes rounding the mall, the new Purgatory, recuperating from things like hip replacements, heart attacks, and quadruple bypass surgeries, radical mastectomies, prostate and colon cancers—hacked-up survivors of biology and time. A reporter asked them what they thought about what had happened. Most didn't even stop, keeping up their heart rates, too engrossed in their own survival.